The scream came without warning.

Wyatt sat straight up in bed, trying to convince himself that he'd been dreaming. But it had sounded so *real.*

He made his way through the house and headed for the kitchen to get a drink. He wasn't particularly thirsty, but at the moment, crawling back into bed did not hold much interest. His heart was still pounding as he took a glass from the cabinet and filled it.

The water tasted good going down, and his panic was subsiding. If he stretched the truth, he could convince himself that his heart rate was back to normal. It was just a bad dream. That was all. Just a bad dream.

Wyatt…

He spun toward the doorway, expecting someone to be standing there. There was no one.

When the voice came again, he knew this was no dream.

Wyatt…Wyatt Hatfield… Help me….

Dear Reader,

We've got a terrific lineup of books to start off the New Year. I hope you'll enjoy each and every one. Start things off with our newest Intimate Moments Extra, Kathryn Jensen's *Time and Again.* This book is time travel with a twist—but you'll have to read it to see what I mean. One thing I can promise you: you won't regret the time you spend turning these pages.

Next up, Marie Ferrarella's cross-line miniseries, The Baby of the Month Club, comes to Intimate Moments with *Happy New Year—Baby!* Of course, this time we're talking *babies* of the month, because Nicole Logan is having twins—and it's up to Dennis Lincoln to prove that a family of four is better than a family of three. Sharon Sala's *When You Call My Name* brings back Wyatt Hatfield from her last book, *The Miracle Man.* This time, Wyatt's looking for a miracle of his own, both to save his life and heal his heart. Beverly Barton continues her miniseries, The Protectors, with *Guarding Jeannie,* Sam Dundee's story. Alexandra Sellers gives the ever-popular secret-baby plot line a whirl in *Roughneck,* and I know you'll want to come along for the ride. Finally, welcome new author Kate Hathaway, whose *His Wedding Ring* will earn a spot on your keeper shelf.

Until next month—happy reading!

Yours,

Leslie J. Wainger
Senior Editor and Editorial Coordinator

Please address questions and book requests to:
Silhouette Reader Service
U.S.: 3010 Walden Ave., P.O. Box 1325, Buffalo, NY 14269
Canadian: P.O. Box 609, Fort Erie, Ont. L2A 5X3

SHARON SALA

WHEN YOU CALL MY NAME

Published by Silhouette Books

America's Publisher of Contemporary Romance

ISBN 0-373-07687-8

WHEN YOU CALL MY NAME

This edition published by arrangement with Harlequin Books S.A.

Printed in U.S.A.

Books by Sharon Sala

Silhouette Intimate Moments

Annie and the Outlaw #597
The Miracle Man #650
When You Call My Name #687

SHARON SALA

is a child of the country. As a farmer's daughter, her vivid imagination made solitude a thing to cherish. As a farmer's wife, she learned to take each day as it came, without worrying about the next. After she and her husband, Bill, raised two children and too many crops to count, she went from clotheslines to deadlines with a smile on her face. Writing is nothing more than the fulfillment of a lifelong habit of daydreaming. Giving birth to characters in her mind and then sharing them with those who like to read is the thing she loves best.

Once, in the middle of the night, I heard my sister, Diane, call my name. I sat alone in the dark, listening for hours for the sound of her voice. It never came again.

I do not believe that death breaks the bonds of love. And because of that, sometimes I still listen, just to see if she will call for me again.

Diane, if you're listening, this book is dedicated to you, and to the love that we shared.

Chapter 1

It's all your fault. You let me down... let me down.

Wyatt Hatfield shifted in his seat and gripped the steering wheel a little tighter, trying to see through the falling snow to the road ahead, doing everything he could to ignore the memories of his ex-wife's accusations. Shirley and his years with the military were things of the past.

This soul-searching journey he'd embarked upon months earlier was for the sole purpose of finding a new direction for himself. He'd fixed what was wrong with Antonette's life with little more than a phone call. Why, he wondered, couldn't he find a way to fix his own? And then he grinned, remembering how mad his sister had been when he'd interfered.

"At least I'm in her good graces now," he muttered, then cursed beneath his breath when his car suddenly fishtailed.

His heartbeat was still on high as he reminded himself to concentrate on the more pressing issues at hand, namely, the blizzard into which he'd driven. The windshield wipers scratched across the icy film covering the glass, scattering the snow in their paths like a dry, whirling flurry, while the heater and defroster did what they could to keep the interior of his car warm.

But as hard as he tried to concentrate on driving, her voice kept ringing in his ear, complaining that when she'd needed him, he was never there.

"Damn it, Shirley, give me a break," Wyatt muttered. "I was wrong. You were right. That should be enough satisfaction for you to let go of my mind."

The car skidded sideways on a patch of ice and Wyatt eased off on the gas, riding with the skid and sighing in relief as the car finally righted itself.

He'd made the wrong decision when he hadn't stopped back in the last town, and he knew it. Then the weather hadn't been this bad, and getting to Lexington, Kentucky, tonight had seemed more important then than it did now. To make things worse, because of the severity of the snowstorm, he wasn't even sure he was on the right road anymore. The weak yellow beam of the headlights did little to illuminate what was left of the road, leaving Wyatt with nothing more than instinct to keep him from driving off the side of the mountain.

And then out of nowhere, the dark, hulking shape of a truck came barreling around a curve and into the beam of light, slipping and sliding as Wyatt had done only moments before, and there was no more time to dwell upon past mistakes. It was too late to do anything but react.

Wyatt gripped the steering wheel, trying desperately to turn away from the truck gone out of control, but he knew before impact that they were going to crash.

"God help us all," Wyatt murmured, knowing there was no earthly way to prevent what was about to happen.

And then the truck's bumper and fender connected with the side of Wyatt's car. Bulk and weight superseded driving skill. Impact sent Wyatt and his car careening across the road and then down the side of the snowpacked mountain.

The last thing he saw was the picture-perfect beauty of lofty pines, heavy with snow and glistening in the headlights of his car. Blessedly, he never felt the car's impact into the first stand of trees...or the next...or the next, or knew when it rolled sideways, then end over end, coming to a steaming, hissing halt against a fifty-foot pine.

He didn't hear the frantic cries of the truck driver, standing at the edge of the road, calling down the mountain and praying for an answer that never came.

The wind from the blizzard whistled beneath the crack in the windowsill across the room. Even in her sleep, Glory heard the high-pitched moan and unconsciously pulled the covers a little higher around her neck. She could hear the warm, familiar grumble of her father, Rafe, snoring. It signified home, protection and family. Directly across from Glory's room, her brother, J.C., slept to the accompaniment of an all-night music station. Mixing with the wail of the wind and the low rumble of an old man's sleep, the melodies seemed somehow appropriate. Glory's long flannel gown added to the cocoon of warmth beneath the mound of covers under which she slept. She shifted, then sighed, and just as her subconscious slipped into dream sleep, she jerked. There was no escape for what came next, even in sleep.

Eyes! Wide, dark, shocked! Red shirt! No... white shirt covered in blood! Blood was everywhere. Pain sifted, filtering through unconsciousness, too terrible to be borne!

Glory's eyelids fluttered and then flew open as suddenly as if someone had thrown open shutters to the world. She sat straight up in bed, unaware of the familiarity of her room, or the snow splattering against the windowpanes. Her gaze was wide, fixed, frozen to the picture inside her mind, seeing... but not seeing... someone else's horror.

White. Cold, so cold! Snow everywhere... in everything. Can't breathe! Can't see! Can't feel! Oh, God, don't let me die!

Glory shuddered as her body went limp. She leaned forward and, covering her face with her hands, she began to sob. Suddenly the warmth of her room and the comfort of knowing she was safe seemed obscene in the face of what she'd just witnessed. And then as suddenly as the vision had come upon her, the knowledge followed of what she must do next.

She threw back the covers, stumbling on the tail of her nightgown as she crawled out of bed. As she flipped the switch, her bedroom was instantly bathed in the glow of a pale yellow light that gave off a false warmth.

The floor was cold beneath her bare feet as she ran down the hall to the room where her father lay sleeping. For a moment, she stood in his doorway in the dark, listening to the soft, even sound of his snore, and regretted what she was about to do. Yet ignoring her instinct was as impossible for Glory to do as denying the fact that she was a woman.

"Daddy..."

Rafe Dixon woke with a start. He'd heard that sound in his daughter's voice a thousand times before. He rolled over in bed like a hibernating bear coming out of a sleep, and dug at his eyes with the heels of his hands.

"Glory girl, what's wrong?"

"We've got to go, Daddy. He's dying...and I've got to help."

Rafe groaned. He knew better than to deny what Glory was telling him, but he also knew that there was a near blizzard in force, and getting down off this mountain and into Larner's Mill might prove deadly for them all.

"But honey...the storm."

"We'll make it, Daddy, but he won't."

The certainty in her voice was all Rafe Dixon needed to hear. He rolled out of bed with a thump and started reaching for his clothes.

"Go wake your brother," he said.

"I'm here, Daddy. I heard."

J.C. slipped a comforting arm across his baby sister's shoulders and hugged her. "Was it bad, Sis?"

The look on her face was all he needed to know. He headed back down the hall to his room, calling over his shoulder as he went. "I'll go start the truck."

"Dress warm, girl," Rafe growled. "It's a bitch outside."

Glory nodded, and flew back to her room, pulling on clothes with wild abandon. The urgency within her made her shake, but her resolve was firm.

Minutes later, they walked out of the house into a blast of snow that stung their faces, but Glory didn't falter. As she was about to step off the porch, J.C. appeared out of nowhere and lifted her off her feet, carrying her through the snow to the waiting vehicle. She shuddered as she clung to his broad shoulders, still locked into the vision before her. And as she saw...she prayed.

"We're not gonna make it," the ambulance driver groaned, as he fought the steering wheel and the vehicle's urge to slide.

"Damn it, Farley, just quit talking and drive. We have to make it! If we don't, this fellow sure won't."

Luke Dennis, the emergency medical technician whose fortune it had been to be on duty this night, was up to his elbows in blood. His clothes were soaking wet, and his boots were filled to the tops with melting snow. The last thing he wanted to hear was another negative. They'd worked too long and too hard just getting this victim out of his car and up the side of the mountain to give up now.

"Come on, buddy, hang with me," Dennis muttered, as he traded a fresh container of D5W for the one going empty on the other end of the IV.

An unceasing flow of blood ran out of the victim's dark hair and across his face, mapping his once-handsome features with a crazy quilt of red. It was impossible to guess how many bones this man had broken, and to be honest, those were the least of Dennis's worries. If they couldn't get him back to the hospital in time, it was the internal injuries that would kill him.

"I see lights!" Farley shouted.

Thank God, Dennis thought, and then grabbed his patient and the stretcher, holding on to it, and to him, as the ambulance took the street corner sideways. Moments later they were at the hospital, unloading a man whose chance of a future depended upon the skills of the people awaiting him inside.

Before he was a doctor, Amos Steading had been a medic in Vietnam. When he saw Wyatt Hatfield being wheeled into his ER, he realized he might have been practicing medicine longer than this patient had been alive. It hurt to lose a patient, but the younger ones were much harder to accept.

"What have we got?" Amos growled, lowering his bushy eyebrows as his attention instantly focused upon the injuries.

"Trouble, Doc," Dennis said. "Thirty-four-year-old male. Recently discharged from the Marines. He's still wearing his ID tags. He got sideswiped by a truck and went over the side of Tulley's Mountain. Didn't think we'd ever get him up and out. He's got head injuries, and from the feel of his belly, internal bleeding as well. From external exam, I'd guess at least four broken ribs, and, his right leg has quite a bit of damage, although it's hard to tell what, if anything, is broken. We had to saw a tree and move it off him to get him out of the car." He took a deep breath as the stretcher slid to a halt. As they transferred the victim to the gurney, he added, "This is his third bag of D5W."

Steading's eyebrows arched as he yanked his stethoscope from around his neck and slipped it into place. This man was bleeding to death before their eyes. Moments later, he began firing orders to the nurse and the other doctor on call.

"Get me a blood type," Steading shouted, and a nurse ran to do his bidding.

It was then that EMT Luke Dennis added the last bit of information about the victim, which made them all pause.

"According to his dog tags, he's AB negative," Dennis said.

A low curse slid out of Amos's mouth as he continued to work. Rare blood types didn't belong in this backwater town of eighteen hundred people. There was no way their blood bank was going to have anything like that, and the plasma they had on hand was sparse.

"Type it anyway," Steading ordered. "And get me some plasma, goddamn it! This man's going to die before I can get him stable enough for surgery."

The once quiet hospital instantly became a flurry of shouts, curses and noise. Luke Dennis stepped out of the way, aware that he'd done his job. The rest was up to the doc and his staff... and God.

He started back toward the door to restock the ambulance, aware that the night was far from over. It was entirely possible that more than one fool might decide to venture out in a storm like this. He just hoped that if they plowed themselves into the snow—or into someone else—they were nowhere near a mountain when it happened. But before he could leave, the outside door burst open right before him, and three people blew in, along with a blinding gust of snow.

Glory breathed a shaky sigh of relief. One hurdle crossed. Another yet to come. She burst free of her father's grasp and ran toward the EMT who'd stepped aside to let them pass.

"Mister! Please! Take me to the soldier's doctor."

Dennis couldn't quit staring at the young woman clutching his coat. Her voice was frantic, her behavior strange, but it was her request that startled him. How could she know that the man they'd just brought in was—or at least had been—a soldier?

"Are you a relative?" Dennis asked.

"No! Who I am doesn't matter, but he does," Glory cried, gripping his coat a little tighter. And then she felt her father's hand move across her shoulder.

"Ease up, Glory. You got to explain yourself a little, honey."

She blinked, and Dennis watched focus returning to her expression, thinking as he did that he'd never seen eyes quite that shade of blue. In a certain light, they almost looked silver...as silver as her hair, which clung to her face and coat like strands of wet taffy.

She took a deep breath and started over.

"Please," she said softly. "I came to give blood."

Dennis shook his head. "I don't know how you heard about the accident, but I'm afraid coming out in this storm was a waste of time for you. He's got a rare—"

Glory dug through her purse, her fingers shaking as she searched the contents of her wallet.

"Here," she said, thrusting a card into the man's hands. "Show the doctor. Tell him I can help—that it's urgent that he wait no longer. The man won't live through the night without me."

As Dennis looked down at the card, the hair crawled on the back of his neck. He glanced back up at the woman, then at the card again, and suddenly grabbed her by the arm, pulling her down the hall toward the room where Steading was working.

"Doc, we just got ourselves a miracle," Dennis shouted as he ran into the room.

Amos Steading frowned at the woman Dennis was dragging into their midst.

"Get her out of here, Dennis! You know better than to bring—"

"She's AB negative, Doc, and she's come to give blood."

Steading's hands froze above the tear in the flesh on Wyatt Hatfield's leg.

"You're full of bull," he growled.

Dennis shook his head. "No, I swear to God, Doc. Here's her donor card."

Steading's eyes narrowed and then he barked at a nurse on the other side of the room. "Get her typed and cross-matched. Now!"

She flew to do his bidding.

"And get me some more saline, damn it! This man's losing more fluids than I can pump in him." He cursed softly, then added beneath his breath, fully expecting someone to hear and obey, "And call down to X ray and find out why his films aren't back!" As he leaned back over the patient, he began to mumble again, more to himself than to anyone else. "Now where the hell is that bleeder?"

There was a moment, in the midst of all the doctor's orders, when Glory looked upon the injured man's face. It wasn't often that she had a physical connection to the people in her mind.

"What's his name?" she whispered, as a nurse grabbed her by the arm and all but dragged her down the hall to the lab.

"Who, Dr. Steading?"

"No," Glory said. "The man who was hurt."

"Oh…uh…Hatfield. William…no, uh…Wyatt. Yes, that's right. Wyatt Hatfield. It's a shame, too," the nurse muttered, more to herself than to Glory. "He looks like he was real handsome…and so young. Just got out of the service. From his identification, some sort of special forces. It's sort of ironic, isn't it?"

"What's ironic?" Glory asked, and then they entered the lab, and the scents that assailed her threatened to overwhelm. She swayed on her feet, and the nurse quickly seated her in a chair.

The nurse grimaced. "Why, the fact that he could survive God knows what during his stint in the military, and then come to this, and all because of a snowstorm on a mountain road." Suddenly she was all business. "Stuart, type and cross-match this woman's blood, stat! If she comes up AB negative, and a match to the man in ER, then draw blood. She's a donor."

As the lab tech began, Glory relaxed. At least they were on the right track.

Three o'clock in the morning had come and gone, and the waiting room in ER was quiet. Rafe Dixon glanced at his son, then at his daughter, who seemed to be dozing beside him. How he'd fathered two such different children was beyond him, but his pride in each was unbounded. It just took more effort to keep up with Glory than it did J.C.

He understood his son and his love for their land. He didn't understand one thing about his daughter's gift, but he believed in it, and he believed in her. What worried him most was, who would take care of Glory when he was gone? J.C. was nearly thirty and he couldn't be expected to watch over his sister for the rest of his life. Besides, if he were to marry, a wife might resent the attention J.C. unstintingly gave his baby sister. Although Glory was twenty-five, she looked little more than eighteen. Her delicate features and her fragile build often gave her the appearance of a child...until one looked into her eyes and saw the ancient soul looking back.

Glory child...who will take care of you when I am gone?

Suddenly Glory stood and looked down the hall. Rafe stirred, expecting to see someone open and walk through the doors at the far end. But nothing happened, and no one came.

She slipped her fingers in the palm of her brother's hand and then stood. "We can go home now."

J.C. yawned, and looked up at his father. Their eyes met in a moment of instant understanding. For whatever her reasons, Glory seemed satisfied within herself, and for them, that was all that mattered.

"Are you sure, girl?" Rafe asked, as he helped Glory on with her coat.

She nodded, her head bobbing wearily upon her shoulders. "I'm sure, Daddy."

"You don't want to wait and talk to the doctor?"

She smiled. "There's no need."

As suddenly as they'd arrived, they were gone.

Within the hour, Amos Steading came out of surgery, tossing surgical gloves and blood-splattered clothing in their respective hampers. Later, when he went to look for the unexpected blood donor, to his surprise, she was nowhere to be found. And while he thought it strange that she'd not stayed to hear the results of the surgery, he was too tired and too elated to worry about her odd exodus. Tonight he'd fought the Grim Reaper and won. And while he knew his skill as a surgeon was nothing at which to scoff, his patient still lived because of a girl who'd come out of the storm.

Steading dropped into a chair at his desk and began working up Hatfield's chart, adding notes of the surgery to what had been done in ER. A nurse entered, then gave him a cup of hot coffee and an understanding smile. As the heat from the cup warmed his hand, he sighed in satisfaction.

"Did you locate his next of kin?" Steading asked.

The nurse nodded. "Yes, sir, a sister. Her name is Antonette Monday. She said that she and her husband will come as soon as weather permits."

Steading nodded, and sipped the steaming brew. "It's good to have family."

High up on the mountain above Larner's Mill, Glory Dixon would have agreed with him. When they finally pulled into the yard of their home, it was only a few hours before daybreak, and yet she knew a sense of satisfaction for a job well done. It wasn't always that good came of what she *saw,* but tonight, she'd been able to make a difference.

She reached over and patted her father's knee. "Thank you, Daddy," she said quietly.

"For what?" he asked.

"For believing me."

He slid a long arm across her shoulder, giving her a hug. There was nothing more that needed to be said.

"Looks like the snow's about stopped," he said, gauging the sparse spit of snowflakes dancing before the headlights of their truck.

"Who's hungry?" Glory asked.

J.C. grinned. "Wanna guess?"

She laughed. It was a perfect ending to a very bad beginning.

Back in recovery, Wyatt Hatfield wasn't laughing, but if he'd been conscious, he would have been counting his blessings. He had a cut on his cheek that would probably scar, and had survived a lung that had collapsed, a concussion that should have put him into a coma and hadn't, five broken ribs and two cracked ones, more stitches in his left leg than he would be able to count and, had he been able to feel them, bruises in every joint.

He could thank a seat belt, a trucker who hadn't kept going after causing the wreck, a rescue crew that went above and beyond the call of duty to get him off of the mountain and an EMT who didn't know the meaning of the word *quit*. And it was extremely good luck on Wyatt's part that, after all that, he wound up in the skilled hands of Amos Steading.

Yet it was fate that had delivered him to Glory Dixon. And had she not given of the blood from her body, the cold and simple fact was that he would have died. But Wyatt didn't know his good fortune. It would be days before he would know his own name.

All day long, the sun kept trying to shine. Wyatt paced the floor of his hospital room, ignoring the muscle twinges in his injured leg, and the pull of sore muscles across his belly.

He didn't give a damn about pain. Today he was going home, or a reasonable facsimile thereof. While he didn't have a home of his own, he still had roots in the land on which he'd been raised. If he had refused to accompany his sister, Toni, back to Tennessee, he suspected that her husband, Lane Monday, would have slung him over his shoulder and taken him anyway. Few but Toni dared argue with Lane Monday. At six feet, seven inches, he was a powerful, imposing man. As a United States Marshal, he was formidable. In Wyatt's eyes, he'd come through for Toni like a real man should. There was little else to be said.

Outside his door, he could hear his sister's voice at the nurses' station while she signed the papers that would check him out. He leaned his forehead against the window, surprised that in spite of the sun's rays it felt cold, and then remembered that winter sun, at its best, was rarely warm.

"Are you ready, Wyatt?"

Wyatt turned. Lane filled the doorway with his size and his presence.

He shrugged. "I guess." He turned back to the window as Lane crossed the room.

For a while, both men were silent, and then Lane gave Wyatt a quick pat on the back before he spoke. "I think maybe I know how you feel," Lane said.

Wyatt shrugged. "Then I wish to hell you'd tell me, because I don't understand. Don't get me wrong. I'm happy to be alive." He tried to grin. "Hell, and if truth be told, a little surprised. When I went over the mountain, in the space of time it took to hit the first stand of trees, I more or less made my peace with God. I never expected to wake up."

Lane listened without commenting, knowing that something was bothering Wyatt that he needed to get said.

"As for my family, I consider myself lucky to have people who are willing to take me in, but I feel so...so..."

"Rootless?"

For a moment Wyatt was silent, and then he nodded. "Exactly. I feel rootless. And...I feel like leaving here will be taking a step backward in what I was searching for. I know it's weird, but I keep thinking that I was *this* close to the end of a journey, and now—"

Toni broke the moment of confiding as she came into the room.

"You're all checked out!" When Wyatt started toward the door, she held up her hand. "Don't get in too big a hurry. They're bringing a wheelchair. Lane, honey, why don't you pull the car up to the curb? Wyatt, are you all packed?"

Both men looked at each other and then grinned. "She was your sister before she was my wife," Lane warned him. "So you can't be surprised by all this."

Toni ignored them. It was her nature to organize. She'd spent too long on her own, running a farm and caring for aging parents, to wait for someone else to make a decision.

"Why don't I go get the car?" Lane said, and stole a kiss from his Toni as he passed.

"I'm packed," Wyatt said.

"I brought one of Justin's coats for you to wear. The clothes you had on were ruined," Toni said, her eyes tearing as she remembered his condition upon their arrival right after the accident. She held out the coat for him to put on. Wyatt slipped one arm in his brother's coat, and then the other, then turned and hugged her, letting himself absorb the care . . . and the love.

"Now all I need is my ride," Wyatt teased, and pulled at a loose curl hanging across Toni's forehead.

On cue, a nurse came in pushing a wheelchair, and within minutes, Wyatt was on his way.

The air outside was a welcome respite from the recirculated air inside his room. And the cold, fresh scent of snow was infinitely better than the aroma of antiseptic. Wyatt gripped the arms of the wheelchair in anticipation of going home.

Just outside the doors, Toni turned away to speak to the nurse, and Lane had yet to arrive. For a brief moment, Wyatt was left to his own devices. He braced himself, angling his sore leg until he was able to stand, and then lifted his face and inhaled, letting the brisk draft of air circling the corner of the hospital have its way with the cobwebs in his mind. He'd been inside far too long.

A pharmacy across the street was doing a booming business, and Wyatt watched absently as customers came and went. As a van loaded with senior citizens backed up and drove away, a dark blue pickup truck pulled into the recently vacated parking space. He tried not to stare at the three people who got out, but they were such a range of sizes, he couldn't quit looking.

The older man was tall and broad beneath the heavy winter coat he wore. A red sock cap covered a thatch of thick graying hair, and a brush of mustache across his upper lip was several shades darker than the gray. The younger man was just as tall, and in spite of his own heavy clothing, obviously fit. His face was creased with laugh lines, and he moved with the grace and assurance of youth and good health.

It was the girl between them who caught Wyatt's eye. At first he thought she was little more than a child, and then the wind caught the front of her unbuttoned coat, and he got a glimpse of womanly breast and shapely hips before she pulled it together.

Her hair was the color of spun honey. Almost gold. Not quite white. Her lips were full and tilted in a grin at something one of the men just said, and Wyatt had a sudden wish that he'd been the one to make her smile.

No sooner had he thought it than she paused at the door, then stopped completely. He held his breath as she began to turn. When she caught his gaze, he imagined he felt her gasp, although he knew it was a foolish thing to consider. His mind wandered as he let himself feast upon her face.

So beautiful, Wyatt thought.

Why, thank you.

Wyatt was so locked into her gaze that he felt no surprise at the thoughts that suddenly drifted through his mind, or that he was answering them back in an unusual fashion.

You are welcome.

So, Wyatt Hatfield, you're going home?

Yes.

God be with you, soldier.

I'm no longer a soldier.

You will always fight for those you love.

"Here comes Lane!"

At the sound of Toni's voice, Wyatt blinked, then turned and stepped back as Lane pulled up to the curb. When he remembered to look up, the trio had disappeared into the store. He felt an odd sense of loss, as if he'd been disconnected from something he needed to know.

Bowing to the demands of his family's concerns, he let himself be plied with pillows and blankets. By the time they had him comfortable in the roomy back seat of their car, he was more than ready for the long journey home to begin.

They were past the boundary of Larner's Mill, heading out of Kentucky and toward Tennessee, when Wyatt's thoughts wandered back to the girl he'd seen on the street.

And as suddenly as he remembered her, he froze. His heart began to hammer inside his chest as he slowly sat up and stared out the back window at the small mountain town that was swiftly disappearing from sight.

"Dear God," he whispered, and wiped a shaky hand across his face.

"Wyatt, darling, are you all right?"

His sister's tone of voice was worried, the touch of her hand upon his shoulder gentle and concerned. Lane began to ease off the accelerator, thinking that Wyatt might be getting sick.

"I'm fine. I'm fine," he muttered, and dropped back onto the bed they'd made for him in the back seat.

There was no way he could tell them what he'd suddenly realized. There wasn't even any way he could explain it to himself. But he knew, as well as he knew his own name, that the conversation he'd had with that girl had been real. And yet understanding how it had happened was another thing altogether. He'd heard of silent communication, but this... this... thing that just happened... it was impossible.

"Then how did she know my name?" he murmured.

"What did you say?" Toni asked.

Wyatt turned his head into the pillow and closed his eyes. "Nothing, Sis. Nothing at all."

Chapter 2

Clouds moved in wild, scattered patterns above the Hatfield homestead, giving way to the swift air current blasting through the upper atmosphere. The clouds looked as unsettled as Wyatt felt. In his mind, it had taken forever to get back his health, and then even longer to gain strength. But now, except for a scar on his cheek and a leg that would probably ache for the rest of his life every time it rained, he was fine.

Problem was, he'd been here too long. He leaned forward, bracing his hands upon the windowsill and gazing out at the yard that spilled toward the banks of Chaney Creek, while his blood stirred to be on the move.

"The grass is beginning to green."

The longing in Wyatt's voice was obvious, but for what, Toni didn't know. Was he missing the companionship of his ex-wife, or was there something missing from his own inner self that he didn't know how to find?

"I know," Toni said, and shifted Joy to her other hip, trying not to mind that Wyatt was restless. He was her brother, and this *was* his home, but he was no longer the boy who'd chased her through the woods. He'd been a man alone for a long, long time.

She could hear the longing in his voice, and sensed his need to be on the move, but she feared that once gone, he would fall back into the depression in which they'd brought him home. Her mind whirled as she tried to think of something to cheer him up. Her daughter fidgeted in her arms, reaching for anything she could lay her hands on. Toni smiled, and kissed Joy on her cheek, thinking what they'd been doing this time last year, and the telegram that Wyatt had sent.

"Remember last year...when you sent the telegram? It came on Easter. Did you know that?"

Wyatt nodded, then grinned, also remembering how mad Toni had been at him when he'd interfered in her personal life.

"In a few weeks, it will be Easter again. Last year, someone gave us a little jumpsuit for Joy, complete with long pink ears on the outside of the hood. It made her look like a baby rabbit. The kids carried her around all day, fussing over who was going to have their picture taken next with the Easter Bunny."

Wyatt smiled, and when Joy leaned over, trying to stick her hand in the pot on the stove, he took the toddler from his sister's arms, freeing her to finish the pudding she was stirring.

Joy instantly grabbed a fistful of his hair in each hand and began to pull. Wyatt winced, then laughed, as he started to unwind her tiny hands from the grip they had on his head.

"Hey, puddin' face. Don't pull all of Uncle Wyatt's hair out. He's going to need it for when he's an old man."

Joy chortled gleefully as it quickly became a game, and for a time, Wyatt's restlessness was forgotten in his delight with the child.

It was long into the night when the old, uneasy feelings began to return. Wyatt paced the floor beside his bed until he was sick of the room, then slipped out of the house to stand on the porch. The moonless night was so thick and dark that it seemed airless. Absorbing the quiet, he let it surround him. As a kind of peace began to settle, he sat down on the steps, listening to the night life that abounded in their woods.

He kept telling himself that it was the memories of the wreck, and the lost days in between, that kept him out of bed. If he lay down, he would sleep. If he slept, he would dream. Nightmares of snow and blood, of pain and confusion. But that wasn't exactly true. It was the memory of a woman's voice that wouldn't let go of his mind.

You will always fight for those you love.

Eliminating the obvious, which he took to mean his own family, exactly what did that mean? Even more important, how the hell had that...that thing...happened between them?

Toni had told him more than once that he'd survived the wreck for a reason, and that one day he'd know why. But Wyatt wanted answers to questions he didn't even know how to ask. In effect, he felt as though he were living in a vacuum, waiting for someone to break the seal.

Yet Wyatt Hatfield wasn't the only man that night at a breaking point. Back in Larner's Mill, Kentucky, a man named Carter Foster was at the point of no return, trying to hold on to his sanity and his wife, and doing a poor job of both.

Carter paced the space in front of their bed, watching with growing dismay as Betty Jo began to put on another layer of makeup. As if the dress she was wearing wasn't revealing enough, she was making herself look like a whore. Her actions of late seemed to dare him to complain.

"Now, sweetheart, I'm not trying to control you, but I think I have a right to know where you're going. How is it going to look to the townspeople if you keep going out at night without me?"

He hated the whine in his voice, but couldn't find another way to approach his wife of eleven years about her latest affair. That she was having them was no secret. That the people of Larner's Mill must never find out was of the utmost importance to him. In his profession, appearances were everything.

Betty Jo arched her perfectly painted eyebrows and then stabbed a hair pick into her hair, lifting the back-combed nest she'd made of her dark red tresses to add necessary inches to her height. Ignoring Carter's complaint, she stepped back from the full-length mirror, running her hands lightly down her buxom figure in silent appreciation. That white knit dress she'd bought yesterday looked even better on than it had on the hanger.

"Betty Jo, you didn't answer me," Carter said, unaware that his voice had risen a couple of notes.

Silence prevailed as she ran her little finger across her upper, then lower lip, smoothing out the Dixie Red lipstick she'd applied with a flourish. When she rubbed her lips together to even out the color, Carter shuddered, hating himself for still wanting her. He couldn't remember the last time she put those lips anywhere on him.

"Carter, honey, you know a woman like me needs her space. With you stuck in that stuffy old courtroom all day, and in your office here at home all night, what am I to do?"

The pout on her lips made him furious. At this stage of their marriage, that baby-faced attitude would get her nowhere.

"But you're *my* wife," Carter argued. "It just isn't right that you... that men..." He took a deep breath and then puffed out his cheeks in frustration, unaware that it made him look like a bullfrog.

Betty Jo pivoted toward him, then stepped into her shoes, relishing the power that the added height of the three-inch heels gave her. She knew that if she had had college to do over again, she would have married the jock, not the brain. This poor excuse for a man was losing his hair and sporting a belly that disgusted her. When he walked, it swayed lightly from side to side like the big breasts of a woman who wore no support. She liked tight, firm bellies and hard muscles. There was nothing hard on Carter Foster. Not even periodically. To put it bluntly, Betty Jo Foster was an unsatisfied woman in the prime of her life.

Ignoring his petulant complaints as nothing but more of the same, she picked up her purse. To her surprise, he grabbed her by the forearm and all but shook her. The purse fell between them, lost in the unexpected shuffle of feet.

"Damn it, Betty Jo! You heard me! This just isn't right!"

"Hey!" she said, then frowned. She couldn't remember the last time Carter had raised his voice to her. She yanked, trying to pull herself free from his grasp, but to her dismay, his fingers tightened.

"Carter! You're hurting me!"

"So what?" he snarled, and shoved her backward onto their bed. "You're hurting me."

A slight panic began to surface. He never got angry. At least he never *used* to. Without thinking, she rolled over on her stomach to keep from messing up her hair, and started to crawl off of the bed. But turning her back on him was her first and last mistake. Before she could get up, Carter came down on top of her, pushing her into the mattress, calling her names she didn't even know he knew.

Betty Jo screamed, but the sound had nowhere to go. The weight of his body kept pushing her deeper and deeper into the mattress, and when the bulk of him settled across her hips, and his shoes began snagging runs in her panty hose, she realized that he was sitting on her. In shock, she began to fight.

Flailing helplessly, her hands clenched in the bedspread as she tried unsuccessfully to maneuver herself out from under him. Panic became horror as his hands suddenly circled her neck. The more she kicked and bounced, the tighter he squeezed.

A wayward thought crossed her mind that he'd messed up her hair and that Dixie Red lipstick would not wash out of the bedspread. It was the last of her worries as tiny bursts of lights began to go off behind her eyelids. Bright, bright, brighter, they burned until they shattered into one great, blinding-white explosion.

As suddenly as it had come, the rage that had taken him into another dimension began to subside. Carter shuddered and shuddered as his hands slowly loosened, and when he went limp atop her body, guilt at his unexpected burst of temper began to surface. He'd never been a physical sort of man, and didn't quite know how to explain this side of himself.

"Damn it, Betty Jo, I'm real sorry this happened, but you've been driving me to it for years."

Oddly enough, Betty Jo had nothing to say about his emotional outburst, and he wondered, as he crawled off her butt, why he hadn't done this years earlier? Maybe if he'd asserted himself when all of her misbehaving began, brute force would never have been necessary.

He smoothed down his hair, then wiped his sweaty palms against the legs of his slacks. Even from here, he could still smell the scent of her perfume upon his skin.

"Get up, Betty Jo. There's no need to pout. You always get your way, whether I like it or not."

Again, she remained silent. Carter's gaze ran up, then down her body, noting as it did, that he'd ruined her hose and smudged her dress. When she saw what he'd done to the back of her skirt, she would be furious.

"Okay, fine," Carter said, and started to walk away.

As he passed the foot of the bed, one of her shoes suddenly popped off the end of her heel and stabbed itself into the spread. He paused, starting to make an ugly comment about the fact that she was undressing for the wrong man, when something about her position struck him as odd. He leaned over the bed frame and tentatively ran his forefinger across the bottom of her foot. Her immobility scared the hell out of him. Betty Jo was as ticklish as they came.

"Oh, God," Carter muttered, and ran around to the edge of the bed, grabbing her by the shoulder. "Betty Jo, this isn't funny!"

He rolled her onto her back, and when he got a firsthand look at the dark, red smear of lipstick across her face and her wide, sightless eyes staring up at him, he began to shake.

"Betty, honey..."

She didn't move.

He thumped her in the middle of the chest, noting absently that she was not wearing a bra, and then started to sweat.

"Betty Jo, wake up!" he screamed, and pushed up and down between her breasts, trying to emulate CPR techniques he didn't actually know.

The only motion he got out of her was a lilt and a sway from her buxom bosom as he hammered about her chest, trying to make her breathe.

"No! God, no!"

Suddenly he jerked his hands to his stomach, as if he'd been burned by the touch of her skin. To his utter dismay, he felt bile rising, and barely made it to the bathroom before it spewed.

Several hours later, he heard the hall clock strike two times, and realized that, in four hours, it would be time to get up. He giggled at the thought, then buried his face in his hands. That was silly. How could one get up, when one had never been down? Betty Jo's body lay right where he'd left it, half-on, half-off the bed, as if he wasn't sure what to do next.

And therein lay Carter's problem. He *didn't* know what to do next. Twice since the deed, he'd reached for the phone to call the police, and each time he'd paused, remembering what would happen when they came. There was no way he could explain that it was really all her fault. That she'd ruined him and his reputation by tarnishing her own.

And that was when it struck him. It *was* her fault. And by God, he shouldn't have to pay!

Suddenly, a way out presented itself, and he bolted from the chair and began rolling her up in the stained bedspread, then fastening it in place with two of his belts. One he buckled just above her head, the other at her ankles. He stepped back to survey his work, and had an absent thought that Betty Jo would hate knowing that she was going to her Maker looking like a tamale. Without giving himself time to reconsider, he threw her over his shoulder and carried her, fireman style, out of the kitchen and into the attached garage, dumping her into the trunk of his car.

Grabbing a suitcase from the back of a closet, he raced to their bedroom and began throwing items of her clothing haphazardly into the bag, before returning to the car. As he tossed the suitcase in the trunk with her body, he took great satisfaction in the fact that he had to lie on the trunk to get it closed.

As he backed from the garage and headed uptown toward an all-night money machine, the deviousness of his own thoughts surprised him. He would never have imagined himself being able to carry off something like this, yet it was happening just the same. If he was going to make this work, it had to look like Betty Jo took money with her when she ran. With this in mind, he continued toward the town's only ATM.

As he pulled up, the spotlight above the money machine glared in his eyes. He jumped out of the car, and with a sharp blow of his fist, knocked out the Plexiglas and the bulb, leaving himself in the bank drive-through in sudden darkness. Minutes later, with the cash in his pocket, he was back in the car and heading out of town toward the city dump.

Ever thankful that Larner's Mill was too small-town in its thinking to ever put up a gate or a lock, Carter drove right through and up to the pit without having to brake for anything more than a possum ambling across the road in the dark.

When he got out, he was shaking with a mixture of exertion and excitement. As he threw the suitcase over the edge, he took a deep breath, watching it bounce end over end, down the steep embankment. When he lifted his wife from the trunk and sent her after it, he started to grin. But the white bedspread in which she was wrapped stood out like a beacon in the night. He could just imagine what would hit the fan if Betty Jo turned up in this condition. He had to cover up the spread.

It was while he was turning in a circle, looking for something with which to shovel, that he saw the bulldozer off to the side.

That's it, he thought. All he needed to do was shove some dirt down on top. Tomorrow was trash day. By the time the trash trucks made the rounds and dumped the loads, she'd be right where she belonged, buried with the rest of the garbage.

It took a bit for him to figure out how to work the bulldozer's controls, but desperation was a shrewd taskmaster, and Carter Foster was as desperate as they came. Within the hour, a goodly portion of dirt had been pushed in on top of the latest addition to the city dump, and Betty Jo Foster's burial was slightly less dignified than she would have hoped.

Minutes later, Carter was on his way home to shower and change. As he pulled into his garage, he pressed the remote control and breathed a great sigh of satisfaction as the door dropped shut behind him.

It was over!

His feet were dragging as he went inside, but his lawyer mind was already preparing the case he would present to his co-workers. Exactly how much he would be willing to humble himself was still in the planning stage. If they made fun of him behind his back because he'd been dumped, he didn't think he would care. The last laugh would be his.

Days later, while Betty Jo rotted along with the rest of the garbage in Larner's Mill, Glory Dixon was making her second sweep through the house, looking behind chairs and under cushions, trying to find her keys. But the harder she looked the more certain she was that someone else and not her carelessness was to blame.

Her brother came into the kitchen just as she dumped the trash onto the floor and began sorting through the papers. "J.C., have you seen my keys? I can't find them anywhere."

"Nope." He pulled the long braid she'd made of her hair. "Why don't you just psych them out?"

Glory ignored the casual slander he made of her psychic ability and removed her braid from his hand. "You know it doesn't work like that. I never know what I'm going to *see*. If I did, I would have told on you years ago for filching Granny's blackberry pies."

He was still laughing as their father entered the house by the back door.

"Honey, are you ready to go?" Rafe asked. "We've got a full morning and then some before we're through in town."

She threw up her hands in frustration. "I can't find my keys."

Her father shrugged, then had a thought. "Did you let that pup in the house last night?"

The guilty expression on her face was answer enough.

"Then there's your answer," he muttered. "What that blamed pooch hasn't already chewed up, he's buried. You'll be lucky if you ever see them again."

"Shoot," Glory muttered, and started out the door in search of the dog.

"Let it wait until we come home," Rafe said. "I've got keys galore. If you don't find yours, we'll get copies made of mine. Now grab your grocery list. Time's a'wastin'."

"Don't forget my Twinkies," J.C. said, and slammed the kitchen door behind him as he exited the house.

Glory grinned at her brother's request, then did as her father asked. As she and Rafe drove out of the yard, they could see the back end of the John Deere tractor turning the corner in the lane. J.C. was on his way to the south forty. It was time to work ground for spring planting.

Carter was playing the abandoned husband to the hilt, and oddly enough, enjoying the unexpected sympathy he was receiving from the townspeople. It seemed that they'd known about Betty Jo's high jinks for years, and were not the least surprised by this latest stunt.

As he stood in line at the teller's window at the bank, he was congratulating himself on the brilliance of his latest plan. This would be the icing on the cake.

"I need to withdraw some money from my savings account and deposit it into checking," he told the teller. "Betty Jo nearly cleaned me out."

The teller clucked sympathetically. "I'll need your account numbers," she said.

Carter looked slightly appalled. "I forgot to bring them."

"Don't you worry," the teller said. "I can look them up on the computer. It won't take but a minute."

As the teller hurried away, Carter relaxed, gazing absently around the room, taking note of who was begging and who was borrowing, when he saw a woman across the lobby staring at him as if he'd suddenly grown horns and warts. So intent was her interest, that he instinctively glanced down to see if his fly was unzipped, and then covertly brushed at his face, then his tie, checking for something that didn't belong. Except for her interest, all was as it should be.

Twice he looked away, thinking that when he would turn back, she'd surely be doing something else. To his dismay, her expression never wavered. By the time the teller came back, his impatience had turned to curiosity.

He leaned toward the teller, whispering in a low, urgent tone. "Who is that woman?"

The teller looked up as he pointed across the room at Glory.

"What woman?" she asked.

"The blonde beside that old man. The one who keeps staring this way."

The teller rolled her eyes and then snorted softly through her nostrils.

"Oh! Her! That's that crazy Glory Dixon and her father."

Dixon...I know that man. I hunted quail on his place last year with Tollet Faye and his boys.

The teller kept talking, unaware that Carter was turning pale. He was remembering the gossip he'd heard about the girl, and imagined she could see blood on him that wasn't really there.

"She fancies herself some sort of psychic. Claims that she can *see* into the future, or some such nonsense. Personally, I don't believe in that garbage. Now then . . . how much did you want to transfer?"

Carter was shaking. He told himself that he didn't believe in such things either, but his guilty conscience and Betty Jo's rotting body were hard to get past. He had visions of Glory Dixon standing up from her chair, pointing an accusing finger toward him, and screaming "murderer" to all who cared to hear.

And no sooner had the thought come than Glory uncrossed her legs. Believing her to be on the verge of a revelation, he panicked.

"I just remembered an appointment," he told the teller. "I'll have to come back later."

With that, he bolted out of the bank and across the street into an alley, leaving the teller to think what she chose. Moments later, the Dixons came out of the bank and drove away. He watched until he saw them turn into the parking lot of the diner on the corner, and then relaxed.

Okay, okay, maybe I made a big deal out of nothing, he told himself, and brushed at the front of his suit coat as he started back to his office. But the farther he walked, the more convinced he became that he was playing with fire if he didn't tie up his loose ends. Before he gave himself time to reconsider, he got into his car and drove out of town. He had no plan in mind. Only a destination.

The small frame house was nestled against a backdrop of Pine Mountain. A black-and-white pup lay on the front porch, gnawing on a stick. Carter watched until the puppy ambled off toward the barn, and then he waited a while longer, just to make sure that there was no one in sight. Off in the distance, the sound of a tractor could be heard as it plowed up and down a field. As he started toward the house, a light breeze lifted the tail of his suit coat.

He didn't know what he was going to do, but he told himself that something *must* be done, or all of his careful planning would be for nothing. If he was going to ignore the fact that Glory Dixon could reveal his secret, then he might as well have called the police the night of the crime, instead of going to all the trouble to conceal it.

Planks creaked upon the porch as it gave beneath his weight. He knocked, then waited, wondering what on earth he would say if someone actually answered. Then he knocked again and again, but no one came. He looked around the yard, assuring himself that he was still unobserved, and then threw his weight against the door. It popped like a cork out of a bottle, and before Carter could think to brace himself, he fell through the doorway and onto the floor before scrambling to his feet.

Now that he was inside, his thoughts scattered. Betty Jo's death had been an accident. What he was thinking of doing was premeditated murder. Yet the problem remained, how to hide one without committing the other. He stood in place, letting himself absorb the thought of the deed. And as he gazed around the room, his attention caught and then focused on the small heating stove in the corner.

It was fueled with gas.

He began to smile.

An idea was forming as he headed for the kitchen. His hands were shaking as he began to investigate the inner workings of the Dixons' cookstove. It didn't take long to find and then blow out the pilot light. As he turned on all the jets, he held his breath. The unmistakable hiss of escaping gas filled the quiet room.

With a sharp turn of his wrist, he turned even harder until one of the controls broke off in his hands. Let them try to turn that baby off, he thought, and hurried out of the kitchen.

Carter wasn't stupid. He knew that almost anything could ignite this—from a ringing telephone to the simple flick of a light switch when someone entered a room. And while he had no control over who came in the house first, he could at least make sure the house didn't blow with no one in it.

With his thumb and forefinger, he carefully lifted the receiver from the cradle and set it to one side. The loud, intermittent buzz of a phone off the hook mingled with the deadly hiss behind him.

Now that it was done, an anxiety to escape was overwhelming. Carter ran through the house and out onto the porch. Careful to pull the front door shut behind him, he jumped into his car and drove away while death filtered slowly throughout the rooms.

It was dusk. Dew was already settling upon the grass, and the sun, like Humpty-Dumpty, was about to fall beyond the horizon as Rafe Dixon drove into the yard and parked beneath the tree near the back door.

J.C. came out of the barn just as Rafe crawled out of the cab. Glory swung her legs out and then slid out of the seat, stretching wearily from the long ride. It felt good to be home. She couldn't wait to get in the house and trade her ropers for slippers, her blue jeans for shorts and the long-sleeved pink shirt she was wearing for one of J.C.'s old T-shirts. They went down past her knees, and felt soft as butter against her skin. They were her favorite items of clothing.

Their errands had taken longer than she'd expected, and she'd told herself more than once during the day that if she'd known all her father had planned to do, she wouldn't have gone. She leaned over the side of the truck bed and lifted the nearest sack into her arms.

"Right on time," Rafe shouted, and motioned his son to the sacks of groceries yet to be unloaded from the back of their truck. "Hey, boy, give us a hand."

J.C. came running. "Daddy! Look! I found another arrowhead today."

Both Rafe and Glory turned to admire his latest find. Collecting them had been J.C.'s passion since he'd found his first years ago. Now he was an avid collector and had more than one hundred of them mounted in frames and hanging on the walls of his room.

"That's a good one," Glory said, running her fingers over the hand-chipped edge, and marveling at the skill of the one who had made it. In spite of its obvious age, it was perfectly symmetrical in form.

"Groceries are gonna melt," Rafe warned.

J.C. grinned and winked at his little sister, then dropped the arrowhead into his pocket. He obliged his father by picking up a sack and then stopping to dig through the one Glory was holding.

"Hey, Morning Glory, did you remember my Twinkies?"

The childhood nickname made her smile as she took the package from her sack and dropped it into the one he was holding. But the urge to laugh faded as quickly as the world that began to slip out of focus.

Common sense told her that she was standing in the yard surrounded by those who loved her best, but it wasn't how she felt. She could barely hear her father's voice above the sound of her own heart breaking. Every breath that she took was a struggle, and although she tried over and over to talk, the words wouldn't come.

Struggling to come out of the fugue, she grabbed hold of the truck bed, desperate to regain her sense of self. Vaguely, she could hear her brother and father arguing over whose turn it was to do the dishes after supper. When sanity returned and she found the words to speak, they were at the back porch steps.

"Daddy! Wait," Glory shouted, as her father slipped the key in the lock.

Even from where she stood, she knew it was going to be too late.

"Hey, look! I think I just found your keys!" J.C. shouted, laughing and pointing at the puppy, coming out of the barn behind them.

It was reflex that made Glory turn. Sure enough, keys dangled from the corner of the pup's mouth as he chewed on the braided leather strap dangling from the ring.

And then it seemed as if everything happened in slow motion. She spun, her father's name on her lips as she started toward the house. In a corner of her mind, she was vaguely aware of J.C.'s surprised shout, and then the back door flew off the hinges and into the bed of the truck. The impact of the explosion threw Glory across the yard where she lay, unconscious.

When reason returned, the first things she felt were heat on her back, and the puppy licking her face. She groaned, unable to remember how she'd come to this position, and crawled to her knees before staggering to her feet. Something wet slid down her cheek, and when she touched it, her fingers came away covered in blood. And then she remembered the blast and spun.

She kept telling herself that this was all a bad dream, and that her brother would come out of the door with one Twinkie in his mouth and another in his hand. But it was impossible to ignore the thick, black coils of smoke snaking up from the burning timbers, marking the spot that had once been home.

Still unable to believe her eyes, she took several shaky steps forward.

"Daddy?" He didn't answer. Her voice rose and trembled as she repeated the cry. "Daaddee! No! No! God, no! Somebody help me!"

Something inside the inferno exploded. A fire within a fire. It was then that she began to scream.

Terror. Horror. Despair.

There were no words for what she felt. Only the devastating knowledge that she'd *seen* the end of those she loved most and had not been able to stop it.

She fell to her knees as gut-wrenching tears tore up her throat and out into the night. Heat seared her skin and scorched her hair as she considered walking into what was left of the pyre. All of her life she'd been separated from the crowd by the fact that she was different, and the only people who'd accepted and loved her for herself had been her father and brother. If they were gone, who would love her now?

And while she stared blindly at the orange and yellow tongues licking at what was left of her home, another image superimposed itself over the flames, and Glory found herself straining toward it, unable to believe what she saw.

A man! Walking through their house, running from room to room. She saw the backs of his hands as they hovered above the stove. Saw them twist...saw them turn...saw them kill. And then he ran, and all that she saw was the silhouette of his back as he moved out the door. The hair crawled on the back of her neck as a reality only Glory understood suddenly surfaced.

Oh, my God! This wasn't an accident!

It was a gut reaction, but she spun in fear, searching for a place to hide. In the dark, she stumbled, falling to her knees. Still in a panic to hide, she crawled, then ran, aiming for the dark, yawning maw of the barn door. Only when she was inside did she turn to look behind her, imagining him still out there...somewhere.

Why would someone want us dead? And no sooner had the thought come, than her answer followed. *It wasn't them. It was me who was supposed to die.*

She slipped even farther inside the barn, staring wide-eyed out into the night, unable to believe what her mind already knew. The guilt that came with the knowledge could have driven Glory over the edge of reason. But it didn't. She couldn't let her father and brother's killer get away with this.

But who...and why? Who could possibly care if she lived or died?

Instinct told her that it wasn't a stranger. But instinct was a poor substitute for facts, and Glory had none. The only thing she knew for sure was that she needed a plan, and she needed time.

There was no way of knowing how long she'd been unconscious, but neighbors were bound to see the fire and could be arriving any minute. A sense of self-preservation warned her that she must hide until she found someone she could trust. Within a day or so, the killer would know that two, not three people, had died in the fire, and then whoever had tried to hurt her would come looking again.

"Oh, God, I need help," she moaned, and then jumped with fright as something furry rubbed up against her leg. She knelt, wrapping her arms around the puppy's neck, and sobbed. "You're not what I needed, but you're all I've got, aren't you, fella?"

A wet tongue slid across her cheek, and Glory moaned as the puppy instinctively licked at the blood on her face. She pushed him away, then stood. Her eyes narrowed above lashes spiked with tears, her lips firmed, her chin tilted as she stared at the fire.

Daddy...J.C....I swear on Mother's grave...and on yours, that I will find him. All I need is a little help.

No sooner had that thought come than an image followed. A man's face centered within her mind. A man who had been a soldier. A man who understood killing. A stranger who, right now, Glory trusted more than friends.

If I knew where you were, Wyatt Hatfield, I would call in a debt.

But the fantasy of finding a stranger in a world full of people was more than she could cope with. Right now she had to hide, and there was no family left alive to help her.

Except...

She took a deep breath. "Granny."

The puppy heard the tone of her voice, and whined softly from somewhere behind her, uncertain what it was that she wanted, yet aware that a word had been uttered it did not understand.

Granny Dixon's house sat just across the hollow as it had for the past one hundred years, a small shelter carved out of a dense wilderness of trees and bush. As a child, Granny had been Glory's only link with another female, and she had often spent the day in her lap, lulled by the sound of her voice and the stories she would tell.

Glory took a deep breath and closed her eyes, imagining she could hear her granny's voice now.

When you tire of them menfolks, child, you just come to old Granny. We women hafta stick together, now, don't we?

Her saving grace was that Granny Dixon's cabin was just as she'd left it. Its presence could be the answer to her prayer. She was counting on the fact that few would remember its existence. Rafe had promised his mother that he wouldn't touch or change a single thing in her home until they'd put her in the ground. In a way, Glory was thankful that Granny's mind was almost gone. At least she would be spared the grief of knowing that her only son and grandson had beat her to heaven.

And while the cabin was there, food was not. Glory made a quick trip through the root cellar, using the light from the fire as a guide, she ran her fingers along the jars until she found what she wanted. She came up and out with a jar of peaches in one hand and a quart of soup in the other. It would be enough to keep her going until she figured out what to do.

And then she and the puppy vanished into the darkness of the tree line. Minutes later, the sounds of cars and trucks could be heard grinding up the hill. Someone had seen the fire. Someone else would rescue what was left of her loved ones. Glory had disappeared.

Chapter 3

The scream came without warning. Right in the middle of a dream he could no longer remember. Wyatt sat straight up in bed, his instinct for survival working overtime as he imagined Toni or the baby in dire need of help. In seconds, he was pulling on a pair of jeans and running in an all-out sprint as he flew out of the door.

He slid to a stop in the hallway outside the baby's room and then looked inside. Nothing was amiss. He sighed with relief at the sight of the toddler asleep on her tummy with her blanket clutched tightly in one fist. She was fine, so Toni hadn't screamed about her. That meant...

Fearing the worst, he crept farther down the hall, praying that he wouldn't surprise a burglar in the act of murder, and wondering why on earth Lane Monday wasn't raising all kinds of hell in response to his wife's screams.

More than a year ago, Lane had taken down a man the size of a mountain to save his sister's life. He couldn't imagine Lane letting someone sneak up on them and do his family harm. Yet in Wyatt's mind, he knew that whatever had made Toni scream couldn't have been good.

The door was ajar so Lane or Toni could hear the baby if she cried. Wyatt pushed it aside and looked in. Lane was flat on his back and sound asleep, with Toni held gently, but firmly, within the shelter of one arm. Even from here, Wyatt could hear the soft, even sounds of their breathing.

"Thank God," he muttered, and eased out of their room the same way he'd come in, trying to convince himself that he'd been dreaming. *But it sounded so real.*

He made his way through the house, careful not to step on the boards that creaked, and headed for the kitchen to get a drink. He wasn't particularly thirsty, but at the moment, crawling back in that bed did not hold much interest. His heart was still pounding as he took a glass from the cabinet and ran water in the sink, letting it cool in the pipes before filling a glass.

The water tasted good going down, and panic was subsiding. If he stretched the facts, he could convince himself that his heart rate was almost back to normal. It was just a bad dream. That was all. Just a bad dream.

Wyatt.

"What?"

He spun toward the doorway, expecting Toni to be standing there with a worried expression on her face. There was nothing but a reflection of the outside security light glancing off the living room window and onto the floor.

Wyatt... Wyatt Hatfield.

His stomach muscles clenched, and he took a deep breath. "Jesus Christ."

Help me.

He started to shake. "This isn't happening."

God... Oh, God... help. I need help.

He slammed the glass onto the cabinet and stalked out of the kitchen and onto the back porch, inhaling one after the other of deep, lung-chilling breaths of cool night air. When he could think without wanting to throw up, he sat down on the steps with a thump and buried his face in his hands, then instantly yanked them off his face, unable to believe what he'd felt.

His hands were cold...and they were wet. He lifted his fingers to his cheeks and traced the tracks of his tears.

"I'm crying? For God's sake, I'm crying? What's wrong with me? I don't cry, and when I do, I will sure as hell need a reason."

But anger could not replace the overwhelming sense of despair that was seeping into his system. He felt weak and drained, hopeless and helpless. The last time he'd felt this down had been the day he'd regained consciousness in a Kentucky hospital and seen the vague image of his sister's face hovering somewhere above his bed.

He remembered thinking that he'd known his sister was an angel to have put up with so many brothers all of her life, but he'd never imagined that all angels in heaven looked like her. It was the next day before he realized that he hadn't died, and by that time, worrying about the faces of angels had become secondary to the mind-bending pain that had come to stay.

Out of the silence of the night, a dog suddenly bugled in a hollow somewhere below Chaney Creek. The sound was familiar. He shuddered, trying to relax as his nerves began to settle. This was something to which he could relate. Someone was running hounds. Whether it was raccoon, bobcat or something else that they hunted, it rarely mattered. To the hunters, the dogs and the hunt were what counted.

He listened, remembering days far in his past when he and his brothers had done the same, nights when they'd sat around a campfire swapping lies that sounded good in the dark, drinking coffee made in a pot that they wouldn't have fed the pigs out of in the light of day and listening to their hounds running far and wide across the hills and in the deep valleys.

He sighed, then dropped his head in his hands, wishing for simpler times, saner times. He wondered where he'd gone wrong. He'd married Shirley full of good intent, then screwed up her life, as well as his own.

And now this!

He didn't know what to think. He'd survived a wreck that should have killed him. But if it had messed with his head in a way they hadn't expected, then making a new life for himself had suddenly become more complicated than he'd planned.

Help. I need help.

He lifted his head, like an animal sniffing the air. His nostrils flared, his eyes narrowed to dark, gleaming slits. This time, he knew he wasn't dreaming. He was wide-awake and barefoot on his sister's back porch. And he knew what he heard. The voice was inside his head. He shivered, then shifted his gaze, looking out at the darkness, listening... waiting.

When the first weak rays of sunlight changed the sky from black to baby blue, Wyatt got to his feet and walked into the house. It had taken all night, and more soul-searching than he'd realized he had in him, but he knew what he had to do.

Somewhere down the hall, Joy babbled, and Toni laughed. Lane smiled to himself at the sound, buttoning his shirt on his way to the kitchen to start the coffee. He walked in just in time to see Wyatt closing the back door.

"Up kinda early, aren't you, buddy?" Lane asked, and then froze at the expression on Wyatt's face, grabbing him by the arm. "What's wrong?"

Wyatt tried to explain, but it just wouldn't come. "I need to borrow one of your cars."

Lane headed for the coffeepot, giving himself time to absorb the unexpected request, and wondering about the intensity of Wyatt's voice. Yet refusing him was not a consideration.

"It's yours," he said.

Measuring his words, along with coffee and water, Lane turned on the coffeemaker before taking Wyatt to task. "Mind telling me where you're going so early in the morning? This isn't exactly Memphis, and to my knowledge there's no McDonald's on the next corner cooking up sausage biscuits."

"I've got to go," Wyatt repeated. "Someone needs me."

Lane's posture went from easy to erect. "Why didn't you say so? I'll help."

Wyatt shook his head. "No, you don't understand. Hell, for that matter, I don't understand. All I know is, last night while I was wide-awake and watching dark turn to day, someone kept calling my name."

The oddity of the remark was not lost on Lane, but trespassing on another man's business was not his way.

"Do you know where you're going?" Lane asked.

Wyatt eyed his brother-in-law, wondering if he would understand what he was about to say.

"I think, back to where it all started," Wyatt said quietly, remembering the woman outside of the hospital and the way he'd heard her voice...and she, his. He'd ignored it then. He couldn't ignore it any longer.

"Back to Kentucky?" Lane asked, unable to keep surprise out of his voice.

Wyatt nodded.

Wisely, Lane stifled the rest of his concerns. While he didn't understand what Wyatt was trying to say, he trusted the man implicitly. He swung a wide hand across his shoulder and thumped him lightly on the back.

"Then let's get you packed," Lane said. "It's an all-day drive."

Wyatt had been on this road before. Last winter. And with no destination in mind. This time, he knew where he was going. He even knew why. What he didn't understand was the pull that drew him down the road. The closer he came to the great Pine Mountain, the more certain he became that he was on the right track. He drove relentlessly, stopping only when necessary, compelled to reach Larner's Mill before nightfall. He couldn't get past the increasing panic he felt, or the fact that he was listening for a voice that had suddenly gone silent.

The sun was halfway between zenith and horizon when he pulled into Larner's Mill, but the relief he imagined he would feel was not there. In fact, the urgency of his quest seemed to have taken on darker overtones. An unsettled feeling had taken root in his belly, and try as he might, there was no rational explanation for the emotion, other than the uncertainty of his quest.

When he pulled into the parking lot of the small community hospital and got out, he found himself wanting to run. But to where? Instead, he took a deep breath and entered through the emergency room doors.

A nurse glanced up from a desk near the door. "May I help you, sir?"

"I want to talk to one of your doctors," Wyatt said.

She slipped a fresh page on a clipboard and held a pen poised above the lines.

"Your name?" she asked.

"Wyatt Hatfield," he said.

"And what are your symptoms?"

"I'm not sick. But I was here before. Last winter, in fact. I had a car wreck during a blizzard. I was..."

"I remember you," she cried, and jumped to her feet. "Dr. Steading was your doctor. You were the talk of the hospital for some time."

"Why was that?" Wyatt asked.

"You know," she said. "About how lucky you were to have had that donor show up when she did. With such a rare blood type, and the blizzard and all, there was no way we could access the blood banks in the bigger cities as we normally might have done."

The expression on Wyatt's face stilled as he absorbed the nurse's unwitting revelation.

"Yes, I suppose you're right. I am one lucky man." He gave her a smile he didn't feel. "So, could I talk to Dr. Steading? There are some things about the accident that I don't remember. I thought maybe he could give me some help."

"I'll see," she said, and shortly thereafter, Wyatt found himself on the way through the corridors to an office in the other wing. When he saw the name on the door, his pulse accelerated. He knocked and then entered.

"Dr. Steading?"

Amos Steading arched one bushy eyebrow, and then stood and reached over his desk, his hand outstretched.

"You, sir, look a damn sight healthier than the last time I saw you," he said, his gravelly voice booming within the small confines of the office.

Wyatt caught the handshake and grinned. "I suppose I feel better, too," he said.

Steading frowned. "Suppose?"

Wyatt took the chair offered him, and tried not to show his uneasiness, but it seemed it was impossible to hide anything, including an emotion, from the grizzled veteran.

Steading persisted. "So, did you come all this way just to shake my hand, or are you going to spit it out?"

Wyatt took a deep breath, and then started talking.

"I know I was in serious condition when I was brought in here," he said.

"No," Steading interrupted. "You were dying, boy."

Wyatt paled, but persisted. "The reason I came is...I need to know if, in your opinion, I could have suffered any residual brain damage."

Steading frowned. That was the last thing he expected to hear this man say. His eyes were clear and bright, his manner straightforward, and he'd walked into his office like a man with a purpose. None of this hinted at any sort of mental disability.

"Why?" Steading asked. "Are you suffering memory loss, or..."

Wyatt shook his head. "No, nothing like that."

"So...?"

"So, I want to know what exactly happened to my head," Wyatt growled.

"You had one hell of a concussion. I wouldn't have been surprised if you'd gone into a coma."

Wyatt started to relax. Maybe this would explain what he thought he'd heard. Maybe his head was still lost in some sort of fugue.

"But you didn't," Steading added. "After surgery, you pretty much sailed through recovery. There's a lot to be said for a young, healthy body."

"Damn," Wyatt muttered beneath his breath. One theory shot to hell.

This time, both of Steading's eyebrows arched. "You're disappointed?"

Wyatt shrugged. "It would have explained a lot."

"Like what?" Steading persisted.

The last thing he intended to admit, especially to a doctor, was that he was hearing voices. They'd lock him up in a New York minute. He changed the subject.

"I understand that I was given transfusions."

"Transfusion," Steading corrected. "And damned lucky to have that one. Whole blood made the difference. I'm good, but I don't think I could have pulled you through surgery without it, and that's the gospel truth."

"I'd like to thank the person who cared enough to come out in such a storm. If it wouldn't be against hospital policy, could you give me a name?"

Amos Steading's face fell. He rocked backward in his chair, and gazed at a corner of the ceiling, trying to find the right way to say the words.

"If that's a problem," Wyatt said, "I'll understand. It's just that I'm trying to make sense of some things in my life, and I thought that retracing my steps through that night might help."

"It isn't that," Steading finally said. "It's just that you're about a day too late."

Wyatt straightened. An inner warning was going off that told him he wasn't going to like this.

"That young woman . . . the one who gave you blood . . . she, along with her family, died sometime last night. I heard about it when I came in to work this morning."

Oh, God! Oh, no! Was that what I heard... the sound of someone crying out for help?

Wyatt's voice broke, and he had to clear his throat to get out the words. "How did it happen? Was it a car accident?"

"No, a fire at the home."

Wyatt shuddered, trying not to think of the horror of burning alive.

"Yes, and a real shame, too, what with her and her brother so young and all. That night when the EMT dragged her into the room where I was working on you, I remember thinking she was just a kid. Wasn't any bigger than a minute, and all that white blond hair and those big blue eyes, it's no wonder I misjudged her age."

It was the description that caught Wyatt's attention. He'd seen a woman who looked like that. A woman with hair like angel's wings, whom *he'd* mistaken for a girl until an errant wind had moved her coat, revealing a womanly figure.

He blanched, and covered his face in his hands. There was something else about that woman that had been unique, and only Wyatt was privy to the fact.

Somehow, when his guard had been down and his defenses weak, she'd insinuated herself within his thoughts. He didn't know how it had happened, but after what he'd just heard, he was firmly convinced that she'd done it again last night, presumably at the point of her death.

"My God," he muttered. Leaning forward, he rested his elbows upon his knees and stared at a pattern on the carpet until the colors all ran together.

"Sorry to be the bearer of such bad news," Steading said. "Are you all right?"

Wyatt shrugged. "I didn't really know her. It was her kindness that I wanted to acknowledge. It's a damn shame I came too late." And then he had a thought. "I'd like to see. Where she lived, I mean. Do you know?"

"Nope, I can't say that I do. But you could ask at the police department. Anders Conway could tell you."

Wyatt stood. "I've taken up enough of your time, Dr. Steading. Thanks for your help."

Steading shrugged.

Wyatt was at the door, when he paused and then turned. "Doctor?"

"Yes?"

"What was her name?"

"Dixon. Glory Dixon."

A twist of pain spiked, and then centered in the region of Wyatt's heart. "Glory," he repeated, more to himself than to the doctor, then closed the door behind him.

"Damn," Amos muttered. "In fact...damn it all to hell."

Wyatt navigated the winding road with absentminded skill. He'd gone over the side of one Kentucky mountain. It was enough. Remembering the directions he'd been given, he kept a sharp watch for a twisted pine, aware that he was to turn left just beyond it. As he rounded a bend, the last rays of the setting sun suddenly spiked through a cloud and the waning light hit the top of a tree. Wyatt eased off the gas. It was the pine. He began looking for the road, and sure enough, a few yards beyond, a narrow, one-laned dirt road took a sharp turn to the left. Wyatt followed it to its destination.

The clearing came without warning. One minute the road was shadowed and treelined, and then suddenly he was braking to a sliding halt as his fingers tightened upon the steering wheel, and his breath came in short, painful gasps.

"Dear God."

There was little else to say as he got out of the car and walked toward the blackened timbers. Yellow police tape was tied from tree to tree and then from fence post to the bumper of what was left of a pickup truck—a vivid reminder that death had occurred here.

The fact that the shell of a washing machine and dryer still stood, while a house was gone, seemed obscene, too vivid a reminder of how frail human life truly was. Smoke continued to rise from several locations as cross beams and a stack of something no longer identifiable smoldered. An unnatural heat lingered in the cooler evening air.

Wyatt stuffed his hands in his pockets and hunched his shoulders against the weight of despair that hung over the area. Last night he'd heard a cry for help and had been unable to respond, and yet when *he'd* needed help most, she had come. The burden of his guilt was almost more than he could bear.

"Ah, God, Glory Dixon. It *was* you, wasn't it? I am so, so sorry. If I had known, I would have helped."

"Do you swear?"

Wyatt spun. This time the voice he just heard had been behind him, not in his head. And when a young woman walked out of the trees, he thought he was seeing a ghost. It was her! The woman from the street!

He looked over his shoulder at the ruins, and then back at her, unable to believe his own eyes. Suddenly, a puppy darted out of the woods behind her and began pouncing around her feet. Wyatt stared. He'd never heard of a ghost with a dog.

He stood his ground, fighting the urge to run. "Are you real?"

Glory sighed, and Wyatt imagined he felt the air stir from her breath. And then she was standing before him, and he looked down and got lost in a silver-blue gaze. An errant breeze lifted the hair from her neck and shoulders, and for a moment, it seemed to float on the air like wings. Once again, Wyatt was reminded of angels.

"Why did you come?" Glory whispered. "How did you know?"

The sound of her voice broke the spell, and Wyatt blinked, trying to regain a true focus on the world around him. Unable to believe his eyes, he grasped a portion of her hair between his fingers. Although it was silken in texture, there was nothing unearthly about it.

"I heard you call my name," he muttered, as he watched the hair curl around his finger.

Glory gasped, startled by what he'd revealed, and stepped back. *Dear God, did I give him more than my blood? Have I given away part of myself?*

Then drawn by the horror she couldn't ignore, her gaze shifted to the pile of blackened timbers, and without warning, tears pooled and then tracked down her cheeks in silent misery. Wyatt groaned and opened his arms, and to his surprise, she walked into his embrace with no hesitation.

In his mind, holding her was like trying to hold sunshine. She was light, fragile, and seemed to sway within his arms with every beat of his heart. Her shoulders shook with grief, and yet her sobs were silent, as if the agony just wouldn't let go.

"I'm so sorry about your family," Wyatt said softly, and closed the gap between his hands until she stood locked firmly within his grasp. "But everyone's going to be so happy to learn that you survived. As soon as you're able, I'll take you back to town."

She went limp, and for a moment, he thought she was going to faint. Instead, it seemed more of a physical retreat. Sensing her uneasiness, he immediately turned her loose.

"I can't go back. Not yet," Glory said quietly.

Wyatt couldn't hide his surprise. "Why ever not?"

"Because this wasn't an accident. Because someone tried to kill me, and my daddy and brother suffered for it."

Before he thought, Wyatt had her by the arms. "What the hell do you mean, 'someone tried to kill me'? Are you saying that this fire was set?"

"At first it wasn't a fire, it was an explosion. The fire came afterward."

Unable to look at him, she turned away. He was bound to doubt. Everyone always did.

"Well, hell," Wyatt muttered. "Then you need to tell the police chief. He'll know what to do."

Glory spun, and for the first time since she'd walked out of the woods, Wyatt saw a light in her eyes and heard fire in her voice.

"No! You don't understand! They'll come tomorrow... or the next day... to go through the ruins. When they do, they're only going to find two bodies, not three. And then whoever it was that did this will try again. I need time to try and figure out what to do."

Wyatt frowned. "What do you mean, whoever did this? I thought you knew."

She shook her head.

"Then how do you know it wasn't an accident?"

Glory lifted her chin, silencing his argument with a piercing look he couldn't ignore.

"I *see* things. Sometimes I know things before they happen, sometimes I see them happen. But however my knowledge comes... I know what I know."

Wyatt took a deep breath. He knew for a fact that he'd been hearing some things of his own. Right now, it wasn't in him to doubt that she might... just might... be able to do more than hear. What if she could see? What if she was for real?

"Are you telling me that you're psychic?"

"Some people call it that."

Wyatt went quiet as he considered the ramifications of her admission.

"Why did you come to the hospital to help me?"

Her chin trembled, but her words were sure. "I *saw* your accident as it happened. I heard your cry for help... and because I could come, I did."

Daring the risk of rejection, Wyatt reached out and cupped her face with his hand. To his joy, she withstood his familiarity, in fact, even seemed to take strength from the comfort.

"How can I thank you, Glory Dixon?"

"By not giving me away. By helping me stay alive until I can figure out why... and who... and..."

"It's done. Tell me what to do first."

Again, she swayed on her feet. Wyatt reached out, but she pushed him away. Her gaze searched the boundary of trees around the rubble, constantly on the lookout for a hidden menace. Fear that she would be found before it was time was a constant companion.

"You need to hide your car. Maybe drive it around behind the barn, out in the pasture."

"Where are you...uh...?"

"Hiding?"

He nodded.

"When you've parked your car, I'll show you, but we need to hurry. There'll be no moon tonight, and the woods are dense and dark."

Wyatt headed for his car, and as he followed her directions through the narrow lanes, wondered what on earth he'd let himself in for. Yet as the beam of his headlights caught and then held on the beauty of her face and the pain he saw hidden in her eyes, he knew he didn't give a damn. She'd helped him. The least he could do was repay the debt.

A few minutes later, they walked away from the site, following what was left of a road overgrown with bushes and weeds. The air was already damp. Dew was heavy on the grass, blotching the legs of their jeans and seeping into the soles of their shoes. The bag Wyatt was carrying kept getting caught on low-hanging limbs, but Glory seemed to pass through the brush without leaving a trace. It would seem that her fragile, delicate appearance was deceiving. He suspected that she moved through life as she did through these trees—with purpose.

The pup ran between their legs, barking once from the delight of just being alive. He ran with his nose to the ground and his long, puppy ears flopping, yet a single word from Glory and he hushed.

Something silent and dark came out of a tree overhead and sailed across their line of vision. Instinctively, Glory threw up her hands and gasped. Wyatt caught her as she started to run.

"I think it was an owl," he said gently, and held her until she had calmed.

"Sorry," she said. "I'm not usually so jumpy. It's just that..." Tears were thick in her voice as she pushed herself out of his arms and resumed their trek.

Visibility was nearly zero, yet Glory moved with a sure sense of direction and Wyatt followed without question. Night creatures hid as the pair walked past, then scurried back into their holes, suddenly unsure of their world. Wyatt heard the rustling in the deep, thick grass, and even though he knew what it was that he heard, he couldn't prevent a shiver of anxiety. This was a far cry from the safety and comfort of the Tennessee home where he'd been recuperating. It reminded him too much of secret maneuvers he'd been on in places he'd rather forget.

He clutched at the bag over his shoulder and caught himself wishing it was a gun in his hands, and not a duffel bag. Twice as they walked, Glory paused, listening carefully to the sounds of the woods through which they walked, judging what she heard against what she knew should be there. After a time, she would resume the trek without looking back, trusting that because Wyatt had come, he would still follow.

Just when he was wondering if they would walk all night, they entered a clearing. Again Glory paused, this time clutching the sleeve of his shirt as she stared through the darkness, searching for something that would feel out of place.

The instinct that had carried Wyatt safely through several tours of duty told him that all was well.

"It's okay," he said, and this time he took her by the hand and led the way toward the cabin on the other side of the yard.

The night could not disguise the humble quality of the tiny abode. It was no more than four walls and a slanted, shingle roof, a rock chimney that angled up from the corner of the roof, with two narrow windows at the front of the cabin that stared back at them like a pair of dark, accusing eyes.

Glory shivered apprehensively, then slipped the key from her jeans. As her fingers closed around it, she was thankful that her daddy had kept this one hidden at the cabin, or she would have been unable to get inside the night before.

Wyatt listened to the woods around them as she worked the lock, and when the door swung open with a slight, warning squeak, she took his hand and led him through with an odd little welcome.

"We're home," she said.

As he followed her inside, he had the oddest sensation that what she said was true.

Chapter 4

"Don't turn on the light."

Wyatt's fingers paused on the edge of the switch. The panic in her voice was too real to ignore.

"You're serious about this, aren't you?"

Glory nodded, then realized that in the dark, Wyatt Hatfield couldn't see her face.

"Yes, I'm serious. Please wait here. I have a candle."

Wyatt did as he was told. He set down his duffel bag and then closed the door behind him, thinking that the dark in here was as thick as the woods through which they'd just walked. Moments later, he heard the rasp of a match to wood, focused on the swift flare of light and watched a wick catch and burn. And then she turned, bathed in the gentle glow of candlelight. Once again, Wyatt was struck by her fragile beauty.

"Will the pup be all right outside?"

"Yes," Glory said. "Follow me." Wyatt picked up his bag. "This is where you'll sleep," she said, and held the candle above her head, giving him a dim view of the tiny room and the single bed. "I'm just across the hall in Granny's bed."

"Granny?"

"My father's mother. This was her cabin. She's all the family I have left." And then her face crumpled as tears shimmered in her eyes. "The only problem is, she's ninety-one years old and in a nursing home. Half the time she doesn't remember her name, let alone me."

As she turned away, Wyatt set his bag inside the room and followed her across the hall, watching as she set the candle on a bedside table, then ran across the room to check the curtains, making sure that no light would be visible from outside.

"Glory?"

She stilled, then slowly turned. "What?"

"Talk to me."

She understood his confusion, but wasn't sure she could make him understand. With a defeated sigh, she dropped to the corner of the bed, running her fingers lightly across the stitching on the handmade quilt, drawing strength from the woman who'd sewn it, and then bent over to pull off her boots. She tugged once, then twice, and without warning, started to cry quiet tears of heartbreak.

Wyatt flinched as her misery filled the tiny space. Without thinking, he knelt at her feet. Grasping her foot, he pulled one boot off and then the other before turning back the bed upon which she sat.

"Lie down."

The gentleness in his voice was her undoing. Glory rolled over, then into a ball, and when the weight of the covers fell upon her shoulders, she began to sob.

"He was laughing," she whispered.

Wyatt frowned. "Who was laughing, honey?"

"My brother, J.C. One minute he was digging through the grocery sack for Twinkies and laughing at something the pup had done, and then everything exploded." She took a deep, shaky breath, trying to talk past the sobs. "I should have been with them."

Wyatt cursed beneath his breath. Her pain was more than he could bear. He wanted to hold her, yet the unfamiliarity of their odd connection held him back. Slowly, she rolled over, looking at him through those silver-blue eyes while the skin crawled on the back of his neck.

"I was the first female born to the Dixon family in more than five generations. They say that my eyes were open when I was born, and that when Granny laid me on my mother's stomach, I lifted my head, looked at my mother's face and smiled. An hour later, my mother suddenly hemorrhaged, then died, and although I was in another room, Granny says that the moment she took her last breath, I started to cry. Granny called it 'the sight.' I consider it more of a curse."

Wyatt brushed the tangle of hair from her eyes, smoothing it from her forehead and off her shoulders. "It saved me," he said quietly.

She closed her eyes. A tear slipped out of each corner and ran down her temples and into her hair.

"I know." Her mouth twisted as she tried to talk around the pain. "But why couldn't I save Daddy and J.C.? Why, Wyatt Hatfield? Tell me why."

Unable to stay unattached from her pain, Wyatt slid his hands beneath her shoulders and lifted her from the covers, then into his lap. As he nestled his chin in her hair, he held her against him.

"I don't know the whys of the world, Glory Dixon. I only know the hows. And I swear to you, I will keep you safe until they find the man responsible."

It was the promise he made and the honesty with which it was said that gave her hope. Maybe together they could get it done.

I'm so glad he's here, Glory thought.

"I'm glad I came, too," Wyatt whispered.

Glory froze. Without realizing it, he'd read her thoughts and answered. And as she let herself draw from his strength, she faced the fact that she'd given more than just blood to this man. It seemed impossible, and it shouldn't have happened, but it was the only explanation that made sense.

A dog ran across the street in front of the car as Wyatt turned a corner in Larner's Mill, aiming for the local police department down the street. He knew where it was. He'd been there yesterday when asking directions to the Dixon home. The people were friendly enough, but he wasn't sure if one small-town police chief and two part-time deputies were going to be up to finding a killer. When they'd driven out of the yard earlier that morning, no one had even bothered to stop them and ask why they were near the scene. On the surface, they seemed geared more toward drunks and traffic violations than tracking criminals. He hoped he was wrong. As he pulled to the curb and parked, Glory's nervousness was impossible to ignore any longer.

"It's going to be all right," he said.

Her eyes were wide and on the verge of tears, her mouth set. He could tell she was hovering on the edge of panic.

"They're not going to believe me," she said, but when Wyatt slipped his hand over hers and squeezed, the fear receded.

"It doesn't really matter whether they believe you or not, as long as they proceed with some kind of investigation. Besides, don't forget Lane's coming."

Glory nodded, remembering their earlier phone call to Wyatt's brother-in-law.

"Having a U.S. marshal on our side isn't going to hurt," Wyatt added, then glanced down at his watch. "In fact, I'd lay odds that he'll be here before dark."

Glory bit her lip and then looked away.

"You have to trust me, girl."

She turned, and Wyatt found himself looking into her eyes and fighting the sensation of falling deeper and deeper into a place with no way out. And then she blinked, and he realized he'd been holding his breath. Muttering to himself, he helped her out of the car.

Glory took heart in the fact that as they walked through the door, he was right beside her all the way.

"God Almighty!"

Anders Conway jumped to his feet and stumbled backward as the couple came in the door. He'd been police chief of Larner's Mill for twenty-nine years, but it was his first time seeing a ghost.

Wyatt felt Glory flinch, and instinctively slipped a hand across her shoulder, just to remind her that he was there.

"Chief Conway, I came to report a murder," Glory said softly.

He was so shocked by her appearance that her remark went right over his head. "We thought you were dead," he said. "Where on earth have you been, girl?"

"Hiding."

"Whatever for? No one's gonna hurt you."

Glory looked to Wyatt for reassurance. The glint in his eye was enough to keep her going.

"The fire at my house was not an accident. Someone deliberately turned on the gas jets. I saw them. When Daddy and J.C. walked in the back door with our groceries, it was nearly dusk and the house must have been full of gas. Wyatt says that one of them probably turned on the light, and that was what sparked the explosion."

Conway frowned. Apparently, none of this was making much sense. "If you saw someone turning on the gas, why didn't you tell your family? Why would your father knowingly go into a house set to blow?"

This was where it got rough. Glory braced herself, readying for the derision that was bound to come.

"I didn't actually *see* what had been done until the house was already burning, I just knew that something was wrong. I tried to stop them from going inside. I called out, but it was too late. They were already there."

The look on Conway's face was changing from shock to confusion. Afraid that he'd run her out before she got a chance to explain, she started talking faster, anxious to get it all said.

"I know it was a man who did it. I could see him in my mind. I saw the back of his hands as he turned on the jets on the stove. He even broke one of them so that it couldn't be turned off. I saw the back of his pant legs as he ran through the other rooms, doing the same to our heat stoves. One in the living room . . . and one in the bathroom, too."

"In your mind. You saw this *in your mind.*"

She nodded.

Conway made no attempt to hide his disbelief. "Exactly *who* did you see? In your mind, of course."

Glory wanted to hide. The simple fact of her father's presence in her life had prevented most people from displaying any out-and-out derision they might have felt. This was the first time that she'd experienced it alone. Suddenly, Wyatt's hand slid under her hair and cupped the back of her neck. She relaxed. *I forgot. I'm not alone.*

"No, honey, you're not," Wyatt said, still unaware that he was reading her thoughts and answering them aloud.

Glory looked startled, but not as surprised as Anders Conway, who turned his focus to the man at her side.

"You're the fellow who was asking directions to the Dixon place yesterday, aren't you?"

Wyatt nodded.

"Are you kin?"

Wyatt glanced down at Glory and winked, then gave the policeman a look he couldn't ignore.

"I'm a friend. Miss Dixon saved my life last year. I'm simply returning a favor."

"How did . . . ?"

"None of that matters," Wyatt said. "The point is, Glory Dixon knows that someone tried to kill her. And, obviously, they did not succeed. The fact remains that when it's made known that she's still alive, he will obviously try again." And then he added, as if it were an afterthought, although he knew what an impact his announcement would make, "you should also know that there's a U.S. marshal on his way here to help with the investigation. He's my brother-in-law. I called him this morning."

Conway's jaw dropped as Wyatt continued. "And I suppose you've already called the state fire marshal about the incident. When is he coming?"

Conway started to fidget. "Well, I...uh, I mean..." Then he slapped his hand on the desk, trying to regain control of the situation. "Look! Everyone knows that fire was an accident. A terrible accident. The coroner should be on his way out there by now to recover the bodies. They tried once yesterday and the wreckage was still too hot."

He ran a hand through his thinning hair and tried to make them see his point.

"I'm real sorry that Miss Dixon lost her family. It has to be a shock, and that's probably what's making her imagine all of this. What you need to do is get her to a doctor and..."

"You didn't answer my question," Wyatt said. "When is the fire marshal coming?"

"I didn't call him . . . yet," Conway added.

Wyatt gave a pointed look toward the phone and then back at the lawman's face. "We'll wait," he said shortly.

Before they had time to sit down, a dispatcher came in from the back of the department with a note in his hand.

"Chief, you won't believe this. They just radioed in from the site of the Dixon fire and said they only found two bodies in the..." At this point, he noticed the couple seated across the room and froze. The note fluttered from his fingers to the floor. "Well, my Gawd! No wonder they didn't find a third body. There you are!"

Glory felt like a bug on a pin, displayed for everyone to see, and listening to them speak of her father and brother as mere "bodies" was almost more than she could bear. She bit her lip and looked away, fighting the urge to scream. And then Wyatt unexpectedly clasped her hand and wouldn't let go. Hysteria settled as she absorbed his warmth.

"Tell them to get on back here with what they've got," Conway growled. "I'm dealing with the rest. And tell them not to do any more than remove the remains. The fire marshal is going to come out and investigate the site."

"Yes, sir!" the dispatcher said, and hurried out of the room.

Wyatt stood. "I guess we'll be going now," he said.

"How can I reach you?" Conway said.

Wyatt heard Glory's swift intake of breath, and knew that while her whereabouts wouldn't be a secret for long, she wasn't ready to reveal them just now.

"We'll be in touch," Wyatt said. "For now, I think the fewer who know where she is, the better. Don't you agree?"

Conway's face turned red. The man had all but accused him of not being able to maintain confidentiality in his own department. And then he relented. If they wanted to make a big deal out of this, he wasn't going to stop them. Everyone knew that Rafe Dixon's girl was a little bit nuts. This so-called friend of the family would learn the truth soon enough, or turn out to be just like them. Either way, it didn't matter to him.

"Yeah. Right," Conway said. "Keep in touch."

The smirk in his voice was impossible to ignore. When they walked outside, Glory wilted. "He doesn't believe me, you know," she whispered.

"I know," Wyatt said. "But I do."

His words were an anchor in Glory's unsettled world, and the touch of his hand was balm to her broken heart.

"Are you up to some shopping?" Wyatt asked. "I expect you would like some changes of clothing, and we definitely need to buy food. Is there anything else you can think of?"

Glory's lip trembled as she worked up the nerve to say it aloud.

"Funeral arrangements. I need to see about..." Her voice caught, and she knew this time, she wasn't going to be able to stop the tears.

Wyatt pulled her into his arms, cupping the back of her head as she buried her face against the front of his shirt.

"I'm sorry, Glory. I'm so sorry you're having to go through this, but you need to remember something. It's *we,* honey, not *I*. Don't forget, you're not alone in this anymore. We'll do whatever it is you want. You're calling the shots."

He seated her in the car and then slid behind the steering wheel, waiting for her to settle.

Oh, God, I don't want to be in charge. I just want this to be over, Glory thought.

Wyatt raked her pale face with a dark, brooding look. "It will be, and sooner than you think. Now then, I don't know about you, but I'm hungry as hell. Where's the best place to eat?"

"How do you do that?" Glory asked.

Wyatt grinned as he began to back out of the parking space. "Do what?"

"You're reading my thoughts, and then answering my questions, even though I haven't said them aloud."

The smile on his face stilled. "No, I'm not."

Yes, you are.

He braked in the middle of the street. Fortunately, no one was behind them. He went as pale as the shirt on his back as he looked at her face.

"What did you say?"

I said... you are reading my thoughts.

"Oh, Lord." His belly began to turn, and he could feel the muscles in his face tightening. He gripped the steering wheel until his knuckles turned white, and try as he might, he couldn't make himself move.

"You didn't know it was happening, did you?" Glory asked.

He shook his head. "It just seemed so..."

"Natural?"

His breath escaped in one long sigh. Finally he nodded. "Yes, natural. That's exactly what it feels like."

Glory nodded. "I know." Suddenly, she smiled. "You're the first person I've ever known who can understand my gift."

It wasn't much, but it was the first time he'd seen what a hint of joy could do to her face. And in that moment, before she redirected his attention to a restaurant down the street, Wyatt Hatfield feared he might be falling in love. It wasn't planned. And it definitely wasn't what he'd had in mind when he started this journey.

In the same instant that he had the revelation, he shut it out of his mind, afraid that she'd be able to see what was in his thoughts. He reminded himself that it was too soon in their relationship for anything like this. Besides, he needed to focus on keeping her alive, not finding ways to steal, then break her heart.

Carter Foster was trying to concentrate on the legal brief on which he was working, but his mind kept wandering to the different scenarios he might use to bring up his next lie. Should he say that Betty Jo had *called* and asked for a divorce, or should he just say she'd *written?* His legal mind instantly settled on the call. That way, he would never be asked to show proof of a letter. And then the moment he thought it, he scoffed. Why should he worry about ever having to showing proof? There was no one left to question his story. Not since the Dixon family perished in that terrible fire.

He'd commiserated along with the rest of the town about the tragedy, and listened to the different explanations circulating. They ranged from a faulty water heater to a leaking gas connection beneath the house. Carter didn't care what people thought. He had done what he'd intended. Glory Dixon was dead and his secret was safe, and...he had few regrets. The fact that he hadn't actually pulled a trigger kept his conscience clear enough to bear.

He had reminded himself that it wasn't his fault the Dixons hadn't detected the scent of gas in time to open some windows. It wasn't his fault that they'd come home so late that it was almost dark and automatically turned on a light upon entering the house. None of that was his fault. All he'd done was twist a few knobs. The results had been in the hands of fate. Obviously, fate was on his side.

"Oh, Mr. Carter! Did you hear?"

He frowned as his secretary flew into his office, clutching the burger and fries that he'd asked her to get.

"Hear what?" he asked, snatching the sack from her arms before she flattened the food beyond description. As he opened it, he sniffed the enticing aroma and then began unwrapping the paper from around the bun.

"Some man found that Dixon girl! She's alive!"

Mustard squeezed out from between his fingers and dripped onto the pad on his desk. A hot, burning pain shot across his chest and then down into his belly, and for a minute he thought he was going to faint.

"What do you mean...alive? How could she survive such a fire?"

"Oh, that's the best part! She wasn't inside after all. Someone said she'd spent the night in the woods, although I don't know why in the world she didn't come home with the firemen when it was over." Then she added, "Of course, you know what they say."

Carter shook his head, anxious to hear what *they* said.

"They say," the secretary said, "that she's a little off in the head. That she claims to be able to 'see things' and 'hear voices,' or some such garbage. It's a shame, too, what with her folks dead and all. Who's going to look after a grown woman whose mind is off plumb?"

Carter shrugged, pretending he didn't know and couldn't care less, and began wiping the mustard from between his fingers and then off of his desk.

"I'm sure it will all work out," he said, and handed her the notes he'd been making on the brief. "Here. Type these up please. I'll probably be out of the office for the rest of the afternoon."

"Yes, sir. Is there some place you can be reached?"

"Home. I'm going home."

She nodded, then left.

Carter stared down at the grease congealing on the paper beneath his burger and then down at the mustard that had dropped on his pants. Cursing beneath his breath, he swiped at it angrily, knowing that he'd have to take these to the cleaners again when they'd just come out. The mustard came away on the napkin, leaving behind an even darker stain on the dark fabric of his slacks.

Suddenly, another stain popped into his mind. The smear of Dixie Red lipstick across Betty Jo's face, and a matching one on the bedspread in which he'd wrapped her. His stomach rolled, and he closed his eyes and leaned back in his chair, telling himself not to panic.

Without taking a bite, he dumped his food in the sack and grabbed his briefcase. Moments later, he was on the street, inhaling the warm, spring air and telling himself to calm down. Just because one plan had failed, didn't mean he couldn't try again. He tossed the sack into a garbage can on the corner and ran across the street to the parking lot to get his car. There were things he needed to do, and they required privacy...and solitude, and a more criminal frame of mind.

A whippoorwill called from across the small clearing in front of Granny's cabin. The pup whined in its sleep, and then was silenced when Glory leaned over and gently patted it on the head.

"It will be dark in an hour or so," Glory said.

"He'll be here," Wyatt said.

"Granny's cabin is hard to find unless you know that it's here."

"Don't forget that they were still digging through the ashes when we came back from town. Chances are there will be someone at the site who Lane can ask. If not, I gave him pretty good directions over the phone." Then he smiled. "You don't know Lane Monday. If he says he'll be here, then he will, and God help the man who gets in his way."

Glory stood up, suddenly restless in the face of nothing to do, and started to go inside.

"I think I'll start supper," she said.

Wyatt caught her at the door. "Glory..."

She looked up, shocked at herself that she was aware of his thumb pressing against the side of her breast. She waited for him to finish.

Suddenly the pup began to bark. Wyatt dropped Glory's arm and thrust her behind him as he spun. In the space of a heartbeat, Glory saw him as the soldier that he'd been. His posture was defensive, his eyes raking the dense line of trees beyond the small yard, and as quickly as he stiffened, he began to relax.

"It's Lane."

Glory took a step sideways, giving herself a better view of the man who was coming out of the trees, and then gasped. *He's a giant.*

Wyatt grinned at her. "Yeah, squirt, from where you stand, I guess he is."

"You're doing it again," she muttered, and punched him on the arm. "What I'd like to know is, if I'm the psychic, why is it you're the one who keeps reading my mind? Why can't I see into yours?"

He shrugged. "Maybe it's the soldier in me. I was trained not to let down my guard." *And the day I let you into my head, I'm in trouble,* he thought, and then focused on the big man, who was coming their way.

Glory held her breath, watching the motion of man and muscle, and wondered who on earth would be brave enough to live with a man of that size.

"My sister," Wyatt answered, and then grinned. "Sorry. That slipped."

Ignoring him, Glory stepped forward and extended her hand as if welcoming Lane into a fine home, instead of a tiny cabin lost among the trees.

"Mr. Monday, I'm Glory Dixon. I thank you for coming." Then she watched as her hand disappeared in his palm.

Lane smiled, and Glory saw the gentleness in him, in spite of his size.

"Well, I sort of owe old Wyatt here," he said. "And from what he said, you're outnumbered. I thought I'd come even the odds."

"I was about to put supper on the table," she said.

"We'll help," Wyatt said, and took Lane's bag from his hand. "Follow me, and duck when you enter."

A coyote howled far in the distance and a night owl hooted from a tree in the yard, sending the puppy into a frenzy of barking that made Wyatt nervous. He knew within reason that the night sounds had set the dog off, but visions of an attacker creeping through the forest would not go away.

"Want me to check it out?" Lane asked.

"Glory says it's just the night. That if it was a man, the pup wouldn't bother to bark at all and would probably lick him to death."

Lane accepted his explanation without comment, watching intently as Wyatt paced the floor between window and chair while Glory was down the hall, taking a bath.

"Do you think she's on the up-and-up?" Lane asked.

Wyatt froze, then turned. "Yes."

"Just like that?"

"Just like that," Wyatt said.

Lane shrugged. "So tell me what you know."

Wyatt's eyes darkened, and the scar across his cheek turned red.

"She says that someone turned on the gas in her house on purpose. I know her father and brother are dead. I hear what she's thinking and I don't know how to explain it."

Lane's mouth dropped, but only slightly. "You're telling me that you can read her mind?"

"Don't look at me like that!" Wyatt growled. "I know how that sounds. But I know what I know. Blame it on the fact that I nearly died. Blame it on the fact that her blood runs in my veins. Just believe me!"

"Wyatt, don't be mad at him."

Both men turned. Glory stood in the doorway to the living room, holding a towel clutched to her breasts while her granny's nightgown lightly dusted the floor. At first glance, she looked like a child, until one noticed the swell of breast beneath the white flannel, and the curve of her hip beneath the fabric as she walked across the room.

"Your feet will get cold," Wyatt muttered, and wanted to bury his fists in the silver-blond sway of her hair brushing close to her waist.

Glory paused, then looked up at both men. The plea in her eyes was impossible to deny.

"We're not fighting, honey," Lane said gently, and watched how she moved toward Wyatt, settling within the shelter of his arms as if she'd done it countless times before. He didn't think he'd ever seen a more gentle, trusting woman in his life.

"It's not his fault he doesn't understand," Glory continued, as if Lane had not even spoken.

"I don't have to understand to help," Lane said. "And I will help. Tomorrow, I'm going to do some investigating of my own at the fire site. One of the men I talked to earlier said the fire marshal was due around nine in the morning. You can come if you want to."

Glory's voice shook, but she managed to maintain her poise. "Tomorrow I bury my family. Maybe later." And then she gave them a smile that didn't quite reach her eyes. "If you don't mind, I think I'll go on to bed. Do you have everything you need?"

Unable to let her go without touching her one last time, Wyatt brushed at a stray strand of hair that was too near her eye. "We'll manage. Just sleep. Remember, whatever happens tomorrow, you won't be alone."

She nodded, and then went into her room and shut the door.

For several minutes, neither man spoke, and when the silence was broken, it was by Lane.

"I hope you don't think that I'm sleeping with *you,*" he muttered.

Wyatt grinned. "I hope you don't think that I'm giving up my bed."

Lane grinned back. "Do you know if there are any extra quilts? I'm thinking that floor looks better all the time."

The tension of the moment was past, and by the time Lane's pallet was made and Wyatt was in the shower, there was nothing to do but watch and wait to see what tomorrow would bring.

Meanwhile, Carter Foster was at home, racking his brain for a solution. Before he'd gone two blocks from the office, he'd heard enough gossip on the street to choke a horse. The fact that Glory Dixon had brought an ex-marine with her to the police department, and that a U.S. marshal was on his way, made him nervous. He was out of his element. What he needed was muscle. Hired muscle. He wondered which, if any, of his ex-clients would be capable of murder, and then wondered what the going rate on hit men was these days.

He slumped into an easy chair, contemplating the rug beneath his toes, fearing that the cost of Betty Jo's burial was bound to increase, and cursed the day he'd ever said "I do."

Chapter 5

The scent of the bacon they'd had for breakfast still lingered in the air of the cabin as Wyatt watched Lane disappear into the trees beyond the small yard, already on his way to the site of the fire. Through the dense growth of leaves overhead, sunlight dappled the ground in uneven patterns, giving an effect similar to the crazy quilt that covered his bed. The pup was in a patch of sunshine worrying a bone, while a blue jay sat on a tree branch above the pup's head, scolding it for its mere presence.

To the eye, it would seem an idyllic day, and yet today Glory was to put to rest her entire family, leaving her, virtually, alone on the face of the earth.

He could hear her moving about in her room, presumably getting dressed for the memorial services later that morning. He knew it couldn't possibly take her long to decide what to wear. She only had the one dress that she'd bought yesterday. His own clothing choices were limited, as well. When he'd left Tennessee, he'd had no inkling of what he would find. If he had, he might have planned accordingly. As it was, boots, clean jeans, a white shirt and his jacket would have to serve as proper dress. His only suit was on a hanger back at the farm above Chaney Creek.

Blindly, he looked through the window without seeing, concentrating instead on the woman he'd found at the end of his search. What was happening between them didn't make sense. It was as crazy as the fact that, seemingly, and for no apparent reason, two people had been murdered. She knew of nothing that would warrant the elimination of everyone she held dear, and yet all was gone. And she said it wasn't over.

Wyatt shuddered. Gut feeling told him she wasn't wrong, and he'd relied too many years on his instinct to ignore it now.

"Wyatt, I'm ready."

He pivoted, a half-voiced thought hanging at the edge of his lips, and then froze, forgetting what he'd been about to say as he beheld the woman before him. All images of the childlike waif were gone, hidden beneath the soft, blue folds of the dress she was wearing. The bodice molded itself to the fullness of her breasts, and the narrowness of her waist only accentuated the gentle flare of hips beneath the ankle length of her skirt. Even her hair had undergone a transformation. Forgoing her normal style of letting it fall where it may, Glory had pulled it away from her face and then anchored it all on top in a white-gold spiral. Escaping strands fell around her face and down her neck, weeping from the silky crown atop her head.

"I know it's not the standard black dress," she said. "But it was Daddy's favorite color. I did it for him, not for tradition."

Wyatt cleared his throat, moved by her beauty as well as her grace.

"I saw them once," he said softly.

"Who?"

"Your father... and your brother."

Her eyebrows arched with surprise.

"Remember, outside the hospital, the day I was being released?"

Understanding dawned, and she almost smiled. "That's right! You did."

It gave her an odd sort of pleasure to know that in this, her day of greatest sorrow, he had faces to go with the names of those she loved best.

"I think they would be proud of you," he said.

She nodded, and then her chin trembled, but her voice was firm. "I wish this was over."

Her pain was so thick that he imagined he could feel it. He crossed the room and then stood before her, wanting to touch her in so many places, to test the new waters of Glory Dixon, but this wasn't the time. Today she must mourn. Tomorrow was another day.

He offered her his arm instead, and when her fingers moved across the fabric of his shirt and then locked into the bend of his elbow, Wyatt paused, savoring the contact, as well as her trust.

"Are you ready to go?" he asked.

She nodded, and together they walked out the door. It was only after she shut it behind her that Wyatt realized they were going to have to walk the quarter of a mile up the overgrown path to where his car was parked. He looked down at her shoes, worrying if she would be able to make it. The narrow strap that held the two-inch heels on her feet seemed too delicate for the rough underbrush that had overtaken the unused road.

No sooner had the worry occurred, than a tall, dark-haired young man emerged from the woods, leading a horse behind him. His freshly starched and ironed overalls were shiny, and every button on his long-sleeved white shirt was fastened right up to the collar. Before Wyatt had time to ask, Glory gasped, her voice shaking as she quickly explained.

"Oh... oh, my! It's Edward Lee."

"He's a friend?" Wyatt asked sharply.

Glory nodded. "He lives about two miles from our house, as the crow flies. J.C. always took him fishing. He's shy of strangers, so don't expect much conversation. He's simple, you see."

"He's wh...?" And then suddenly Wyatt understood, although it had been years since he'd heard the old hill name for mental retardation.

Glory patted his arm. "Don't worry. Edward Lee knows he's different. He won't embarrass you."

That wasn't what Wyatt had been thinking, but it was too late to explain himself now. The young man was nearly at their feet.

"Hey, Mornin' Glory, I brought you my horse. You shouldn't be walkin' in the brush today."

The black gelding stood quietly at the end of the reins, as if it understood the limitations of its master quite well. The old saddle on its back was gleaming with polish, the metal studs on the halter glittered in the sunlight like polished silver. For Edward Lee, the work had been a labor of love.

Glory touched his arm in a gentle, easy manner. "Why, Edward Lee. How did you know?"

He ducked his head as tears ran unashamedly down his face. "I know that your pa and J.C. got burned up. Ma said the buryin' is today and I knew where you was stayin', and that the old road is all grown up with weeds and such." And then he lifted his head, as if proud of the assumption he had made, and continued. "I knew you'd be all pretty today, Mornin' Glory. I wanted to help you."

Morning Glory. Somehow that fits her, Wyatt thought, and suddenly resented Edward Lee for sharing a past with Glory that he had not. He saw the sweetness of Glory's expression as she accepted the young man's gift, recognized the adoration in Edward Lee's eyes, and knew that, but for a quirk of fate that had rendered Edward Lee less than other men, he would have been a fierce suitor for Glory Dixon's hand. Jealousy came without warning, and the moment he recognized it for what it was, he was ashamed of having felt it.

"Edward Lee, I want you to meet my friend, Wyatt."

Edward Lee glanced at Wyatt, his expression suddenly strained, his behavior nervous, as if expecting a negative reaction that must have happened all too many times before.

As Wyatt watched, he realized how special the bond was between Edward Lee and Glory. In their own way, they'd each experienced the judgement of a prejudiced and uneducated society. A society that seemed bound to ridicule that which it did not understand. Edward Lee was as different in his own right as Glory was in hers.

Wyatt smiled and extended his hand. "Any friend of Glory's is a friend of mine."

The grin that broke across Edward Lee's face was magnificent. He grabbed Wyatt's hand and pumped it fiercely as he started to explain.

"You can leave Rabbit in Mr. Dixon's barn," Edward Lee offered. "Then when you come home, you can ride him back here. When you don't need him no more, just lay the reins across the saddle and turn him loose. He'll come home."

Wyatt's smile widened. "Rabbit?"

Edward Lee nodded. "'Cause he runs like one."

Glory's small laugh broke the peace of the glade, and both men turned, each wearing a different expression as they gazed at the woman before them. Edward Lee's was one of devotion. Wyatt's was one of pure want.

Glory saw neither. All she knew was that two people who meant something to her seemed at ease with each other. It gave her joy in this day of distress.

"I can't thank you enough for your kindness, Edward Lee. Tell your mother I said hello," she said.

He nodded, and then turned and walked away, moving with unnatural grace for one with so crippled a mind.

"Can you ride?" Glory asked, eyeing the saddle and remembering her dress, and wondering how she was going to accomplish this feat with any amount of dignity.

Wyatt grinned, then lifted her off her feet and set her sideways in the saddle, leaving her legs to dangle off to one side.

"That's almost an insult, honey. I'm a Tennessee boy, born and bred, remember."

And with one smooth motion, he swung up on the horse, settling just behind the saddle on which Glory was perched, and slipped his long legs into the stirrups.

Glory shivered as Wyatt's breath moved across her cheek, and his arms fenced her close against his chest.

"Glory?"

"What?"

"Why did he call you Morning Glory?"

A sharp pain pierced and then settled around the region of her heart. She took a deep breath, knowing that it was something to which she must become accustomed.

"It was J.C.'s nickname for me...and they were Daddy's favorite flowers. They grow—" her breath caught on another pain as she amended "—grew, on trellises on both sides of our front porch. That's how I got my name. Daddy said when I was born my eyes were as blue as the morning glory."

Impulsively, Wyatt hugged her, and feathered a kiss near her eyebrow.

"I'm sorry. I didn't know it would cause you pain."

She looked up at him, her eyes filling with unshed tears. "It wasn't so bad," she said quietly. "In fact, it almost felt good to remember."

Wyatt watched her mouth forming around the words, and wanted to bend just a little bit closer and taste that pearly sheen of lip gloss painted on her mouth. But he couldn't... and he didn't...and the urge slowly passed. The horse moved sideways beneath them, ready for a command. He gripped the reins firmly, and settled Glory a little bit closer to his chest.

"Can you hold on?" he asked.

"As long as you're behind me," she warned, trying to find an easy way to sit without sliding too far backward or forward.

As long as I'm behind you. The words hung in Wyatt's mind, fostering another set of hopes that he didn't dare acknowledge. *What if I never left you, little Morning Glory? How would you feel about that? Even more to the point, how do I feel? Are you what I was looking for when I started on this journey last fall... or am I just kidding myself, looking for easy answers to the emptiness inside myself?*

He shrugged off the thoughts, unwilling to pursue them while she was this up close and personal. He had to be careful. The last thing he wanted to do was ruin another woman's life as he'd ruined his and Shirley's. If he ever took a woman again, it would be forever. Wyatt Hatfield didn't make the same mistake twice.

The trip up the overgrown road was much easier on a horse, and done in the bright light of day. As they passed through the woods, Wyatt wondered how on earth they'd managed to get through it the other night without tearing their clothing to shreds.

For an old horse, Rabbit pranced, as if aware of his fine appearance and the precious cargo that he carried. In spite of the seriousness of the day, Glory smiled more than once at what they saw as they rode.

Once her hand suddenly clutched at Wyatt's thigh and then she pointed into the trees. He followed the direction of her finger, and saw the disappearing tail of a tiny red fox. And then a few minutes later, she pointed upward, watching as a hawk rode the air currents high above their heads.

"This is a fine place to live," Wyatt said.

The words gave solace to Glory's pain. It was a sentiment she'd heard her father offer more than once.

Wyatt felt some of the tension slipping out of her body, and she almost relaxed against him as they rode. Almost... until her homesite came into view, and the scent of something having been burned replaced the fresh mountain air.

Death seemed to hover above the spot where her house once stood. As they passed the ruins on their way to the barn to get his car, Wyatt noticed she turned away. In spite of the unusual activity taking place there, she was unable to look at the place she'd once lived.

Men hard at work paused at the sight of the pair's arrival on horseback. When they realized who it was, to a man, they took off their hats, standing with eyes down, sharing her sorrow and her loss.

Glory's breath caught on a sob.

"I'm sorry, honey," Wyatt said softly.

Tears were thick in her voice as she answered. "Oh, God, Wyatt Hatfield. So am I. So am I."

A short time later, as they passed the boundary sign on the north edge of town, Wyatt began easing up on the gas. It wouldn't do to get a ticket for speeding on the way to a funeral, but he'd been lost in thought.

While Glory had been unwilling to look at the men on her property, Wyatt had looked long and hard. Satisfied that Lane was right in the middle of what was being done, he'd left with an easy conscience. Whatever was found there today, whatever conclusion they came to, it would be fair, or Lane Monday would know the reason why.

"Are you all right?" Wyatt asked.

She nodded, her eyes wide and fixed upon the road before them. And then she asked, "Do you remember the turnoff to the cemetery we took to pick out grave sites yesterday?"

"I remember."

"I thought graveside services were appropriate for Daddy and J.C., considering their...uh...their condition." And then she hesitated, suddenly unsure of the decision she'd made yesterday. "Don't you?"

"I think whatever you decided is right. They were your family. Remember?"

She sighed and covered her face with her hands. Her voice was shaky, her fingers trembling as she let them drop in her lap.

"Oh, God, just let me get through this with my dignity."

"To hell with dignity, Glory. Grief is healthy. It's what you hold back that will eat you alive. Believe me, I'm the ultimate stiff upper lip, and look what a mess I've made of my life."

"I don't see it as such a mess," she offered.

He grimaced. "Yeah, right! I got married to a perfectly good woman, and then gave my heart... and attention... to the military instead of her. It took me years to figure out why."

She listened quietly, afraid to speak for fear he'd stop the confidences he'd suddenly begun to share.

"The military didn't demand anything from me except loyalty and a strong back. What my wife wanted from me was something I didn't know how to share."

And that was...

Wyatt answered her thought before he realized it had just been a thought.

"Me. I was too big and strong and tough to let someone see inside *my* soul. I suppose I thought it wasn't manly." A corner of his mouth turned up in a wry, self-effacing grin. "I think that idiot notion came from having too many older brothers. They used to beat the hell out of me just to see how long it would take me to bleed, and then laugh. But let anyone else try the same stunt, and they'd take them apart." He shrugged as the cemetery gates came into view. "Brotherly love is a strange, strange thing. It doesn't always lay the best of groundwork for making a good husband out of a strong man."

Glory shook her head. "You're wrong," she said quietly. "It wasn't that you were the wrong kind of man. I think it was the wrong time for you to have married. Maybe if you'd waited..." She shrugged, and then unbuckled her seat belt as he pulled to a stop.

For you?

The thought came and went so quickly that Wyatt almost didn't know it had been there. But the feeling it left behind was enough to keep him close at her side as they circled tombstones, walking across the close-clipped grass toward a tent in the distance.

When they were almost there, Glory paused in midstep and stared. Wyatt followed her gaze. Realizing that she'd at the propane tank, there would have been no way to its escape."

Wyatt shrugged. "I'm not surprised."

Lane grinned. "That Conway fellow isn't much of a cop. wanted to suggest that Glory had turned them all on self after the fire was over, just to back up her story. The e marshal almost laughed in his face, and then asked him try and turn one of the valves himself. Old Conway nearly isted a gut trying to break the knob loose."

"Did it happen?" Wyatt asked.

"Hell, no," Lane muttered, and scooped a piece of cherry ie on his fork. "The fire fused them in place. You couldn't udge one with a blowtorch."

"So, the official conclusion is in," Wyatt muttered. 'Arson that resulted in two innocent deaths. The bottom ine is, whoever did it is guilty of murder."

"Thank God," Glory said.

Both men turned at the sound of her voice. "At least now they *have* to believe me."

Lane grinned again. "Yes, ma'am, they do at that. Not hat I didn't believe you myself... but hard proof is always good to have."

"So, where do I go from here?" she asked.

"Nowhere, unless I'm with you," Wyatt said. "Because you're right about that, then you're right about why. Un- il they catch the man who's trying to hurt you, you will ave twenty-four-hour protection."

Glory looked startled. *What do I do with two men the size f small horses in Granny's little cabin?*

Wyatt laughed aloud, startling Lane and making Glory ush. She'd forgotten his ability to read her thoughts.

"Well," she said, daring Wyatt to answer.

Lane wondered if he looked as lost as he felt. "I know en I've missed something, but the honest to God truth is, ever saw it go by. What's going on?"

Glory frowned, and pointed at Wyatt. "Ask him. He's . Know-it-all."

spotted the single casket bearing what was left of both men, he reached down and clasped her hand in his.

Her chin lifted, her eyes glittering in the midmorning sunlight as she looked up at Wyatt. A slight breeze teased the thick, dark hair above his forehead, scattering it with the temerity of an unabashed flirt. His dark eyes were filled with concern, his strong, handsome features solemn in the face of what she was about to endure. The scar on his cheek was a vivid reminder of what he'd endured, and as Glory saw, she remembered, and took hope from the fact that he'd survived.... So, then, could she.

Glory made it through the service with composure that would have made her father proud. Not once did she give way to the angry shrieks of denial that threatened to boil over. The only signs of her pain were the tears, constant and silent, that fell from her eyes and down her cheeks as the minister spoke.

It was afterward, when the people who'd come to pay their respects started to file past the chairs in which she and Wyatt were sitting, that she realized she wasn't as alone in this world as she'd thought.

The first woman who came was elderly. Her voice shook more than her hands, but her intention was plain as she paused at Glory's chair, resting her weight on the cane in one hand, while she laid a small picture in Glory's lap.

"I'm eighty-nine years old," she said. "I been burned out once and flooded out twice in my lifetime. In all them times, I never lost no family, and in that I reckon I was lucky. But I remembered the thing that I missed most of all that I'd lost, and it was my pictures. We talked about it at church last night. We've all knowed your family long before you was born, girl. The ones of us who had these, have decided to give 'em you."

Glory stared at the picture, dumbfounded. It was an old black-and-white print of a young dark-haired woman with a baby on her hip.

"It's your granny," the old woman said. "And that there's your daddy, when he was just a young'un. I don't remember how I come by it, but me and Faith Dixon are near the same age."

Glory ran her finger lightly across the surface, absorbing the joy caught on their faces. Her voice was shaking when she looked up.

"I don't know how to thank you," she whispered.

"No need . . . no need," the old woman said. "Just don't you ever be so scairt that you go and hide in no woods alone again. That plumb near broke my heart. We won't hurt you, girl. You're one of us."

And one after the other, people filed past, giving their condolences for her loss, along with another piece of her family to treasure. A girl from her high school class gave her an annual of their senior year of school.

The man who owned the feed store had two photographs of J.C., taken years ago at a livestock show.

The newspaperman had old photos on file of the year her father had bagged a twelve-point buck.

And so they came, people and pictures of times she'd forgotten, and places to which she'd forgotten they'd been. And when they were gone, Glory sat in silence, clutching the mementos to her breast, unable to speak.

"They've made a dinner for you and your man at the church," the minister said, as he started to take his leave. "I know it's hard, Miss Dixon, but letting them help you grieve will help you, as well."

"I don't know if I can," she whispered, then turned her face to Wyatt's shoulder and wept.

"Just give us a bit," Wyatt said. "We'll be along."

The minister nodded. "That's fine. Real fine. I'll let them know you're coming."

And finally, except for the casket waiting to be lowered, they were alone.

"Oh, Wyatt. I knew that people thought a lot of Daddy and J.C., but I didn't think they liked me."

Her pain broke his heart. "Cry, Glory. Cry it all out, and then let it go." With that, he pulled her a little bit closer to

his chest and held her as she mourned for
lost . . . and rejoiced for what she had gained.

Food was everywhere inside the tiny cabin. C
cabinet space, overflowing in the refrigerator, s
deep in aluminum foil dishes on the table and wa
eaten.

It had been impossible to refuse the kindness
dies who'd prepared the meal, because when it wa
was the custom of the country, the bereaved famil
ways to take home the leftover food.

Insisting that she could never use it up, Glory succ
to their admonition that she had company to feed.
declared that, at the very least, she shouldn't have t
for others in her time of grief.

Wyatt had been fully prepared to make several
through the woods with the leftovers, because he h
intention of getting on Rabbit while trying to hold
Glory and a handful of pies.

But when they drove into the yard, expecting Rabbit
the next ride, they saw that while they were gone, son
had cleared the old road between their houses.

Thankful for the unexpected reprieve, Wyatt t
Rabbit loose as Edward Lee had instructed, and h
Glory drove up to Granny Dixon's cabin in comf
wasn't until later, when Lane was helping them unlo
food from the car, that they learned one of Glory's
bors had taken his tractor and front-end loader and
two hours what would have taken a road crew two
accomplish.

Glory disappeared into her room to change, and L
happily through the covered dishes, eating his fi
homemade food as he filled Wyatt in on all that
curred while they were gone.

"She was right, you know," Lane said, as he t
ond helping of scalloped potatoes. "Every gas
house was opened wide. And one of the contr
kitchen stove had been broken off. Short of turn

Wyatt grinned even wider. "Maybe you could bed one down in your daddy's barn, and the other outside with the pup."

She raised an eyebrow, refusing to be baited by his words or his wit. "One of these days, you're going to eavesdrop on something you won't have an answer for," she said. Then she sat down beside Lane and began shuffling through the stack of pictures she'd left on the table.

The cryptic statement hit home as the smile slid off Wyatt's face. He knew she was right. Right in the middle of a new set of worries, Glory suddenly changed the subject.

"Lane, would you like to see my pictures?"

"Yes, ma'am, I would be honored."

Food and the future were forgotten as Glory led both men through her past, and as she talked, she absently caressed the pictures because it was all she had left to touch.

But while Glory was learning to heal, Carter Foster was festering into one big sore. His first choice for hit man was languishing in the state penitentiary. His second had moved to another state. He'd gone through the past seven years of his legal practice, trying without success to find a name to go with the game. It wasn't until he started on the files of his first year that he remembered Bo Marker.

It had been Carter's first big win in court. He'd successfully defended a man he knew was guilty as sin. Remembering the photographs he'd seen of Marker's victim, he was certain that this might be his man. Surely a man who was capable of killing a man with his fists was equal to pulling a trigger. He read through the file, making notes of the address and phone number he'd had at the time. He was certain that he'd have to do a little detective work on the side to find Marker, but it would all be worth it in the end.

He wrote quickly, returning the file as soon as he was through. Time was of the essence. The longer Glory Dixon remained alive, the shorter his own days of freedom. He'd lived in hell with Betty Jo long enough, and her death had, after all, been an accident. He deserved a break. Then he winced and ran his finger along his neck, loosening his collar and his tie. Just not the kind Betty Jo had gotten.

Chapter 6

Wyatt sat across the table from Glory, nursing a cup of coffee and watching the play of emotions upon her face as she went through the photographs she'd been given yesterday. At least they gave her pleasure, which was more than he could do. He'd lain in bed last night right across the hall from her door, listening for nearly an hour to her muffled sobs. It had been all he could do not to cross the hall and yank her out of that bed and into his arms. No one should have to cry like that alone.

Glory knew that Wyatt was watching her. Those dark eyes of his did things to her fantasies they had no business doing. They made her think things she shouldn't, and want things she couldn't have. She should be thinking of him as nothing but a kind stranger, yet with each passing hour, he became more of a permanent fixture in her thoughts.

She sighed.

Thinking like that could get her hurt . . . very, very badly, and losing her family had been hurt enough. This man had already admitted to having doubts about himself. She didn't need to be falling for a man who would be here today and gone tomorrow. Glory was a forever kind of woman. She needed a forever kind of man.

The pictures slipped from her fingers and into her lap as she closed her eyes and leaned back against the couch, letting herself imagine what forever with Wyatt Hatfield might be like.

As her eyes closed and her head tilted backward, Wyatt froze. The delicate arch of her bare neck and the flutter of those gold-tinged eyelashes upon her cheeks were a taunting temptation to a man with deep need. He set his cup aside then got up, intent on walking out of the room before he got himself in trouble, wishing he'd gone to run the errands instead of Lane. But when he reached the doorway, he made a mistake. He looked back and got caught in a silver-blue spell.

There was a question in her eyes and a stillness in her body, as if she were waiting for something to happen. Wyatt ached for her...and for himself, well aware of just what it might be if he didn't readjust his thinking.

Suddenly, some of the pictures slid out of her lap onto the floor. He reacted before he remembered his intention to keep his distance, and was on his knees at her side, scooping them up and placing them on the table, before she could move.

Glory focused her attention on his hands, seeing strength in the broad palms, tenderness in the long, supple fingers and determination in the man himself as he persisted until every picture that she'd dropped was picked up. Forgetting the fact that he could tap into her thoughts at any given moment, she pictured those hands moving upon her body instead, and softly sighed.

"Here you go," he said, and started to drop the last of the pictures in her lap when an image drifted through his mind. *Skin...smooth to the touch, dampened by a faint sheen of perspiration. A pulse racing beneath it...a heartbeat gone wild beneath his fingertips.* He rocked back on his feet and looked up at her.

Ah, God, Wyatt thought.

Glory saw the tension in his body, heard his swift intake of breath and remembered too late that, once again, she'd let him inside her mind. She held her breath, afraid to speak. How would he react, and what should she do? Ignore it...and him?

And then he lifted the pictures out of her lap and dropped them onto the cushion beside her, taking the decision out of her hands.

Mouths met. The introduction was short. It went from tentative to demanding in three short ticks of a clock.

Her lips were as soft as he'd imagined, yielding to a silent question he did not have the nerve to ask, then begging for more of the same. The sweetness of her compliance and the shock of their connection were more than he'd bargained for. Her breath was swift upon his cheek, her passion unexpected, and when he lifted his head from the kiss, as yet unfulfilled.

Oh, Wyatt!

"My sentiments exactly," he whispered, and ran his thumb across her lips where his mouth had just been. "Lord help us, Glory, but where do we go from here?"

Outside, the pup began to bark. Wyatt was on his feet in an instant, and out the door. The moment had passed.

Glory groaned, then buried her face in her hands. She'd been saved from having to respond. It was a small, but much needed, respite, because she had no answer for Wyatt. Not now, and maybe, not ever.

Lane followed Wyatt back into the house, unaware of what he'd interrupted, and blurted out what had been on his mind all night.

"Glory, can you turn that psychic business of yours on at will?"

She seemed startled by the question, yet understanding dawned as to where he was leading.

"I've never tried. In fact, it's been quite the opposite. I've tried more than once to stop what I see, but I've never tried to start it."

"Don't you think now might be a good time to practice?" he asked.

Wyatt wanted to argue. Instinct told him this was too much too soon, but it was Glory's life that was on the line. It was her family who'd died. The least he could do was let her make the decision. Yet when she nodded, he frowned.

"Are you sure?" Wyatt asked.

She looked at him with a clear gaze. "About some things, no. About this, yes."

He didn't have to be a genius to read between the lines of her answer. She wasn't sure about what had just happened between them, but she was ready to try anything in order to find the person responsible for her father's and brother's deaths. All in all, he had to admit that her answer was more than fair.

"Then let's go," Lane said.

"Where to?" she asked.

"To where it all started."

Glory blanched, and in a panic, looked to Wyatt for support.

"I'm with you all the way," he said softly. "Want to walk, or ride?"

"Ride, I think. The sooner we get there, the sooner it's over."

The drive was short, but the silence between the trio was long. When Glory got out of the car, she had to make herself look at the spot where her house had been standing. The blackened timbers and the rock foundation more resembled some prehistoric skeleton than the remnants of a home. It hurt to look at it and remember what had happened. But, she reminded herself, that was why she'd come.

Wyatt's hand cupped her shoulder. "How do you want to do this?" he asked.

"I don't know. Just let me walk around a little, maybe something will happen. I told you, I've never tried this before."

Lane had already found himself a seat in the shade. He watched Wyatt and Glory from a distance, thinking to himself that there seemed to be a lot more between them than the simple repayment of a debt. Wyatt hovered like a watchdog, and Glory kept looking to him for more than support.

Lane's eyes narrowed thoughtfully as Wyatt caressed the crown of her head, his fingers lingering longer than necessary in the long, silvery length. When he cupped her face with the palm of his hand, an observer might have supposed it were nothing more than a comforting touch. But Lane knew better. He saw the way Glory leaned into Wyatt's hand, and even from here, he could see a glow on her face that had nothing to do with the heat of the sun. If he wasn't mistaken, there was a slow fire burning beneath those two. Only time would tell whether it caught...or whether it burned out of its own accord.

Wyatt retreated, giving Glory space and time, but watched with a nervous eye as she paused on what was left of the back porch steps.

As she stepped over the block foundation and then down onto the ground below, she stumbled. Instinctively, Wyatt started toward her, but then she caught herself, and so he paused and waited, watching as she started to move through the ash and the rubble.

Wyatt suddenly noticed that something seemed different about the site. It took a few moments for the reality to sink in. "That yellow crime scene tape is gone!"

Lane nodded. "They took it down after the fire marshal left. He said that it was impossible to preserve much of anything out in the open like this, and so he collected all of the evidence that he could. I think they took two or three of the small heating stoves in as evidence and took pictures of the rest."

"This is a hell of a deal, isn't it?" Wyatt muttered, taking consolation from Lane's comforting thump on his back.

Time passed slowly for the men, but Glory was reliving an entire lifetime as she walked through the rubble, and it was all too short a time considering what was now left.

She stood, looking out across the broken foundation, trying to picture the man who'd invaded their home, and instead saw herself as a child, running to meet her father as he came in from milking. Seeing, through her mind, the way the solemnity of his expression always broke when he smiled. Almost feeling his hands as they circled her waist, lifting her high over his head and then spinning her around. Hearing his deep, booming laughter when he set her on his shoulders and she used his ears for an anchor by which to hold.

Oh, God, Glory thought, and swayed on her feet, overwhelmed by the emotion.

Angrily, she turned away, unwilling to savor the memory because of her loss. Black soot and ash coated the legs of her jeans and the tops of her boots as she trudged through what had once been rooms. Without walls to hold the love that had abounded within, the area looked pitifully small.

Again she stumbled, and something crunched beneath her boot. She bent over, sifting through the rubble to see what it had been. When she lifted it out, she choked back a sob. "Oh, no! I broke one of J.C.'s arrowheads."

She looked back down, and then gasped. There were dozens of them everywhere, shattered into remnants of their former beauty. What the explosion and fire hadn't ruined, the men who'd conducted the investigation had.

Tears flooded her eyes, then poured down her face, streaking the faint coat of ash on her skin as rage sifted through the pain.

Damn this all to hell!

She closed her fingers around the broken bits, squeezing until they cut into the palm of her hand. Anger boiled, then spilled, rocking her with its power. On the verge of a scream, she drew back her arm and threw. The broken pieces skipped through the air like rocks on water, and then disappeared in the grass a good distance away.

She was shaking when she turned, swiping angrily at the tears on her face. Crying would get her nowhere. She'd come to try and help find out who killed her family, not feel sorry for herself.

Wyatt could tell something monumental had just occurred. Her pain was as vivid to him as if it was his own. And when she turned toward them with tears running rampant down her face, he jumped to his feet.

"Damn it, that's enough," Wyatt said, and started to go after her.

Lane grabbed him by the arm. "Don't do it, brother. She'll stop when she's ready. Don't underestimate your woman. She survived real good on her own before you came. She's tough enough to do it when you're gone."

The look Wyatt gave him would have stopped a truck. It was somewhere between anger that Lane had dared to limit the time that was between them, and fear that he might be right.

Wyatt turned, unaware that the look he was giving Glory was full of regret. "She's not *my* woman, she's... Oh hell."

He bolted across the yard just as she staggered toward them. He caught her before her legs gave way.

"Glory... sweetheart... are you all right?"

His voice was anxious, his hands gentle as he steadied her on her feet. When she looked up, her face was grim and tinged with defeat, and for the first time since he'd come, he heard surrender in the tone of her voice.

"Damn, damn, damn. Nothing worked. Absolutely nothing. I couldn't think of *him* for remembering Daddy and J.C. I'm sorry. I just couldn't do it."

"To hell with this," he muttered. "I'm taking you home."

Her face was flushed and beaded with sweat, but her mouth twisted angrily as she looked over his shoulder. The dust of death was on her clothes, up her nostrils, coating her skin. At that moment, she hated. She hated her father and brother for leaving her, and herself for having survived. Pain came out cloaked in fury as she pointed to where she'd been.

"I am home, remember?" and she tried to push him away.

Wyatt ignored her anger, understanding it for what it was, and braced her with his hand. She trembled against him like a leaf in a storm.

Lane decided it was a good time to interrupt.

"Look, Glory, don't let it worry you. It was just an idea. I think I'm going to run into town and check on a few things. You just take it easy. We'll find him the good old-fashioned way." And then Lane gave Wyatt a long, considering stare. "I trust you'll take good care of her?"

Wyatt glared at the knowing look in Lane's eyes, then ignored him. When he thought about it, his brother-in-law could be a big fat nuisance.

"You're coming with me, Glory. You need a cool bath, a change of clothes and something to eat."

His proprietary manner was too new . . . and at this time, too much to absorb. She pushed his hand away. "Let me be, Wyatt. Don't you understand? I just want to be left alone."

Frustration was at the source of her anger, but the fact that he'd been indirectly caught in its path, hurt. He stepped back, holding up his hands as if he'd just been arrested, and gave her the space that she obviously needed.

"You don't want help? Fine. You don't want to talk to me? That's fine, too. But you don't get to be alone. You can have distance, but you don't get alone. Not until the son of a bitch is found who set fire to your world. So, do you want to maintain your solitary state in the front seat of my car while I drive, or shall I follow at a discreet distance while you walk?"

Lane hid a grin and headed for his car, thinking he'd be better off gone when the fireworks started. He'd heard that kind of mule-headed attitude before, only it had come out of Toni's mouth, not Wyatt's. Obviously that streak ran deep in the Hatfield clan. He wondered if Glory Dixon was up to the fight.

They were still staring, eye to eye, toe to toe, when the sound of Lane's car could no longer be heard.

Wyatt's eyes glittered darkly. He'd never wanted to swing a woman over his shoulder as badly as he did at this moment. For two cents, he'd . . .

I'm sorry.

"Well, hell," he grumbled, resisting the urge to kiss the droop of her lower lip. "If that's not just like a woman, expecting me to read her sweet mind for an apology."

Glory sighed, and then tried to smile. And when she held out her hand, he caught it, holding tighter than necessary as he pulled her up close.

"Apology accepted," he whispered. "I'm sorry, too."

"For what?" Glory asked. "You didn't do anything wrong."

Wyatt grinned wryly. "I'd like to get that in writing," he said. "I know people who'd beg to differ."

But despair kept pulling her deeper and deeper back into herself. "Dear God, Wyatt, there's nothing left to do but wait for him to try again."

He grabbed her by the arms and shook her, hating her for the fatalistic attitude. "Don't! Don't you even suggest that to me! You can't turn my world upside down, get into my mind and then give up on yourself without a damn fight! Do you hear me?"

After that, for a long, silent moment, neither spoke. And then Glory slowly lifted her finger and traced the path of the scar down the side of his face.

"Such a warrior."

Wyatt's confusion was obvious. "A what?"

Glory smiled, not much, but enough to let him know that he was off the hook. "You make me think of a warrior. For a while there, I forgot that you'd been a soldier. I'm sorry. I won't take you lightly, ever again."

"Well, then," he muttered, at a loss for anything else to say.

Glory nodded, glad she was forgiven, and then turned back to stare at the rubble. Long minutes passed during which the expression on her face never changed, but when she abruptly straightened and put her hands on her hips, there was a glint in her eyes that hadn't been there before. Wyatt didn't know whether to be glad, or get worried.

"Wyatt."

"What?"

"I am going to rebuild."

His heart surged, and then he paled. *Dear God, if only I could be that certain about my life.*

"And, since you're bound and determined to dog my steps, you're about to get as dirty as I am." She headed for the barn with Wyatt right behind her.

"What are you going to do?" he asked, as she began to push back the wide double doors hanging on tracks.

"I am going to clean house," she said. "Help me push this last door back. It always sticks."

Without giving himself time to argue, he did as he was told, and then watched her climb behind the steering wheel of an old one-ton truck that had been parked behind the doors.

"Better move," she shouted, as the starter ground and the engine kicked to life. "The brakes aren't so good. I'll have to coast to a stop."

"The hell you say," he muttered, and then quickly moved aside, uncertain what to think of her newfound determination.

It was long past noon when Wyatt tossed the last board on the truck bed that it could possibly hold. Without thinking, he swiped at the sweat running down his face and then remembered the grime on his gloves and groaned. He yanked them off, but it was too late.

Glory turned to see what had happened, then started to smile. He frowned as she grinned.

"Well?" he grumbled, and she laughed aloud.

"What's so funny?" he said, knowing full well he'd probably smeared ashes all over his face.

Glory closed her eyes and grimaced, pretending to be lost in deep thought, and then started to speak in a high singsong voice.

"I see a man. I see dirt. I see a man with a dirty face. I see..."

Her playful attitude pleased and surprised him, despite the fact that he was the butt of her joke. He grinned, then without warning, scooped her off her feet, threw her over his shoulder and stalked toward the well house near the barn.

Glory was laughing too hard to continue her taunt. The world hung at a crazy angle as her head dangled halfway down his back. The ground kept going in and out of focus as she bobbed with his every step. And then her view shifted, and a corner of her mouth tilted. She knew just how to make him put her down.

Hey, Hatfield... nice buns!

"Lord have mercy, Glory, give a man a break," Wyatt muttered, suddenly thankful that his face was too dirty to reveal his blush. And while she was busy enjoying the point she had scored, he turned on the faucet, picked up the connected garden hose and aimed it directly at her face.

She choked on the water and a laugh, and then fought him for the nozzle. In the middle of the game, her participation suddenly ceased. Wyatt dropped the hose, letting it run into a puddle at their feet as he watched her withdrawal.

"What is it, honey?" he asked.

She started to speak and then covered her face, suddenly ashamed of what she'd been doing.

He grasped her hands and pulled them away. "Talk to me, Glory."

"I shouldn't have been... It isn't right that I..."

Understanding dawned. "You feel guilty for being happy, don't you?"

She nodded, and tried not to cry.

"Oh, honey, I'm sorry," Wyatt said, and wrapped his arms around her. "It's natural, you know. But you can't regret being alive, and I don't believe that your father would have wanted you to die with him... would he?"

She shook her head.

"So, okay then." He picked up the hose, then handed it to her. "Come on, let's wash ourselves off before we go unload. And, after I put some of that brake fluid you found in the truck, I'm driving. You, however, will have to navigate our way to the city dump. It wasn't on your town's tourist map."

She held the hose, watching intently as he washed his hands, then lowered his head, letting the water from the hose run over the back of his hair and down his neck. He straightened quickly, shaking his head and wiping water from his eyes with both hands.

"Now you," he offered, and held the hose while she washed her hands, then cupped several handfuls of water and sluiced them on her face. "Feel better?" he asked, as he handed her his handkerchief.

"Wyatt?"

"What, darlin'?"

"Thank you," she said, and gave the used handkerchief back to him.

His gaze raked the contours of her body, now obviously revealed by the wet clothes clinging to her shape, and reminded himself of the task at hand.

"You're more than welcome."

The sign said Dump—$2.00 Per Load. But there was no one around to collect the fee, and so they drove right in and then backed up as near to the edge of the open pit as Wyatt dared. Taking into account the lack of decent brakes on the truck, he had no intention of going too close and then being unable to stop.

Glory got out of the truck with every intention of helping unload when Wyatt stopped her.

"Let me, okay?"

She relented. Her arms already ached from the strenuous job of loading the debris, and her legs were shaking with weariness.

"Okay, and thanks."

He smiled. "You're welcome. Now go find yourself some shade. This shouldn't take long."

Glory did as she was told, moving away from the side of the truck as Wyatt shed his shirt. She watched from a distance as he climbed up on top of the truck bed and began tossing the rubble, board by board, down into the pit, admiring the fluidity of his body and the grace with which he moved. After a while, she began to stroll around the area, stepping over bits of loose trash that had blown about, and kicking at pieces of metal and stone lying haphazardly about the site.

Down in the pit, a huge, black crow began cawing loudly as it suddenly took flight, and two others followed. Glory turned, watching as they moved through the air on obsidian wings. She looked back to where Wyatt was working and saw that he had paused and was scanning the area with a careful eye. It gave her courage to know that he was ever on the lookout for her welfare.

He turned to her and waved. She started to wave back when his image began to waver like a fading mirage. Believing it to be caused by heat rising from the pit, Glory started to shade her eyes, and then felt the ground go out from under her. It was reflex that sent her to her knees to keep from falling face-first, down in the dirt. And when her heart began to race, and the mirage began to reshape itself, Glory grabbed on to the grass beneath her hands and held on, afraid to let go of the ride through her mind.

Bright sunlight was suddenly gone, as was her father's flatbed truck and Wyatt's image. Another had come to take its place. One stronger... darker... deadlier. She groaned, unaware that she was plunging her fingers deep into the dirt and grass in an effort to hold on.

Panic painted the man's movements, hastening his actions and coloring the short, uneven gasps of his breath. His rapid footsteps were muffled by the loose dirt and grass as he moved from the front of a car to the back.

A faint glow of a quarter moon glinted on the trunk lid of the car as it popped open. He bent down, then straight-

ened, carrying something in his arms. Something heavy... something long... something white.

He staggered to the pit and then dropped it over the edge, watching as it fell, end over end, rolling, tumbling. Panic was beginning to subside. His relief was palpable.

Glory shuddered, trying to pull back from the scene in her mind, yet caught in a web not of her making. She watched, as if through his eyes, unable to see his face. She rode with his thought, moved with his stride, paused with his hesitation. But when he stood on the edge of the pit and looked down, Glory's own horror pulled her out of the fugue. In spite of the realization that it was all in her mind, she began to scream.

The wind tunneled through Wyatt's thick, dark hair, cooling the sweat upon his body and blowing away the ever-present stench of burned wood. Nearly through with the job, he paused and looked up, making certain that they were still alone, and ever careful to keep Glory within constant view.

Watching the wind play havoc with her hair made him smile. She'd already remarked while loading the truck that she should have done more than just tie it at the back of her neck, that it should have been braided to keep from whipping in her face and eyes.

And then he watched in horror as she suddenly dropped to her knees. Her name was on his lips as he jumped from the truck bed. And then he was running as fast as he could run, across the ground, past the edge of the pit, toward the sound of her screams. He yanked her out of the dirt and into his arms.

"Glory! Sweetheart! I'm here! I'm here. Let it go!"

She staggered, then swayed and, without thought, wrapped her arms around Wyatt's waist and held on, because he was her only stability in a world gone wrong.

"Dead. She's dead," Glory moaned. "All in white. And it came undone."

The plaintive wail of her voice sent shivers up his spine. She? Dead? What in God's name had Glory *seen* now?

He cupped her face with both of his hands, tilting it until she had nowhere to look but at him.

"Look at me!" he shouted. "Damn it, Glory, look at *me!*"

Her gaze shifted, and he could actually see cognizance returning. Breath slid from his lungs in a deep, heavy sigh as he wrapped his arms around her shoulders and rocked her within his embrace.

"Tell me, honey. Tell me what you saw."

And as quickly as her terror had come, it passed. There was intensity in her voice, in her manners, in the way she clutched at his bare arms.

"I saw a man take something white from a trunk of a car. I saw him drop it in the pit. It rolled and tumbled and..." She shuddered, then swallowed, trying to find ways to put into words what she saw in her mind. "He watched it fall. I felt him smile. The thing that he'd thrown came open. Like a candy that had come unwrapped. I could see her face. Her eyes were open wide, as if she'd been surprised. Oh, Wyatt, he threw a woman's body into the dump!"

"Good Lord! Are you sure?"

She nodded.

He stared down into the pit, noting the few bags of garbage that had been dumped earlier in the day, and then looking more intently at the huge layers of earth that had already been pushed over weeks of refuse.

"They probably cover this site every night. There's no way of telling how long ago this happened, is there?"

Her face contorted as she tried to remember everything that she'd seen and then she slumped in dejection. "No, it was so dark, I couldn't tell..." She gasped, and then cried. "A quarter moon! There was a quarter moon."

Wyatt tensed, then turned and stared at her face. "That was less than a week ago. I know, because I sat on a porch in Tennessee, watching clouds blowing across a quarter moon and listening for the sound of your voice."

Glory shuddered. "What do we do?"

"We go tell Chief Conway."

She groaned. "He's going to laugh in our faces," she warned.

"Sticks and stones, honey. Sticks and stones. Now let's get the rest of that stuff on the truck unloaded and get back to the cabin. I think we need to look our best when we ask the chief to dig up a dump."

Chapter 7

Lane was waiting for Wyatt and Glory when they pulled up to the curb and parked in front of the police department.

"I got your message," he said. "What's up?"

"After you left, Glory wanted to haul some stuff to the dump. While we were there, she had a . . . uh, she saw . . ."

Glory sighed. Even Wyatt, who claimed to believe, had trouble putting into words what she so took for granted.

"Granny always called them *visions,*" she said.

Lane's attention piqued. "Look, Glory, you've already made a believer out of me, and that's no easy task. So what did you *see?*"

"A woman's body being tossed in the dump."

"Oh, hell," Lane muttered, thinking of the ramifications of convincing the law to act on a psychic's word. "This won't be easy."

After they went inside, he knew he'd been right. The police chief erupted as Glory started to explain, while the deputy slipped out of the room, hovering just out of sight on the other side of the door.

"You saw what?" Conway shouted, rising from his chair and circling his desk to where Glory was standing. "And I suppose you saw this incident *in your mind,* as well?"

Wyatt glared, inserting himself slightly between them. "There's no need to shout," he said.

A vein bulged near Conway's left eye as his face grew redder by the minute. "Let me get this right. You had this *vision,* during which time you saw a man throw a woman's body into the dump. Oh! And she was dressed all in white, right?"

Glory's stomach tightened. She wanted to turn and walk out and forget she'd ever seen what she'd seen. "Yes, I told you I saw her—"

Conway interrupted. "Can you explain why the man who works the bulldozer at the dump didn't see her...or why twelve men who work three different trash trucks on two different routes didn't see her while they were dumping loads?"

"No," Glory muttered.

Conway smirked. "I didn't think so." He glared at Wyatt, as if blaming him for this latest in a series of problems he felt unequipped to deal with. "Look, Hatfield. I deal in facts, and these...uh, impulses she claims to have are not facts. They're dreams. They're imagination. They're..."

The deputy slipped back in the room, unable to resist a comment. "But Chief, she was right about them gas stoves."

"Shut up," he growled, and the deputy wisely retreated again, this time to the back room.

The chief's attitude did not surprise Lane. Law enforcement dealt with rules and givens. There were no rules for what Glory Dixon could do.

"I don't suppose you've had any missing person reports filed recently," Lane asked.

Conway made no attempt to hide his surprise. He apparently couldn't believe that a U.S. marshal would actually take any of this hogwash as fact.

"No, I don't suppose I have," he muttered.

"You're also real certain that none have come in over the wire from surrounding areas."

Conway flushed. He was pretty sure, but not positive. Obviously, however, he wasn't about to say it.

"Look, you two. You think because you're from the big city that the law in a little hill town like Larner's Mill can't cut the mustard, don't you? Well, you're wrong, and I don't like anyone buttin' into *my* business." His glare was directed as much at Lane as it was at Glory.

Before Wyatt or Lane could answer, Glory interrupted.

"I said what I came to say. What you do with the information is strictly up to you. However . . . if I'm right . . . and you're wrong, you've just let a man get away with murder. And that's your business, not mine, isn't it?" She walked out, leaving Wyatt and Lane to do as they chose.

They chose to follow her, and when they were gone, Anders Conway had no one to argue with but himself. It was a brief discussion that ended on a question. Just because Glory Dixon had been right about the fire that killed her folks didn't mean that she was always going to be right about that stuff floating around in her head...did it? He ran a hand through his thinning hair in frustration as he shouted at his deputy.

The deputy came running. "Yes, sir, what do you need?"

"I want to see everything we've got on missing persons in this county, as well as recent faxes along the same line." And when the deputy grinned, Conway glared. "Just because I asked to see the files doesn't mean I believe her," he grumbled. "I'm just doing my job. That's all."

Outside, Wyatt caught Glory by the arm as she walked toward the car.

"What?" she asked, still angry with the sheriff and the world in general.

"You did good," he said quietly.

Surprise colored her expression as Lane agreed.

"Wyatt's right. You said what had to be said. If the chief fails to follow up, then he's the one who's going to look like a fool. Now, if you two think you can make it on your own for a day or two, I'm going home to check on Toni and Joy, then swing by the office. I can access more information there than we're ever going to get out of Conway. Maybe something will turn up on the computer that fits what Glory saw."

"I'm really sorry all of this mess is taking you away from your family," Glory said.

Lane smiled. "My job always takes me away from my family, honey. We're used to it." And then his expression changed as he turned to Wyatt. "I've got some stuff I need to leave with you before I go. Why don't you pop the trunk of the car? I'll toss it in there."

"I'll do it," Glory said, and as she scooted across the seat, missed seeing the look on Wyatt's face as Lane set a handgun and several boxes of ammunition inside, then handed him his portable phone.

"Just so we can keep in touch," Lane said.

"And the other?" Wyatt asked.

"Just in case."

"Damn, I hate this," Wyatt said. "I thought I put all of this behind me when I left the military."

"Just take care of yourself," Lane said, and then gave Wyatt a quick, brotherly hug. "I'll call you as soon as I know something."

Wyatt watched him drive away, then looked back at Glory, who sat patiently inside the car, waiting for him to get in. Her profile was solemn as she stared out a window, obviously lost in thought. Wyatt glanced at the trunk lid, picturing what Lane had put inside, and then looked up at Glory, struck by her repose and innocence.

Oh, Lord, I don't know what I'm afraid of most. Trying to keep you safe, or taking you to bed.

She turned. Their eyes met, and for a second, Wyatt was afraid that she'd read his mind. But when she did nothing but smile, he got in without hesitation, satisfied that his thoughts were still his own.

"Where do we go from here?" Glory asked.

He'd asked her that same question this morning right after the kiss, and like her, he had no answer.

"It's all up to you," he finally said.

"Wyatt?"

"What, honey?"

"Have you ever had so many problems that you just wanted to run away from everything?"

"Unlike you, sweetheart, I've been running all my life. We'll find a way to work this out. Just don't quit on yourself, and better yet, don't quit on me. I would hate to wake up one morning and find you gone."

An odd light glittered in her eyes, and then she turned away. "When it comes time to leave, I won't be the one with a suitcase in hand, and we both know it."

There was no way to argue with what she said and come out on the good side of the truth. Angrily, he started the car. Having done what they came to do, they headed back to Granny Dixon's cabin.

As they drove, Wyatt fought demons of his own that kept tearing at his concentration. Okay, he told himself, he didn't have to love her, and she didn't have to love him. All he had to do was keep her safe. He thought of the gun in the trunk and the look on Lane's face when he left. His stomach turned, imagining Glory in pain or danger, and he wanted to slam on the brakes and take her in his arms. He resisted the urge and kept driving. Yet the farther he drove, the more certain he became that it was too late. He didn't *have* to love her...but he did.

Thunder rumbled beyond the valley, and a streak of lightning crossed the sky. The rocking chair in which Glory was sitting gave an occasional comforting squeak as she kept up the motion by pushing herself off with the toe of her shoe. She looked up as Wyatt came in the door and dropped the magazine she'd been reading into her lap.

"Did you find the puppy?"

He shook his head. "Maybe he's afraid of the storm. He's probably under some bush or even gone back to the barn to a place that's familiar to him."

"Maybe."

But Glory couldn't shake the feeling that something was wrong. The puppy was all she had left of her life before the fire, and she couldn't bear to think of losing him, too. J.C. had adored him, and had sworn he would make a good hunting dog, but with her brother gone, the training sessions were over. If the pup came home at all, the only thing he would be hunting was biscuits. But her attention shifted from the missing pup to Wyatt as she noticed his behavior.

Rain began to pepper the glass behind the curtains, and although it wasn't really cold, she shivered, watching as Wyatt kept pacing from window to window, then to the other side of the house, ever on the lookout for something to come out of the dark. Something...or someone...that didn't belong. His every movement was that of a man on edge.

The more she watched him, the more fascinated she became. She thought back to the night of the blizzard, and the first time she'd seen him, stretched out on a gurney and covered in blood. And then again, the day he'd been released from the hospital. Who would have guessed that one day, he'd be the single person who stood between her and death?

Looking back now, it hurt to remember how good and how simple life had been. Then she'd had a home and a family and a world that made sense. Now she had nothing but her life. And how Wyatt had come to her from across the miles was still a mystery; why he stayed, an even bigger puzzle. As she rocked, he unexpectedly turned and got caught in her stare.

"Glory...what is it?"

"Why don't you doubt me? Everyone else does, except maybe Lane."

She held her breath, afraid to hope, afraid to care...and then the lights went out.

"Wyatt? Is that you?"

"Hell, yes, it's me," he growled. "Who else were you expecting? If anyone else touched you but me right now, I'd kill them with my bare hands."

Even in the dark, she started to smile. She wasn't going to question what had changed his mind, she would just be thankful that he had.

He found her right where he'd left her, and when his ands moved across her body in the darkness of the room, e felt her inhale, then sigh. He groaned with want as her easts pushed against the palms of his hands.

"I didn't think you were coming back."

"I just went to my car...for these."

He caught her hands and flattened them against his rain-attered shirt, guiding them to a shirt pocket to the right is heartbeat.

ncertain what was about to happen, she still followed his feeling the pocket, then the flap, then at his instiga- dipping her hand inside. Thunder rattled the window- as a gust of wind slapped tree limbs against the edge house. She gasped, spinning toward the sound be-hem.

s all right, darlin'. It's just the wind."

then he caught her hand and laid something into her

frowned as her fingers curled around the objects, o identify the sharp, clean edges of the flat, foil

't understand," she said. "What is it?"

protection, sweetheart. I have never made love to in my entire life without it in one form or an- not about to put you at risk."

essed it," he said, and then laughed softly.

His answer was instantaneous, as if he'd thought about it himself, time and time again, and knew all of the words by heart.

"I don't know. All I know is, from the first there's been a connection between us. I don't understand it, but I know that it's there." He looked away, unwilling to say too much.

"Everyone thinks I'm crazy, so why are you different? Why do you stay with a crazy woman, Wyatt Hatfield? Why aren't you running as fast as you can from this mess?"

Now he hesitated. Telling the truth about his growing feelings for her could ruin everything, and yet lying to her was not an option. He had to find an answer somewhere in between. When he looked up, his eyes were full of secrets.

"Maybe I'm just waiting to hear you call my name."

The rocking chair came to an abrupt halt, ending in the middle of a squeak. *Oh, Wyatt. I'm afraid to. I'm afraid to love. I'm afraid that you won't understand me, and I can't change.*

Again, as he had in the past, he tapped into her thoughts and answered without realizing she hadn't spoken them aloud.

"I wouldn't change a thing about you, even if I could," he said. "I'm the one who's all messed up. I don't have it in me to make a good woman happy, because I've already tried and failed."

"No one is perfect, Wyatt. If you wanted to try, I believe that you could make anyone happy." And then her voice faltered, and she had to clear her throat before she could continue. "Even me," she whispered.

He froze. There was no mistaking the invitation, and ignoring it was beyond him. Because she sat waiting, he went to her, then held out his hands.

Glory took them without hesitation. The magazine in her lap fell to the floor when he pulled her to her feet, and when he began threading his fingers through her hair, her focus shifted, as it did when a vision was upon her. As he cupped the back of her head, tracing his thumbs across the arch of her cheekbones, she lost her center of gravity. Had it not been for Wyatt's arms, she would have fallen.

Even though she wanted this and much more from him, yielding to his greater strength was frightening. It was as if she'd suddenly lost her sense of self and was being consumed by his power. His voice rumbled too close to her ear, and instinctively, she shivered. Wyatt read her actions as something other than desire, and began feathering small kisses across her forehead, pleading his case as he drew her closer and closer against him.

"Don't be afraid of me...or of anyone else. Being afraid of love is like hiding from life. Sometimes you have to take a chance to be happy, and taking chances is what life is all about."

When his hands moved from the back of her head to the back of her neck, she sighed, giving way to a greater need within herself.

"Oh, Wyatt, I'm not afraid *of* you, only of *losing* you."

Lord help both of us.

He lifted her off of her feet. With her lips on his mouth and her body in perfect alignment with his, he began to turn, holding her fast within his arms as her feet dangled inches above the floor. Seductively, deliberately, with nothing but passion for music, they slow danced to a tune only they could hear.

Faintly aware of the ceiling spinning above and the lights blinking in and out of focus as they moved about the floor, she wanted to laugh, and she wanted to cry. She'd never known such joy... and such fear. She was hovering on the brink of discovery in Wyatt Hatfield's arms.

Wyatt ached, wanting more, so much more than the brief, stolen kisses that he was taking. Time, I need to take my time. But it was all he could do to heed his own words.

Unable to resist the temptation, he traced the curve of her cheek with his mouth and groaned when he felt her shudder. When he began nuzzling the spot below her ear with his nose, then his lips, savoring the satin texture of her skin, inhaling the essence of the woman that was Glory Dixon,

she sighed, whispering something he couldn't understand. Her voice was soft against his cheek, and she yielded to him like a woman, giving back more than she got.

Clutching her fingers in his short, dark hair, she hid her face beneath the curve of his chin, ashamed of what she was about to ask, but afraid this chance would never com[e] again.

"Oh, Wyatt, I've learned the hard way that life is too [un]certain. This time tomorrow you could be gone, or I c[ould] be dead. Please make love to me. I don't want to die [with]out knowing what that's like."

He froze in the middle of a breath, with his mout[h on] her lips and his hands just below the curve of her hi[ps. Ex]cept for the blood thundering through his veins and hammering against his ear, all movement ceased.

"What did you just say?"

Glory lifted her head. She wouldn't be ashame[d] ... she was. Truth was better said face-to-face.

"I asked you to make love to me," she whisp[ered].

"Not that. The part about dying."

"I've never been with a man, Wyatt. I don['t] ... it feels like to have a man's hands on my bod[y] ... side of me."

"Oh... my... God."

There was little else he could think to s[ay] ... with need, it was all he could do to turn he[r] ... to be done. He'd started something in th[e] ... mind, and had to stop it before it was to[o] ...

"Well, damn," he said quietly, and ... room.

She could hear the front door slam f[...] The fire that he'd started was scaldin[g] ... out. She didn't know whether to cry ... his name, or go after him. She was ... hunger he'd started when she h[...] abruptly, and then slam shut, muti[...] accompanying the rain still poun[...] click of a lock was loud in the su[...]

The sound of his laughter curled her toes and made her weak at the knees. Heat swept across her body, and she realized she was blushing.

"Where were we?" he muttered, and slipped his hands beneath her hips, cupping her body to his, and lowering his mouth in the darkness, searching for the sweetness of a kiss that he knew would be waiting.

The packets dropped to the bed behind them as she wrapped her arms around his neck. And then she moved against his groin, testing the bulge behind his zipper, and whispered against his mouth.

"Right about here... I think."

Moments later, Wyatt lifted her off her feet and laid her on the bed. The quilt shifted beneath her as his body pressed her deeper and deeper into the mattress.

Wyatt gritted his teeth, reminding himself that making love to Glory would be a whole new ball game, and took a long, slow breath to clear his senses. When he felt her shudder, his heart raced in sudden fear.

"Dear God, don't be afraid of me," he said. "I'll stop this right now if that's what you want."

Her hands moved up his thighs, pausing at the sides of his hips. "It's not fear that makes me tremble, Wyatt Hatfield, it's you."

"Have mercy," he said softly.

"Only if you hurry," she answered.

He did.

Clothes went flying in the darkness, landing where they'd been tossed with little care for the decorum. Now there was nothing between them but skin and need. Wyatt moved back across her body, settling the weight of himself upon her, testing the size of himself against her fragility. She was so damned tiny it scared him half to death.

Without wasted motion, he took her in his arms and rolled, taking her with him until he was flat on his back and she was lying upon him, mouth to mouth, breast to chest.

And when his hands cupped her breasts, rolling the hard aching peaks between his fingers with delicate skill, she instinctively arched, her mind blanking on everything but his touch.

Oh?

He smiled in the darkness, moving his hands upon her body, mapping the tiny bones and a waist he could circle with both hands, testing the gentle flare of her hips, then letting his thumbs slide down. . .down.

Oh, Wyatt!

Glory gasped, then moaned as her head fell back and her hips followed the pressure of his fingers. When her body swayed, and the long flow of her hair brushed across his thighs, teasing at the juncture of his turgid manhood, Wyatt shuddered with longing. Not yet, he warned himself.

His hands slid over the quilt top, finding, then opening one of the packets he'd brought in from the car—doing what had to be done, before it was too late to think.

The room spun and the bed tilted. Glory rode with the motion, afraid it would stop, afraid to let go of the man beneath her. He'd built too many fires with the touch of his hands and the sweep of his mouth. Something was building, tightening, spiraling inside her so deep that it had no name. There was no understanding of what would come next, only the mind-bending need for it to be.

"Oh. . . Wyatt."

Her cry was soft, almost unheard, but Wyatt felt it just the same. He was aware of what was happening to her and wished he could be inside of her when it happened. But he couldn't...not the first time...not until she knew that this act came with something besides pain.

"Wyyaatt?"

There was panic in her voice, riding along with a racing heart as he continued to stoke the fires he'd created.

"That's it, Glory. Don't fight it. Don't fight me. Just let it happen."

And then it did, breaking over her in swamping waves of heat, shattering in one spot and then spilling into every other part of her body.

"Ah, Wyatt," she groaned, and would have collapsed, had he not caught her in mid-slump.

"Not yet, sweet lady. There's a thing I must do, and I ask your forgiveness now, before it's too late."

Glory's mind was still swimming in the midst of pure pleasure when he rolled with her once again. Vaguely aware of the bed beneath her bare back and the weight of the man above her, she was unprepared for the spear of manhood that gently shattered the dissipating pleasure. The pain was sharp, burning and, after such joy, unexpected. Unable to stifle a cry, her fingers dug into the sides of his arms as she instinctively arched against the thrust.

"Ah, Glory, I'm sorry, so sorry," he whispered, and gritted his teeth to maintain control.

A sob caught at the back of her throat. Afraid to breathe, she braced herself for the next wave of pain. It didn't come. Only an unexpected fullness she'd never known before. One slow breath after another, she waited for him to move, and only after she began to test the theory herself, did he react.

Bracing himself above her, he shifted slightly, and then smiled in the dark when he heard a soft moan that had nothing to do with pain.

"Sweetheart, are you all right?" he whispered.

Her hands snaked around his shoulders. "I don't know yet. I'll tell you when it's over."

His laughter rocked the walls. When he lowered his head, feeling for her lips in the darkness, the smile was still upon his face. And then he started to move, slowly, tentatively, giving her time to adjust to his presence. Deeper and faster, he took her with him, driving like the rain that blew against the outer walls, losing himself in this woman who held his heart in her hands.

The end came almost without warning. One moment Wyatt was in total control, and then Glory moved unexpectedly, wrapping her legs around his hips and pulling him too far in to stop. Heat washed over him like a wave, sweeping everything from his mind but the feeling they'd created together. And then it was over, and he wanted her more.

Long silent minutes passed while he cradled her in his arms, whispering things in the dark that he could never have said in the light, stroking her body with the flat of his hand, unable to believe that this tiny, tiny woman was capable of such passion and love.

Finally he asked her again. "Glory?"

She sighed, and then slid one leg across his knees. "Hmmm?"

"Now are you all right?"

He felt her smile against his chest, and dug his hands in the long tangle he'd made of her hair.

"Oh, Wyatt...I didn't know, I didn't know."

"Know what, honey?" he whispered, as he continued to cuddle her close.

"That love came in colors."

"That it did what?"

"It's true. When we...I mean when I..."

He grinned. "It's okay, I know the moment you're trying to identify."

"I saw red...and then white."

Touched by her admission, he teased her, trying to alleviate his own emotions. "What...no blue?"

"Red was what I saw just before...when you...when we..."

His voice vibrated with laughter. "Darlin', we're going to have to find a way to get you past this mental roadblock. Just say it. When you lost your sweet mind, right?"

"I suppose it *was* right about then."

This time, he couldn't suppress a chuckle. And then her arms tightened around his chest and when he reached out to stroke her face, he felt tears on her cheeks.

"Tears? Don't tell me I was that bad," he whispered.

"No, Wyatt. I didn't cry because it was bad. I cried because it was so good."

He hugged her, too moved to respond to her praise.

A few seconds passed, and in that time, he felt her restlessness, and knew that there was something else she wanted to say. Then he remembered she hadn't explained the other color.

"So I made you see red. But what about the white?"

Excitement was in her voice as she lifted herself on one elbow and traced the lines of his face with her fingertips.

"Oh, Wyatt...just as everything within me gave way...I saw you... or at least the essence of you. There was no way to tell where I ended and you began. And the light with which you came to me was so bright...so pure...so white!" Her voice faltered, then broke. "That was when I cried."

Oh, my God!

More than once, he tried to respond, but there were no words to express what he felt, only an overwhelming sense of inevitability, as if he'd been on the course all his life, and the outcome was out of his hands.

And so they slept, wrapped in each other's arms while the storm front moved on, and morning dawned to a damp, new day.

The sharp ringing of the telephone near his ear sent Carter Foster scrambling to shut off an alarm. By the time he realized that it was the phone, and not the alarm, he had knocked a stack of papers onto the floor and cracked the plastic housing around his clock.

"Damn it," he muttered, and then picked up the phone. "Foster residence."

"It's Marker."

The skin on the back of Carter's neck crawled as his belly suddenly twisted into a knot. Hiring Bo Marker yesterday had been a last resort, but he hadn't expected to hear from him quite so soon.

"Is it over?" Carter asked.

Marker snorted loudly into the phone, his voice filled with derision. "Hell no, it ain't over. You didn't tell me she had a bodyguard *and* a watchdog."

Carter groaned. He should have known Marker would screw up.

"For all I know, she could have three of everything," Carter snarled. "You're the one who claimed to be an expert. It's up to you to find a way to accomplish what you're being paid to do."

"I want more money," Marker argued. "I done been dog-bit, and that man who hangs on the Dixon woman's arm is no slouch. I seen him take a handful of ammo and a piece out of his trunk that could blow a hole in an elephant."

"What did you think they would do, throw rocks at you?" Carter yelled. "And hell no, you don't get more money. If you don't do what I paid you to do, you don't even get the last half of what I promised."

Then he pinched the bridge of his nose, took a slow, calming breath and stared out of the window at the rising sun. Screaming at Neanderthals was not something to which he was accustomed. Someone was going to have to do the thinking, and obviously, Bo Marker was not going to be it.

"Look, just get rid of the dog and..."

"Already done it."

Carter sighed. "Then why are you bothering me? You know what has to be done. Go the hell out and just do it. And don't call me again until it's over!"

Marker frowned. "Yeah, right," he muttered, and let the phone drop back onto the receiver, well aware that it would echo sharply in Carter Foster's ear.

Carter winced as he disconnected, and then fell backward onto his bed, staring up at the ceiling without seeing the fancy swirls of plaster that Betty Jo had insisted upon, and contemplating how swiftly a man's life could change.

One day he'd had a wife and a business and a fairly normal life. That he no longer had a wife was not strictly his fault. He'd firmly convinced himself that Betty Jo had brought everything upon herself. And, when he thought about it, he regretted the fact that he'd been forced to eliminate other lives in order to maintain his own... but not enough to sway himself from his chosen path. Yet thinking about that Dixon woman and what she could do to his world made him sick with fear.

"Well, damn," he mumbled, and rolled off the bed and headed for the bath. It was time to start another day.

Chapter 8

With daylight came restraint. Glory wasn't versed in morning-afters, and Wyatt looked even bigger and more imposing in the bright light of day as she lay in bed, watching him wake beside her.

The color of his hair was a stark contrast to the pillowcase upon which he lay. Dark to light. Black to white. His eyelashes fluttered as consciousness returned, brushing the cheeks upon which they lay like shadows moving in the night.

Glory shivered with longing as she gazed at his lips, remembering how he'd raked them across her body, and how she'd responded. He stretched, and she followed the path of muscles that contracted along his arms and chest, amazed at the size of him and of his obvious strength, yet remembering how gently he'd held her when they made love.

Nervously, she waited for those dark eyes to open, waited anxiously to see how he would respond, and reminded herself, *I'm the one who started this. I asked him to make love to me.*

Wyatt opened his eyes and turned to face her. An easy smile creased his lips as he scooped her up in his arms.

"And I will be forever grateful."

Glory blushed. "I thought you were asleep," she grumbled. "You could make a woman real nervous, sneaking in on her thoughts like that."

Wyatt grinned, then slid his hands down the length of her back, testing the softness of her skin. Stoking new fires, he began measuring the distance of his restraint between lust and passion. He wanted her to know pleasure before he knew his. But when her eyelids fluttered and her breath began to quicken, he knew it was time to ask.

"I don't want to insist, but I'd like to talk about, uh... losing our minds...just once more...before I get out of this bed."

"Talk's cheap," she said, and ran her hand down his chest, past his belly and beyond.

He grinned again as he caught her hand before she went too far in her exploration and ruined the extent of his plans, and then he paused, remembering last night had been her first time.

"But... I don't want you to do this if it's going to be uncomfortable for you," he whispered, tracing the shape of her mouth with a fingertip.

She raised up on one elbow and began digging through the tangle of bedclothes until she felt one of the flat packets beneath her hand. She handed it to Wyatt with only the faintest of blushes.

"Here. You're the one who feels uncomfortable, not me."

Again, in the midst of a most intimate moment, she had made him laugh by acknowledging that his manhood was hard and, most probably, aching. And in that moment, Wyatt knew a rare truth. Going from laughter to passion, without foreplay in between, was a rare and beautiful thing. Like the bloom of the morning glory, a thing to be treasured.

He took what she offered, and moments later he rolled across the bed, taking her with him until she was firmly in place beneath the weight of his body.

Glory looked up. The breadth of his shoulders swamped her in size. The weight of his body was twice that of her own, and yet she knew that she was in total control.

One word.

That was all it would take to change the drift of Wyatt Hatfield's thoughts. But Glory wasn't a fool. If one word need be uttered, it would be one of compliance, not rejection. The question was in his eyes, the thrust of his body against the juncture of her thighs was all the proof that he could show of his need. The muscles in his arms jerked as he held himself above her, waiting for her decision.

"Glory...sweetheart?"

She lifted her arms and pulled him down. "Yes."

And when he slid between her legs and filled that in her that was empty, she sighed with satisfaction. "Oh, yes."

Wyatt smiled, and then it was the last thought he could manage as morning gave way to love.

Everything was wet. Last night's rain had soaked ground, grass and trees, and the creek below Granny Dixon's old cabin was frothed with mini whitecaps from the swiftly flowing stream. Wyatt stood lookout at the top of the creek bank, watching as Glory searched the thickets below, calling and calling for a missing pup that never came.

"Give it up, honey," he called. "If the pup was anywhere nearby, you know it would come to you."

She looked up, and the sorrow on her face was more than he could bear. He started down the bank toward her when she waved him away, and started up instead.

"We can go up to your house. Maybe the pup spent the night in the barn," he suggested.

She shook her head and all but fell in his arms as she reached the top. "Even if he had, he would have come back this morning begging for something to eat."

Weary in body and heart, she wrapped her arms around his waist and then suddenly gasped, jumping back in shock when her hands accidentally brushed across the pistol he had slipped in the waistband of his jeans. Her eyes widened with shock, turning more silver than blue as she looked up at Wyatt's face. It was all she could do to say his name.

"Why are you carrying a gun?"

His expression flattened. Once again, she saw the soldier that he had been.

"I want you alive. I want you safe. This is the only way I have of helping to keep you that way."

She paled, then spun away, and Wyatt watched as her hair fanned around her like a veil of pale lace. He wanted to touch her, but her posture did not invite intrusion. Instead, he waited for Glory to make the next move.

Glory stared blindly about her at the pristine beauty of the thick, piney woods that had always been her home, searching for the comfort that had always been there. Yet as she looked, the shadows that she'd once sought to play in no longer offered cool solace. Instead, they loomed, ominous by their mere presence. Trees so dense that it would be impossible to drive through no longer seemed a source of refuge. Now they seemed more like a prison. She doubled her fists and started to shake. Anger boiled up from her belly, burning and tearing as it spilled from her lips.

"I hate this," she muttered, and then turned back to Wyatt, her voice rising in increments with each word that she spoke. "I hate this! It isn't fair! My family was taken from me. I no longer have a home. And now J.C.'s puppy is gone." Her voice broke as tears began to fall. "It was the last thing I had from before."

Wyatt reached for her, but she was too fast. Before he knew it, she had started toward what was left of her home, splattering mud up the legs of her jeans and coating her boots as she stalked up the road.

He didn't argue, and he didn't blame her. Fighting mad was a hell of a lot healthier than a silent grief that never healed. He began to follow, never more than a few steps behind.

A slight mist was beginning to rise from the puddles as the midmorning sun beamed down through the trees, evaporating the water that had not soaked into the ground. The cry of a red-tailed hawk broke the silence between them as it circled high above, searching for food. Wyatt shaded his eyes and looked up, and as he did, missed seeing Glory as she suddenly veered from the road and dashed into the edge of the trees.

But when she screamed, he found himself running toward her with the gun in his hand before he realized that he'd even moved. Years of training, and an instinct that had kept him alive in places like Somalia had kicked in without thought.

By the time he reached her, she was coming back to him on the run. He caught her in midstride, holding her close as he trained the gun toward the place she had been, expecting to see someone behind her. Someone who meant her great harm.

"Talk to me," he shouted, shaking her out of hysterics before it got them both killed. He needed to know what was out there before he could help.

She pointed behind her, and then covered her face with her hands and dropped to her knees in the grass.

"The puppy...back there...it's dead."

God! Wyatt ran his hand gently over the crown of her head, then patted her shoulder, his voice was soft with regret and concern. "Wait here, sweetheart. I'll be right back."

It had been dead for some time. That much was obvious, due to the fact that while it had been shot, there was no blood at the scene. Last night's rain had taken care of that...and any other clues that might have led Wyatt to some sort of answer. And yet he knelt near the carcass, searching the ground around it for something, anything, that might lead to an answer.

He stared at the hole in the side of the pup's head, and another just behind one of its front legs. For Wyatt, it was total proof that it hadn't been some sort of hunting accident. One shot maybe, two, no. And then he noticed something beneath the pup's mouth and tested it with the tip of his finger. It was soft and wet and blue. Frowning, he pulled, then rocked back on his heels when a bit of cloth came away in his hands. It had been caught in the pup's teeth.

"Well, I'll be damned," he muttered, fingering the small bit of fabric. "Looks like you got a piece of him before he got to you, didn't you, fella?"

He stuffed the fabric in his pocket, then looked back at Glory. She was only a short distance away, and he could tell by the way she was standing that she'd been watching every move that he'd made.

Damn. He stood, then started toward her.

"Someone shot him, didn't they?"

He nodded.

"What was that you put in your pocket?"

He frowned, yet keeping the truth from her was dangerous. It could very well get her killed.

"I think maybe you had the makings of a good watchdog, honey. There was a piece of fabric caught in its teeth."

The anger that had carried her up the road simply withered and died as she absorbed the ramifications of what that could mean. Had the puppy died defending its territory from a trespasser? Maybe the same man who'd been in her house?

"So what do you think?" she finally asked.

What he was thinking didn't need to be said. He slipped an arm around her shoulder and hugged her gently. "Just that I need a shovel."

Her shoulders drooped. "There's one in the barn."

He held out his hand and then waited. This time, they traveled the rest of the distance hand in hand. But when they came out of the barn, Glory groaned in dismay. Edward Lee was walking toward them up the road, carrying the pup's limp body dangling across his outstretched arms.

"Oh, no," she said softly.

"What?" Wyatt asked.

"Edward Lee gave J.C. the puppy for a birthday present about six months ago. He's not going to take this well."

Sure enough, Glory was right. Edward Lee was sobbing long before he reached them.

"Look, Mornin' Glory, someone went and killed your dog."

"We know, Edward Lee. See, we have a shovel. We were about to bury him. Would you like to pick a place?"

Tears slowed, as the idea centered within the confusion in his brain. He blinked, and then lifted his gaze from the pup to Glory.

He nodded. "I will pick a good place," he said. "A place that James Charles would like."

In spite of her pain, Glory smiled, thinking what a fit J.C. would have had if he'd heard that. Edward Lee was the only person who occasionally insisted upon calling her brother by his full given name. Everyone else had been forced to use the nickname, J.C., which he preferred.

And then Edward Lee looked at Wyatt, suddenly realizing he was there. "Wyatt is my friend," he said, assuring himself that the new relationship still held true.

Wyatt nodded. "Yes, I am, Edward Lee. Now, why don't you tell me where to dig, and we'll make a good place for the puppy to rest."

Glory watched from the shade of the barn while Edward Lee led Wyatt to a nearby lilac bush in full bloom. When he began to dig, she said a quick prayer and let go of her fear. A short time later, there was a new mound of dirt near the thick cover of lavender blossoms. It was a fitting monument for a short, but valiant, life.

They walked with Edward Lee to the end of the road, and then watched as he disappeared into the trees. A few moments later, as they were about to enter the cabin, the persistent ringing of an unanswered phone could be heard.

"Shoot." Wyatt suddenly remembered the phone that he'd tossed on the bed while getting dressed. He darted inside, and then toward the bedroom, answering it in the middle of a ring.

"Hello."

"Where have you been?" Lane growled. "And why didn't you take the damned phone with you? I left it so I could stay in touch. I was just about call out the National Guard."

"Sorry," Wyatt said, and dropped onto the side of his bed. "We were burying a dog."

"You were what?"

"The pup. Someone shot it while we were in town yesterday. We didn't find it until this morning."

"The hell you say. How's Glory taking it?"

"About like you'd imagine. It was her brother's dog."

Lane frowned. He didn't like what he was thinking, but it had to be said. "Look, Wyatt, remember when I was laid up at Toni's after the plane crash and your nephew's dog was killed?"

Wyatt grinned. "Yeah, was that before or after you got my sister pregnant?"

"Just shut up and listen," Lane muttered. "The point I'm trying to make is that the inmate we all thought was dead was actually hiding in the woods. He killed the dog to keep it quiet during one of his trips to forage for food. I'm warning you to be careful. Bad guys have a habit of eliminating all obstacles in their paths, no matter what."

Wyatt dug in his pocket and pulled out the bit of fabric. "Don't think it hasn't already crossed my mind. The pup got a bite of whoever it was that did him in, though. I found a piece of fabric caught between his teeth."

"Well, well! That's real good detective work. Maybe there's hope for you yet," Lane drawled.

Wyatt grinned. "Is there a real reason you called, or were you just checking up on me?"

"Oh, yeah, right! Look, I've been running a check on any or all missing person reports filed in the past two months in a five-hundred-mile radius of Larner's Mill. There are only two, and both of them are males. Glory is real sure the body she visualized was a female?"

"Absolutely," Wyatt said, and heard Lane sigh in his ear.

"Okay. I'll keep searching. Meanwhile, for God's sake, carry the phone with you. You never know when you'll need to reach out and touch someone... understand?"

"Understood," Wyatt said, and disconnected. When he looked up, Glory was standing in the doorway. She'd been listening to their conversation. There was a slight, embarrassed smile on her face, but stifling the question on her mind was impossible.

"Lane got your sister pregnant?"

Wyatt laughed. "It's a long story, honey. But don't feel sorry for my sister. She got exactly what she wanted. In fact, old Lane was the one who got caught in the Hatfield cross fire."

She smiled, trying to imagine anyone as big and forbidding as Lane Monday getting caught by anything.

"You're very lucky," she said.

Wyatt frowned as he tried to follow her line of thinking. "How so, honey?"

"You have a large family. I think it would be wonderful to be a part of that."

"I'll share mine with you," Wyatt muttered. "Sometimes they can be a royal pain in the you-know-what."

If only I could share your family, Wyatt Hatfield. But she didn't say it, and walked away.

Wyatt sat on the side of the bed, calling himself a dozen kinds of a fool for not responding to her wish. But how could he say it, when he wasn't sure what to say? All he knew was that he lived for the sound of her voice, rested easy only when she was within eyesight, and came apart in her arms from their loving. It was definitely passion. But was it true love?

He followed her into the kitchen. "Don't cook. We need to get out of here for a while. Why don't you make a list?

We'll do some shopping and then eat supper out before we come home?"

Glory turned. "I have to change. I'm muddy, and my hair's a mess."

Wyatt dug his hands through the long, silky length, then buried his face in the handful he lifted to his face.

"Your hair is never a mess," he said softly. "It feels like silk, and smells like flowers." And then he leaned down and pressed a swift kiss on her mouth. "And... I love the way it feels on my skin."

And I love the way you feel on my skin, she thought.

Startled, Wyatt dropped her hair, and looked up. Glory arched an eyebrow, unashamed of having been caught.

"Did it again, didn't you?" she asked, and left him wearing a guilty expression as she went to change clothes.

Within the hour, they were in the car and on their way up the road. When they passed the old barn, Glory turned toward the new grave and impulsively pressed her hand against the glass.

"When this is all over, you could get another puppy," Wyatt said.

Glory shrugged. "If I'm still here to care for it, I might."

Wyatt was so angry he was speechless. That she kept referring to the fact that she might not live through all of this made him crazy. He couldn't shake the fear that she might be seeing something of her own future that she wasn't willing to share.

Sundown had come and gone while they were inside Milly's Restaurant on the outskirts of Larner's Mill. They exited the lively establishment into a crowded parking lot as the scent of hickory smoke from the inside grill coated the damp night air.

Glory walked silently beside Wyatt as they wove their way through the unevenly parked cars, absorbing the comfort of his presence even though she was unable to voice what she was feeling. And truth be known, she wasn't certain she could put into words the emotions swirling inside her head.

All she knew was she wanted this man as she'd never wanted another.

A couple got out of a car just ahead of them, and paused and stepped aside, giving Wyatt and Glory room to pass.

Pleasantries were traded, and then they walked on just as someone shouted Wyatt's name. He turned. It was the chief of police.

Anders Conway stepped off the curb and started toward them while Glory's good mood began dissipating.

"Oh, great," she muttered. "I'm not in the mood for any more of that man's sharp-edged doubt. Wyatt, could I please have the keys? I'd rather wait for you in the car."

He slipped his hand beneath the weight of her hair, caressing the back of her neck in a gentle, soothing touch, then handed her the keys without comment.

Beneath a tree a short distance away, Bo Marker sat in a stolen car, well concealed behind the dark tinted windows as the engine idled softly. When he'd seen the Dixon woman and her man come out of Milly's, he'd been satisfied that tonight, he could quite literally kill two birds with one stone, get the rest of his money from Foster, and be out of Kentucky before this night had passed. And then the chief of police had followed them outside.

"Son of a . . . !" he muttered, then shifted in the seat.

But berating himself for bad luck wasn't Bo Marker's style. All he needed was a change of plans, and when Glory Dixon suddenly walked away from her watchdog companion, Marker smiled. It creased his wide, homely face like cracks down the side of a jar. He leaned forward, hunching his great bulk behind the wheel of the car, and when Glory Dixon moved into the open, he quietly shifted from Park to Drive, and then stomped on the gas.

Bo Marker had stolen wisely. The souped-up hot rod could go from zero to sixty in seconds. The engine roared, coming to life like a sleeping lion. Tires squalled, gravel flew, and the car fishtailed slightly as he shot out of a parked position, down the short driveway toward the highway beyond, and right into Glory Dixon's path.

At the sound, Glory looked up and found herself staring straight into the blinding glare of headlights on high beam. Before she could think to react, a weight caught her from behind in a flying tackle, and before she had time to panic, Wyatt's arms surrounded her as they went rolling across the gravel.

Tiny shards of rock stung her leg as the car flew past, and she heard Wyatt grunt in pain as they came to a stop against the bumper of another vehicle. His hands were moving across her body before she could catch her breath to speak. She didn't have to hear the panic in his voice to know how close that had been.

"Glory! Sweetheart! Talk to me! Are you all right?" Before she could answer, she heard a man shouting orders and remembered. Chief Conway had witnessed it all.

"How bad is she hurt?" Conway asked Wyatt, as he knelt beside them.

Wyatt's voice broke. "Oh, God, I don't..."

Glory caught Wyatt's hand as it swept up her neck in search of a pulse. In the second before she spoke, they stared straight into each other's eyes. There were no words for what they felt at that moment, nor were any necessary. He'd saved her life, as surely as she'd saved his all those months ago.

"Thanks to Wyatt, I think I'm all right."

"Damn crazy driver," the chief said. "I am in my personal car, or I'd have given chase myself." And then by way of explanation, he added, "I couldn't catch a rabbit on a hot day in that thing, but at least I had my two-way. My men are already in pursuit."

Even as Wyatt helped Glory from the ground, the sounds of fading sirens could be heard in the distance.

"Oh, damn," Wyatt whispered, as he peered through the faint glow of the security lights to the dark stain coating his hand. "Glory...you're bleeding."

She followed the trail of a burning sensation on her left arm. "I just scraped my elbow." And then she shuddered, and leaned forward, letting Wyatt enfold her within his embrace. "It wasn't an accident, Wyatt."

"I know, honey."

Conway frowned. "Now, it could have been a drunk driver, or a—"

Angry with Conway's persistent blind streak where Glory was concerned, Wyatt interrupted. His voice rose until by the time he was finished, he was shouting in the policeman's face.

"Last week, someone blew up her house, fully expecting her to be in it. Yesterday, someone shot her dog. We found this in his teeth when we went to bury it." Wyatt dug the bit of fabric from his shirt pocket and slapped it into the chief's hand. "Now, tonight, someone tried to run her down. And before you argue, consider the fact that the car wasn't already rolling when Glory stepped into the drive. I heard the motor idling. I heard him shift gears. He was waiting for her. When he had a clear shot, he took it."

Glory shuddered and Wyatt felt it.

"Now I'm going to take her to the hospital to be checked out. If you want to talk more, feel free to come along. Otherwise, I suppose you can file this information and the bit of fabric I just gave you where you've filed the rest of Glory's case."

"No hospital, Wyatt. Just take me home. There's nothing wrong with me that you and some iodine can't fix."

"Are you sure, honey?" he asked.

"I'm sure. Just get me out of here."

Conway felt restless, even guilty, although there was little else he could do right now, other than what he'd just done. He followed them to the car as Wyatt helped Glory into her seat.

"Look, Miss Dixon. We're doing all we can to follow up on what you've told us. Maybe we'll have the man in custody before the night is out."

She didn't answer, and when they drove away, Conway was struck by the quiet acceptance he'd seen in her eyes. As if she knew that what he said was little more than whitewash for the fact that they had nothing to go on, so therefore, they were doing nothing.

"Damn it all to hell," Conway muttered. He looked down at the fabric that Wyatt had handed him, and then stuffed it in his pocket as he ran back to his car. The least he could do was get to the office and follow the pursuit from there.

As they drove through town on their way home, Wyatt couldn't quit watching the play of emotions on Glory's face.

"Honey...are you sure you don't want me to drive by the hospital?" His fingers kept tracing the knuckles of her left hand as he drove, as if he didn't trust himself to ever let her out of his grasp again. "When I took you down, I hit you hard...real hard. I just couldn't think of a quicker way to move you out of danger."

Glory turned sideways, staring at Wyatt's profile, wondering how she would bear it when he left her. Her voice was soft, just above a whisper as she reacted to his concern.

"It's all right, Wyatt. You saved my life tonight, and we both know it." She scooted across the seat and laid her head on his shoulder. "Thank you."

He exhaled slowly, finally able to shake off the panic he'd felt when he'd seen her danger. With his left hand firmly on the steering wheel, he slipped his right arm around her shoulders and held her close. "Now you know how I feel about you."

She sighed, and her breath trembled, thick with tears she wouldn't let go. "Wyatt...oh, Wyatt, what are we going to do?"

God help us, I wish that I knew, Wyatt thought, but didn't voice his own fears. Instead, he pulled her that little bit closer and stared blindly down the road, aware that their fate was as dark and uncertain as what moved through the night beyond the headlights of their car.

Marker cursed loud and long. He knew the moment he sped past that he'd missed. And all because of that man who walked at her side. Instead of the solid thump he'd expected when bumper met body, he'd got nothing for his trouble but a high-speed pursuit that had taken him hours to escape.

Thanks to the fact that the car he'd stolen was faster than the police vehicles, he finally eluded the chase. He dumped the hot rod where he'd hidden his own vehicle hours earlier. When and if they found the car, they'd have nothing to pin it on him.

He'd made sure to leave no fingerprints behind, and he was an old hand at never leaving witnesses to his crimes. It was what had kept him out of prison this far, but cold-blooded murder was a different business and a little bit out of his class. Fed up with the hit-and-miss success of his strikes against Glory Dixon, as he drove, he made plans. New plans. Next time, he wouldn't miss.

Chapter 9

Moonlight lay across Glory's bare shoulders like a silver sheet, broken only by the presence of a long, ivory braid down the middle of her back. Covers bunched around her waist as she struggled with nightmares she couldn't escape.

Wyatt heard her moan, and turned from the window where he stood watch, sickened by the darkening bruises on her shoulder and the bloody scrapes on her elbows. It was all he could do not to crawl in that bed with her and take her in his arms. But he didn't. He'd let down his guard once and it had nearly cost her her life. It wasn't going to happen again.

Even now, the playback of the engine as it accelerated and the tires as they spun out on the gravel was all too real in his mind. He didn't remember moving, only feeling the impact of hitting Glory's body and then rolling with her across the parking lot.

As he watched, a single tear slipped from the corner of her eye and then down her cheek like a translucent pearl. Impulsively he reached out, catching it with the tip of his finger and then tracing its path with his lips, tasting the satin texture of her skin and the salt from the tear.

His breath fanned her cheek as he whispered, "Darlin', don't cry."

Her eyelids fluttered, and then she sighed. Reluctantly, he moved back to his post, took one last look out of the window by her bed, then picked up the phone and headed for the tiny living room.

The view from those windows wasn't much different from the view at the back, and yet he couldn't let go of the notion that something or someone watched them from the woods. Lightly, he ran his fingers across the gun in his waistband, waiting as his eyes adjusted to the dark, and then finally, he began to dial.

Lane Monday's voice was rough and thick with sleep, but he answered abruptly before the second ring.

"Hello?"

"It's Wyatt."

Lane rose on an elbow, leaning over Toni as she slept, to peer at the lighted dial on the alarm. It was nearly one o'clock in the morning. That, plus the tone of Wyatt's voice, gave away the urgency of the call.

"What's wrong?"

"We went out to eat this evening. Someone tried to run Glory down in the parking lot. And before you ask, no, it wasn't an accident."

Lane rolled out of bed. Taking the portable phone with him so as not to wake Toni, he went down the hallway and into the living room where his voice could not easily be heard.

"I can be there in about six hours."

Wyatt cursed softly. "And do what?" he muttered. "I was right there beside her and I was almost too late."

"Is she all right?"

"Except for bruises and scrapes...and some more nightmares to add to the ones she already has...yes." Then Wyatt started to pace. "Look, I didn't call for backup. I just wanted to let you know what's happening. The only positive thing I can tell you is that Anders Conway witnessed the whole thing."

Lane sighed, torn between wanting to help and knowing that there was nothing he could do that Wyatt wasn't already doing.

"Okay, but keep me posted," he muttered, and then added, "Remember, all you have to do is call. If it's an emergency, I can hop a copter and be there in a couple of hours."

The nervousness in Wyatt's belly started to subside, if for no other reason than the fact that someone besides him knew what was going on.

"Thanks," Wyatt said, then added, "Oh...kiss Toni and Joy for me." Then he hung up and began pacing from window to window, afraid to sleep, afraid to turn his back on Glory...ever again.

Sometime before morning, Glory woke with a start, then groaned beneath her breath when aching muscles protested the sudden movement. Seconds later, she realized what was wrong.

Wyatt was gone!

Careful not to insult her injuries, she crawled out of bed, picked up the nightgown and slipped it over her head before leaving the room.

The floor was cool beneath her feet. The old hardwood planks were smooth and polished from years of use and cleaning, and as familiar to Glory as her own home had been. The half-light between night and dawn was just below the horizon as she made her way into the kitchen. He was standing at the window.

"Wyatt?"

Startled by the unexpected sound of her voice, he spun. When she saw the gun in his hand, she wanted to cry. He was holding fast to his promise to keep her safe, even at his own expense. She crossed the room and walked straight into his arms.

"Come to bed," she whispered. "Whatever is going to happen will happen. You can't change fate, Wyatt. No matter how much it hurts."

He cradled her face in the palm of his hand, tracing the curve of her cheek and the edges of her lips with his fingers as a blind man would see.

"You don't understand, Glory. I don't quit. I don't give up. And one of these days, I'm going to get my hands on the bastard who's doing this to you. When it happens..."

Her fingers silenced the anger spilling out of his mouth, and in the quiet of Granny's kitchen, she took the gun from his hand and laid it on the table, then slipped her arms around his neck and whispered softly against his mouth.

"No, Wyatt, there's no room for hate in this house, only love. Now come to bed. It's my turn to take care of you."

Unable to resist her plea, he scooped her up into his arms and carried her back to her bed, making room for himself beside her. Just when Glory thought he was settling down, he suddenly rolled, then bolted from the room, returning only moments later. When she heard a distinctive thump on the bedside table, she knew he'd gone back for the gun.

"Don't say it," he growled, as he crawled in beside her. "Just let me have that much peace of mind."

Tears shimmered across her vision, but she didn't argue. Instead, she wrapped her arms around him and cradled his head on her breasts.

Just sleep, my love. It's my turn to keep watch over you.

For a moment, he forgot to breathe.

Like all the Hatfields, Wyatt had been full grown in size by the time he was sixteen years old. At three inches over six feet, he was a very big man and had been taking care of himself for a very long time. If anything, he was the caregiver, the fixer, the doer. That a little bit of female like Glory Dixon dared suggest she could take care of him might have made him smile...if he'd been able to smile through his tears.

Long after the quiet, even sounds of his breathing were proof of his sleep, Glory still held him close. Wide-eyed and alert, she watched morning dawn and then sunlight come, as it spilled through the slightly parted curtains and onto the man in her arms.

Sunbeams danced in the air above her head, bringing hope with the new day. Wyatt stirred, and Glory shifted, giving him ease and a new place to rest. When he smiled in his sleep, the scar on his cheek shifted slightly, reminding her of what he'd endured and survived. A deep and abiding ache resurfaced. She recognized it for what it was, and while he wasn't looking or listening, let herself feel what was there in her heart.

I love you, Wyatt Hatfield. And then a small, silent prayer to a much greater power. *Dear God, please keep him safe. Don't let me be the instrument of another man's death.*

Hours later, Wyatt rolled over in bed, reached out to pull Glory closer, and then woke as suddenly as she had earlier. He was alone. But before he could panic, the scent of fresh coffee and the familiar sounds of a kitchen in use calmed his nerves.

He got out of bed and headed for the bathroom. A shower and a change of clothes later, he was entering the kitchen just as Glory set a pan of hot biscuits on the table. She looked up with a smile.

"Your timing is impeccable," she said.

Wyatt grinned. "So I've been told."

It took a second for the innuendo to sink in, and when it did, a sweet blush spread across Glory's face and neck.

"You are a menace," she muttered, and turned back to the stove just as his hands slid around her from behind and came to rest just below the fullness of her breasts.

"That, too." He chuckled, and kissed the spot just below her earlobe that he knew made her shiver.

She turned in his arms and let his next kiss center upon her mouth. It was hard and hungry, and just shy of demanding, and then he groaned, letting go as suddenly as he'd swooped.

"Glory...darlin', I almost forgot your bruises. How do you feel?"

"Like I was run over by a..."

"Don't!" His eyes darkened as he pressed a finger over her lips. "Don't joke. Not to me. I was there, remember?"

She smiled. Just a little, but just enough to let him know she was all right with the world.

"The biscuits are getting cold," she said, and aimed him toward the table. "Sit. I'm just finishing up the eggs."

"I should be cooking for you," he muttered.

"Lord help us both." When he smiled, she turned back to the eggs.

Later, Glory fidgeted as they ate, and Wyatt could tell there was something on her mind. But it wasn't until they were almost through with the dishes that she started to talk.

"Wyatt...last night at the restaurant...I nearly died, didn't I?"

"Don't remind me," he muttered, and set a clean glass in Granny's little cupboard.

"Oh...that's not what I was getting at," she explained. "What I meant was...if there had been anything left in this life I still wanted to do...it would have been too late."

"Hellfire, Glory! This is a real bad discussion right after a good meal."

She grinned. "Sorry. What I'm trying to say is..."

He tossed the dish towel on the cabinet and took her by the arm, careful not to touch the places that hurt.

"Look, girl! Just say what's on your mind."

She lifted her chin, pinning him with that silver-blue gaze that always made him feel as if he were floating.

"I need to go see my granny one more time...just in case. Chances are she might not even recognize me, but I don't want her to think that we forgot about her. Daddy always went at least once a month. It's past that time now. She's in a nursing home in Hazard. Will you take me?"

Wyatt felt the room beginning to spin. It scared the hell out of him, just hearing her admit that she might not live another week as casually as she might have announced she wasn't going to plant a garden. Unable to keep his distance, he reached out for her, and when she relaxed against him, he shuddered.

"I'll take you anywhere you want to go. I'll stand on my damned head in the woods for a week if it will make you happy. But so help me God, if you don't stop forecasting so much doom and gloom, I'm going to pack you and your stuff and take you home with me to Tennessee. Then we'll see how far this killer wants to travel to die. I've got enough kin there to mount a small army."

She could tell by the tone of his voice that he was serious. But it was an impossible suggestion.

"No, Wyatt! It's bad enough that you've put your life on the line for me. I couldn't live with myself if any more people were put in danger because of this. I'll try not to be so negative, but truth is hard to ignore."

"The only truth is . . . your killer is a screwup. He tried to kill you and got your family instead, and then even later your dog. The fact that he was stupid enough to try a third time, and right in front of the chief of police, doesn't say much for his brains, only his desperation. Desperate men make mistakes, Glory. Remember that!"

In the face of all she'd lost, what he said shouldn't have helped, but for some reason, it did. She relaxed in his arms.

"Okay! I promise! Now let me change my clothes so we can go. And when we go through Larner's Mill, could we stop at the bakery? Granny loves their gingersnaps."

He nodded, and as she left, he retraced his path to the window, looking out into the bright sunlight of a brand-new day, wondering what it would bring.

As nursing homes went, it wasn't so bad. Like similar institutions across the country, it offered health care and comfort to people with aging bodies and minds. But the reason for its being was still the same. It was where the old went to die.

Wyatt caught himself holding his breath as they walked down the hallway. The scent of incontinence, cleaning solvents, and medication was a blend impossible to ignore.

Somewhere ahead of them, an old man's cries for help echoed in the hall while other residents roamed at will, scooting along on walkers, thumping with their canes and wheeling the occasional wheelchair.

And then Glory touched his arm and paused at an open doorway before stepping inside. He followed. It was, after all, why they'd come.

She sat by a window, rocking back and forth in an uneven rhythm, as if sometimes forgetting to keep a motion going. Her body was withered and stooped, her snow-white hair as fluffy and sparse as wisps of cotton. The yellow robe she was wearing was old and faded to near-white, but new, fuzzy blue slippers covered her feet. She had no memory of how she'd come by them, only that they kept her warm. Her eyes were fixed on something beyond the clear glass, and her mouth was turned up in a soft, toothless smile... quite lost in happier times and happier days.

"Granny?"

At the sound of her name, the rocker stopped, and the smile slid off her face. She turned, staring blankly at the pair in the doorway and frowned.

"Comp'ny? I got comp'ny?"

Glory quickly crossed the distance between them to kneel at her side, covering the gnarled, withered hands with her own. The skirt of her only dress puddled around her as she knelt and kissed her granny's cheek. "Yes, Granny, it's me, Glory."

Wyatt watched while recognition came and went in the old woman's pale, watery eyes, and then suddenly she smiled, and ran her hand across Glory's head, fingering the long pale lengths of her hair. In that moment, he saw her as the woman she once had been.

"Well, Glory girl, it's been a while! I didn't think you was ever comin' to see your granny again. Where's your pa? I swear, that boy of mine is always late. I'm gonna give him a piece of my mind when he shows up, and that's a fact."

There was a knot in Glory's throat that threatened to choke her. Twice she faltered before she could speak, and it was only after Wyatt touched her shoulder that she could find the strength to continue.

"Daddy won't be coming today, Granny. It's just me."

A frown deepened the furrow of wrinkles across her brow, and then she cackled and slapped her knee.

"That's good! That's good! Us women gotta stick together, don't we, little girl?"

Tears shimmered across Glory's eyes, but the smile on her face was as bright as the sunshine warming Granny's lap.

"Yes, ma'am, we sure do."

Granny's attention shifted, as if suddenly realizing that Glory was not alone. She looked up at Wyatt, puckering her mouth as she considered his face, and then waved him toward a nearby chair.

"Sit down, boy!" she ordered. "You be way too tall to look at from down here." Then she cackled again, as if delighted with her own wit.

Wyatt grinned and did as he was told.

"Who's he?" Granny asked, as if Wyatt had suddenly gone deaf.

Glory smiled. "That's Wyatt Hatfield, Granny. He's my friend."

And then in the blunt, tactless manner of the very old, she looked up at Wyatt and asked, "Are you messin' with my girl?"

Glory rolled her eyes at Wyatt, begging him to understand, but it was a silent plea she need never have made.

"No, ma'am, I would never treat Glory lightly. I care for her very much."

Satisfied, Granny Dixon leaned back in her rocker and started to rock. Wyatt handed Glory the box of gingersnaps they'd brought from the bakery in Larner's Mill.

"Look, Granny, we brought you gingersnaps."

She set the box in Granny's lap, then patted her on the knee to remind her that she was still here.

The joy on the old woman's face was a delight to see, and when she opened the lid, the scent of molasses and spice filled the air.

"I do love my gingersnaps," Granny said. "But I reckon I'll save 'em till I get me some milk to sop 'em in. I don't eat so good without my teeth, anymore. Glory girl, you set these by my bed, now, you hear?"

"Yes, ma'am," Glory said, and did as she was told.

When she returned, she knelt back at her Granny's knee. It was such an old, familiar place to be, that before Glory realized what she was doing, she found herself leaning forward. When the rocking chair suddenly paused, she exhaled slowly on a shaky sob and laid her head in Granny's lap, waiting for those long, crippled fingers to stroke through her hair, just as they'd done so many years ago.

Suddenly, Wyatt found himself watching through tears and feeling the isolation that Glory must be feeling. Here she was, the last of her line, caught in a hell not of her making and seeking comfort from a woman who was fighting a losing battle with reality. He had the strongest urge to take both women in his arms and hold them, but reason told him to refrain. Here he was the onlooker. He didn't belong in their world.

Long silent minutes passed while Granny Dixon combed her fingers through the silken lengths of Glory's hair, soothing old fears, calming new pain. And then in the quiet, Granny paused and tilted Glory's face. She looked long and hard, then leaned closer, peering at the tearstained gaze in her granddaughter's eyes. Knuckles swollen and locked with age stroked the soft skin on Glory's cheek, brushing lightly against the halo the sun had made on Glory's hair.

"Such a pretty little thing...Granny's little Morning Glory. You been havin' them visions again, ain't you, girl?"

Glory nodded, unable to speak of the horrors she'd recently survived, unwilling to tell this woman that her only son was dead.

"It'll be all right," Granny said. "You jest got to remember that it's God's gift to you, girl. It ain't no burden that you got to bear...it's a gift. Use it as such."

"Yes, ma'am," Glory said, and when she heard Wyatt's feet shuffle behind her, she knew he was struggling with his own brand of pain.

Then the old woman's attention shifted, and once again, Wyatt found himself being grilled on the spot.

"You know 'bout Glory's gift, don't you, boy?"

"Yes, ma'am, that I do," Wyatt said. "It's because of her that I'm still alive. She saved my life."

Granny beamed, and the sunlight caught and danced in her eyes, giving them life where vacancy had just been. She clapped her hands and then patted Glory on the shoulder.

"That's my girl! You see what I'm a'tellin' you, Glory? You did good with your gift, and it brought you a man. That's good fortune!"

"But Granny, he's not actually my—"

Wyatt interrupted, unwilling to hear Glory put the tenuous part of the relationship into words.

"I consider myself the fortunate one, Mrs. Dixon."

"That's good. That's good. You got yourself a man who has the good sense to know which side his bread is done buttered on."

When Glory blushed, Wyatt laughed, which only pleased her granny more.

"You understand your responsibilities of lovin' a woman as special as my Glory, don't you?"

Wyatt nodded. "Yes, ma'am, I believe that I do."

"Sometimes she'll ask things of you that you'll find hard to 'cept. Sometimes she'll know things you don't want to hear. But she'll be true to you all your life and that's a fact."

"Granny, he doesn't want to hear all about..."

Wyatt leaned forward. His brown eyes darkened, his expression grew solemn.

"Yes I do, Morning Glory, yes, I do."

Glory held her breath as joy slowly filled her heart. She hoped he'd meant what he said, and then suddenly turned away, unwilling to look just in case he did not.

One hour turned into two as Granny Dixon regaled them with stories from Glory's childhood as well as old times before she'd ever been born. And while Wyatt listened, absorbing the love that had spanned all the years, bonding these women in a way no family name could have done, he knew that he'd finally found what had been missing in his own life.

Love.

The love that comes with knowing another as well as you know your own heart. The quiet, certain love that is there when all else has failed. The passionate, binding love that can lift a man up, and keep him afloat all his life.

Before Glory, Wyatt had been running... always on the move... afraid of sinking before he had lived. Now the answer to his own brand of pain was sitting at his feet, and unless they caught the man who was trying to kill her, he could lose it... and her... before they were his. He believed that she loved him. He knew that he loved her. The uncertainty lay in keeping her alive.

And finally, when Granny's head began to nod, Glory motioned that it was time to go. As they stood, Granny reached out and caught Wyatt's hand.

"You'll bring my little Morning Glory back, won't you?"

"Yes, ma'am, I sure will."

Granny's mouth squinched in what might be called a flirtatious smile, although it was hard to tell with so much vacancy between her lips. "Since you're gonna be in the family, I reckon you could be callin' me by my given name."

Wyatt grinned. "I'd be honored. And what would that be?" he asked.

Granny thought and then frowned. "Why, I should be knowin' my own name, now, shouldn't I?" And then a smile spread wide. "Faith! I'm called Faith." She shook her finger in Wyatt's face. "And you'll be needin' a whole lot of faith to love a woman as special as my Glory."

"Yes, ma'am, I suppose that I will."

"Maybe you'd be inclined to name your firstborn girl after me? I'd be pleased to know that my name lived on after I'm gone."

Moved by her innocence, Wyatt knelt, and took the old woman's hands in his own.

"I'm honored, Faith Dixon. And you have my word that it will be done."

Pleased that she'd covered all the bases with her granddaughter's new beau, Granny closed her eyes. Moments later, she began to rock, forgetting that they were even still there.

Wyatt slipped an arm around Glory's shoulder.

"Are you ready?"

Glory looked up, her eyes filled with tears, her lips trembling with the weight of unvoiced love for this man who held her.

"Yes, please."

She took Wyatt's hand, and let him lead her out of this place. When they were in the parking lot, she knew there was one more place she needed to go.

"Since we're in Hazard, I suppose I should go by the lawyer's office. Daddy always said if anything ever happened to him, that J.C. and I were to come here, that Mr. Honeywell would know what to do."

"Then we will," Wyatt promised. "You direct, I'll drive."

A short time later, they were sitting in the office of Elias Honeywell, the senior partner of Honeywell and Honeywell. He was still in shock at what he'd been told. His little round face was twisted with concern.

"Miss Dixon, I'm so sorry for your loss," he said. "But you needn't worry about your position. Your father was a farseeing man. Not only did he leave a will, but there is a sizable insurance policy, of which you are the sole beneficiary."

Glory had known of the will, but had had no idea her father had indulged in life insurance. Their life had been simple. Money had never been easy to come by. That he'd used it for a future he would not participate in surprised her.

"I had no idea," she said.

Elias Honeywell nodded solemnly. "Your father wanted it that way. He was concerned about your welfare after he passed on. I believe I recall him saying something to the effect that his daughter had more to bear than most, and he wanted to make sure you would not suffer unduly."

"Oh, my." It was all Glory could say without breaking into tears. Even in death, her father was still taking care of her.

Wyatt could see that Glory was not in any shape to question him. In spite of his reticence to interfere, he thought it best to ask now, rather than after they were gone.

"Mr. Honeywell, what will you need from Glory to proceed with the probate and claims?"

The little lawyer frowned, then shuffled through the file on his desk. "Why, I believe I have nearly everything I need," he said. "Except..." He hesitated, hating to bring it up. "We will need death certificates for her father as well as her brother before I can apply for the life insurance on her behalf. I have her address. If I need anything more, I will be in touch."

Glory rose with more composure than she felt. Had it not been for Wyatt Hatfield's presence, she would have run screaming to the car. The darkness within her mind kept spreading. She kept thinking this was all a bad dream, and that most any time she would wake, and it would all be over.

But reality was a rude reminder, and when they exited the office to resume the trip home, the only thing that kept her sane was remembering the promise Wyatt made to Granny. The fact that he'd made such a claim of the heart to a woman who would never remember he'd said it, didn't matter to Glory. At least not now. He'd said she was his girl. He'd promised Granny that he would take care of her forever. Glory needed to believe that he meant every word that he'd said.

Long after they were back on Highway 421, driving south toward Pine Mountain and Larner's Mill, which nestled at its base, Glory still had no words for what Wyatt had given her this day. It wasn't until later when he stopped for gas that she managed to say what was in her heart.

"Wyatt?"

"What, darlin'?" he said absently, as he unbuckled his seat belt to get out.

"I will never forget what you said to Granny today. No matter what you really thought, you made an old woman happy."

He paused, halfway out of the car seat, and looked back at her. "What about you, Morning Glory? Did it make you happy, too?"

"What do you mean?" she asked.

"I didn't say anything that wasn't already in my heart."

"Oh, Wyatt! You don't have to pretend with..."

"If you need to go to the little girls' room, now's your time," he said quietly, aware that she looked as scared as he felt. But as Glory had said, who knew what tomorrow would bring? Denying his feelings for her seemed a careless thing to do.

She got out of the car with her head in a whirl, her heart pounding with a hope she thought had died. Was there a chance for her after all? Could she have a future with a man she'd just met? More to the point, would she even want to try it without him?

Chapter 10

Anders Conway entered his office with a beleaguered air. Having to explain to a U.S. marshal why two of his patrol cars had not been able to apprehend a hit-and-run suspect hadn't set well with his lunch. His eardrums were still reverberating from the dressing down he'd gotten over the phone from Lane Monday, and while he wanted to resent the constant interference of Glory Dixon's newfound friends, he couldn't bring himself to blame them. It was obvious they were truly worried about her welfare and afraid for her life.

What surprised him was that they believed her story without a single doubt. She'd lived in Larner's Mill all of her life and had been looked upon as something of an oddity. Why two strangers should suddenly appear in her life and take her every word as gospel was a puzzle.

But the fire marshal's report sitting on his desk was strong evidence that Glory Dixon had something going for her. After reading it, Conway been unable to deny the truth of the young woman's claim. Whether he believed her story of *how* she saw it happen was immaterial. Fact was, someone had meddled with gas stoves, causing the deaths of her father and brother.

Conway paced the room, mentally itemizing the series of events concerning her. Her claim that she'd been the target for the fire was too farfetched for him to buy, and he chalked it up to a guilt complex for not having died along with her family. And then she wanted him to believe that she was still in danger, and had used the accidental shooting of her dog as more proof.

Conway snorted softly, muttering beneath his breath. "This isn't the kind of place where people go around killin' dogs for sport."

He started to pour himself a cup of coffee and then cursed when he realized it was cold. Someone had gone and turned the darn thing off, leaving the black brew to congeal along the sides of the pot.

"To hell with dogs...and coffee," he grumbled, and slammed his cup down with a thump.

But his mind wouldn't let go of his thoughts, and he kept dwelling on the oddity of the pup being killed so soon after all of the other trauma in Glory's life. He hadn't actually viewed the carcass, but he was inclined to believe that if it *had* been shot, it was most likely by accident, and someone hadn't been man enough to own up to the deed.

He fiddled with the papers in the file on his desk, staring long and hard at the evidence bag containing the bit of fabric that was supposed to have been caught in the dog's teeth, certain that it meant nothing either.

Yet as hard as he tried to convince himself that there had to be a reasonable explanation for the things that had been happening to Glory, last night was an altogether different circumstance.

Watching that car take aim at her, and then seeing Wyatt Hatfield suddenly turn and leap, had been like watching a scene out of a bad movie. Although it was an improbable thing to be happening in Larner's Mill, he *had* seen someone purposefully try to run her down.

"But damn it, I can't take the word of a psychic to court. If only my men hadn't lost that damn hot rod on the logging road, I'd have me a bona fide suspect to question. Then maybe I could get to the bottom of this mess."

"You talkin' to me, Chief?" the dispatcher yelled from the other room.

"Hell, no, I am not!" Conway shouted, and then winced at the tone of his own voice. If he didn't get a grip, he was going to wind up a few bales short of a load and they'd be shipping him off in a straitjacket.

He cursed again, only this time beneath his breath, shoved the file back into the drawer and stomped over to his desk, slumping into his easy chair and feeling every day of his sixty-two years. If only his deputies had been able to keep up with that hit-and-run driver. Everything had hinged upon finding the suspect, and he'd gotten away.

His stomach began to hurt. The familiar burning sensation sent him digging into his desk for antacids and wishing he'd taken early retirement. But when he found the bottle, it was empty. With a muttered curse, he tossed it in the trash and then walked back to dispatch.

"I'm going to the drugstore. Be back in a few minutes," he said, and ambled out of the office without waiting for the dispatcher's reply.

As he walked down the street, a car honked. Out of habit, he turned and waved before he even looked to see who had hailed him. Across the street and directly in his line of vision, he saw Carter Foster locking his office and putting the Out to Lunch sign on the office door.

"Now there's another man with problems," Conway muttered, looking at the lawyer's rumpled suit and pale, drawn face. "Poor bastard. I wonder how much Betty Jo took him for when she left?"

Then he shrugged. He didn't have time to worry about cheating women. He had a belly on fire and an office full of trouble just waiting for him to return. Just as he was about to enter the drugstore, an odd thought hit him. He turned, staring back down the street where the lawyer had been, but Carter and his car were nowhere in sight.

Well, I'll be damned. We do have one missing person... of a sort... here in Larner's Mill, after all. Old Carter is missing a wife, isn't he?

But as swiftly as the thought had come, he shoved it aside. "God Almighty, I *am* losing my grip. Everyone knows that Betty Jo would bed a snake if it held still long enough for her to get a grip. When her money runs out, or the old boy she took off with runs out of steam, she'll be back. And poor old Carter will probably be stupid enough to let her."

Satisfied with his conclusion, he entered the store, heading straight for the aisle where antacids were stocked.

Carter drove toward the café, unaware of the chief's discarded theory. Had he known, he might have kept on driving. As it was, he was going through the motions of normalcy while fighting a constant state of panic. He firmly believed that if Bo Marker didn't put Glory Dixon out of the picture, he was a ruined man.

But, Carter kept reminding himself, there was one thing about this entire mess that had worked to his benefit. No one questioned his drawn countenance or his lack of attention to details, like forgetting two court dates and missing an important appointment with a client. It *could* all be attributed to a man who'd been dumped by his wife, and not a man who'd tossed his wife in a dump.

He switched on the turn signal, and began to pull into the parking lot of the café when a deputy stepped in front of his car and waved him to a different location. Surprised by the fact that nothing ever changes in Larner's Mill, he followed the officer's directions. But after he had parked, he couldn't contain his curiosity, and wandered over to the area to see what was going on.

"Hey, buddy, what's with the yellow tape?" Carter asked, and flipped it lightly with his finger as if he were strumming a guitar string.

"We had ourselves a crime here last night!"

Carter watched with some interest as another deputy was measuring some sort of distance between two points.

"What kind of crime? Someone steal hubcaps or something?"

"Nope. We had ourselves a near hit-and-run, and I got in on the chase afterward." And then he frowned and turned away, unwilling to admit how it galled him that the perpetrator had escaped.

Carter grinned. "How do you have a *near* hit-and-run, as opposed to an actual one?"

"Someone deliberately tried to run that Dixon girl over. You know, the one who just buried her daddy and brother?" He was so busy telling the story, that he didn't see the shock that swept across Carter Foster's face. "Anyway…her and her friend was just comin' out of the café when some guy took aim and tried to run her down. If it hadn't been for that man who's stayin' with her, he would have done it, too."

Damn, damn, damn, Carter thought, and then worry had him prodding for more information.

"Have you considered that it might have been just a drunk driver?" he asked, hoping to steer their investigation in a different direction.

The deputy shook his head. "No way. It was deliberate! Chief Conway witnessed the whole thing. We was in fast pursuit within seconds of it happenin', and would have caught him, too, except the guy was driving a stolen car. It was that Marley kid's hot rod. Ain't no one gonna catch that car, I don't care who's drivin' it."

The hunger that had driven Carter to the café was turning to nausea. He couldn't believe what he'd just heard.

"Anders Conway witnessed the incident? He *saw* someone try to run her over?"

"Yes, sir. Now, if you'll excuse me, Mr. Foster, I'd better get back to work. We got ourselves a felon to catch."

Carter stood without moving, watching as the officers picked through the scene. The longer he stared, the more panicked he became. The thought of food turned his stomach, and the thought of Bo Marker made him want to kill all over again. The stupidity of the man, to attempt a crime in front of the chief of police, was beyond belief.

Disgusted with the whole situation, he stomped to his car, then drove toward home while a slow, burning anger built steam. At least there he could eat in peace without watching his life go down the toilet.

He was already inside the kitchen, building a sandwich of mammoth proportions, when realization sank in. So Bo Marker was stupid. Carter had known that when he'd hired him. He'd counted on his dim wit to be the deciding factor when he'd offered him the job of murderer.

Carter dropped into a chair, staring at the triple-decker sandwich on the plate, as well as the knife he was holding, watching as mayonnaise dripped from it and onto his lap.

So, if I hired Bo Marker, knowing his IQ was that of a gnat, what, exactly, does that make me?

He dropped the knife and buried his face in his hands, wishing he could turn back time. A saying his mother once told him did a replay inside his head. It had something to do with how the telling of one lie could weave itself into a whole web of deceit. Carter knew he was proof of his mother's wisdom. He was caught and sinking fast. Unless Bo Marker got his act together and did what he'd been hired to do, he was done for.

Using the trees around Granny Dixon's cabin as cover for the deed he had planned wasn't unique, but Bo Marker didn't have an original thought in his head. He was still mad about missing his mark last night, but had gotten some joy out of the wild ten-mile chase afterward. Running from the cops like that made him feel young again.

He glanced down at his watch, wondering when that Dixon bitch and her lover would come back home, and cursing his luck because he'd come too late this morning to catch them as they'd left. It would have been so easy just to pick them off as they'd walked out to the car.

He sighed, shifting upon the dirt where he was sitting, searching for a softer spot on the tree against which he was leaning. That knothole behind his back was beginning to feel like a brick.

Bo was at the point of boredom with this whole procedure and kept reminding himself what he could do with the money he would get from this job. As he sat, he rested his deer rifle across his knees and then spit, aiming at a line of ants that he'd been watching for some time. It wasn't the first time he'd spit on them, and in fact, as he spit, he was making bets with himself as to which way they'd run when it splattered. But his mind quickly shifted from the game at hand when something moved in the brush behind him. He grabbed the rifle and then stilled, squinting through the brush and searching for a sign of movement.

"Don't you think that rifle's a bit big for huntin' squirrels?"

Startled, Bo rolled to his feet, aiming his gun as he moved. But the man who'd come out of the brush was ready for the action. When Bo moved, the man swung his gun downward, blocking the motion. It took Bo all of five seconds to forget about tangling with the big, bearded mountain man.

The man stood a good four inches taller, and was more than fifty pounds heavier. And while Bo's gun was more powerful, that bead the man had drawn on his belly was all the incentive Bo needed to show some restraint. Being gut-shot wasn't a good way to die.

"Who said anything about hunting squirrels?" Bo muttered, and tried taking a step back. The big man's gun followed his movement like a snake, waiting to strike.

Teeth shone, white and even through the black, bushy beard. It might have passed for a smile if one could ignore the frosty glare in the mountain man's eyes.

Bo had no option but to stand and wait while the man took the rifle from his hands and emptied the shells in the dirt, then tossed back the empty gun.

Bo caught it in midair.

und her neck, hugging her in a happy, childlike
e and Daddy have been waitin' for you."
nodded, and then watched as Edward Lee's father
in hand. Although Liam Fowler was a very big
touch and words were slow and gentle.
s enough, Edward Lee. We came to talk business,
?"
Lee smiled, pleased to be a part of anything his
. And then he remembered Wyatt and pointed.
s Wyatt Hatfield. Wyatt is my friend," he an-

good, son." Liam Fowler's teeth were white
e thickness of his beard, as he acknowledged
a nod. "But we need to do what we came to do,
"
ised. "And that is?"
e to warn you," Liam said. "There's a stranger
s."
ayed. The shock on her face was too new to hide.
nd fell into Wyatt's arms with a muffled moan.
will this never end?"
oney," Wyatt said softly, and wrapped his arms
d her, willing her to feel his strength, because
t he had to give.
e was too weary and heartsick to stand on her
Wyatt hold her, trusting him to face what she

huffled their feet, looking everywhere but at
comfortable with her fear because they had no

ou know about the stranger?" Wyatt asked.
him? Did you talk to him?"
he men chuckled and then they all looked to
to answer. Obviously they knew more than
g.
"You could say that," he said. "Now, back
of why we're here." He gave Wyatt a long,
k. "My son says that you're a good man."

The man grinned again as he spoke. "Now you're not about to tell me you're huntin' out of season...are you? We don't like strangers on our mountain...especially out of season."

Bo paled. The threat was all too real to ignore.

"Well, hell, if that's the way you wanna be, then I'm gone," he muttered, and tried a few steps of retreat.

"You know, that might be the smartest thing you did all day," the man said.

Bo nodded, then took a deep breath. Daring to turn his back on the man with the gun, he began to walk away. Just when he thought he was in the clear, a shot rang out, and he fell to the ground in mortal fear, fully expecting to be shattered by pain. Seconds later, something landed with a heavy thud in the middle of his back.

His face buried in his arms, sucking dirt and old leaves into his mouth, he began to shriek. "God have mercy! Don't kill me! Don't kill me!"

The man cradled his rifle in the bend of his arm and bent over Bo's body. "Now...whatever made you think you was in danger?" he asked.

Bo held his breath as the weight suddenly disappeared from his back. Shocked, he slowly lifted his head and then rolled on his back, staring up in disbelief at the big gray squirrel the man was holding by the tail. Blood dripped from a tiny hole in the side of its neck, and Bo had a vision of his own head in the same condition, and shuddered.

The man waved the squirrel across Bo's line of vision, breaking the thick swirl of his beard with another white smile.

"Got myself a good one, don't you think?"

"Oh, God, I thought you was shootin' at me," Bo groaned. He started to crawl to his feet when the man stuck the barrel of the gun in the middle of Bo's fat belly. "Should I have been?" the man asked quietly.

The tip of the barrel penetrated the fat just enough to hurt. Bo was so scared, that had he been a cat, eight of his nine lives would have been gone on the spot.

"No, hell, no!" Bo groaned. "Now are you gonna let me up, or what?"

"Be my guest," the man said, and waved his arm magnanimously.

Five minutes later, Bo burst out of the woods on the run, sighing with relief to see his truck right where he'd left it.

Considering his bulk, he moved with great speed, his rifle in one hand, his truck keys in another. But his relief turned sour when he noticed the tires. All four were as flat as his old lady's chest, and just as useless. Fury overwhelmed him. He couldn't believe he'd let himself be bullied by some mountain man. And now this. He spun, staring back at the woods.

"For two cents," he muttered, "I'd go back in there and..."

And then the sound of breaking twigs and rustling bushes made him pause. A picture of that squirrel's bloody head and limp body made him want to retch. All of his bravado disappeared as he pivoted. Dragging the empty rifle behind him, he made a wild dash for the truck, and moments later, started down the mountain. The truck steered like a man crawling on his belly, but Bo didn't care.

Putting distance between himself and this place was all he wanted to do.

The sound of flapping rubber and bare rims grinding against the gravel on the road could be heard long after Bo had disappeared. And finally, the rustling in the underbrush ceased.

A short time later, the sounds of the forest began to revive. Birds resumed flight, a blue jay scolded from an overhead branch, and a bobcat slipped quickly across the road and into the trees on the other side.

Pine Mountain was alive and well.

It was close to sundown when Wyatt turned off the main highway and onto the one-lane road leading to the Dixon farm. A soft breeze circled through the car from the half-open windows, stirring through Glory's hair and teasing at

the skirt of her blue dress like a nau
asleep for the better part of an hour v
and without thinking, Wyatt bracec
tumbling as the car took the turn.
He drove without thought, his mi
revelation that he'd had this day. It
ago, he hadn't even known she'd ex
as if he'd known her for years, eve
The years stretched out before h
couldn't see a future without Glory
past the burned-out remnants of he
the old road toward Granny's cal
riage was the last thing he should
now, all that mattered was keepin
His foot was on the brake whe
coming out of the trees. They w
who knew their place on this ea
proud, their shoulders back.
clean-shaven. Some wore jeans
were short, while others towered
what they had in common th
man, they were armed, and fro
definitely looked dangerous.
"God," he said softly, and
point of wondering whether
awoke and stirred.
"Are we home?" She rub
was only after Wyatt grabbe
ized something was wrong.
She looked up. "It's all r
bors." Before Wyatt coul
beckoning for him to follo
When Edward Lee can
hind them, Wyatt began
Glory smiled and moti
"Hey, Mornin' Glory
through the men as if th

arms ar
way. "M
Glory
took hin
man, his
"That
rememb
Edwar
father di
"This
nounced.
"That
through
Wyatt wi
remembe
Wyatt
"We ca
in the wo
Glory s
She turne
"Oh, Goo
"Don't,
firmly aro
it was all t
Because
own, she le
could not.
The men
each other,
way to stop
"How do
"Did you se
Several of
Liam Fowler
they were telli
Liam smiled
to the busines
considering lo

Edward Lee almost strutted with importance. It wasn't often that grown men took anything he said to heart.

Wyatt smiled at him, and then waited.

"He says that you came to take care of Glory," Liam persisted.

"Yes, sir, I did that," Wyatt said.

"We feel right ashamed that it took a stranger to do what we should have done on our own," Liam said. "Glory sort of belongs to us now, what with her family passin' and all."

Wyatt's arms tightened around Glory's shoulders. "No, sir. She doesn't belong to you. Not anymore."

When Glory suddenly stilled then shifted within his embrace, Wyatt tightened his hold and looked down, wondering if she would challenge him here in front of everyone. To his relief, he saw nothing but surprise and a little bit of shock, and knew that she hadn't been prepared for what he'd said.

The men came to attention, each gauging Wyatt with new interest as they heard and accepted the underlying message of his words. He'd laid claim to a woman most of them feared. More than one of them wondered if he knew what he was getting into, but as was their way, no one voiced a concern. Live and let live was a motto that had served them well for several centuries, and they had no reason to change their beliefs. Not even for a stranger.

Finally, it was Liam who broke the silence. "So, it's that way, then?"

Wyatt nodded.

Liam reached out, touching the crown of Glory's head in a gentle caress. "Glory, girl, are you of the same mind?"

Without looking at Wyatt, she turned, facing the men within the safety of Wyatt's arms. "Yes, sir, I suppose that I am."

So great was his joy that Wyatt wanted to grin. But this wasn't the time, and with these somber men judging his every move, it also wasn't the place. Like dark crows on a fence, they watched, unmoving, waiting for the big, bearded man to speak for them all. So he did.

"Then that's fine," Liam said, and offered Wyatt his hand. "Know that while you're on this land, within the boundaries of our hills, you will be safe. We guarantee that to you. But when you take her away from here, her safety is in your hands."

Aware of the solemnity of the moment, Glory stepped aside as Wyatt moved forward, taking the hand that was offered. And then each man passed, sealing their vow with a firm handshake and a long hard look. When it was over, they had new respect for the stranger who'd come into their midst, and Wyatt felt relief that he was no longer in this alone. And then he noticed that Edward Lee had stayed behind.

"Edward Lee, aren't you going to shake my hand, too?"

Wyatt's quiet voice broke the awkward silence, and his request made a friend of Liam Fowler for life. Wyatt had instinctively understood how the young man wanted so badly to belong.

He looked to his father, a poignant plea in his voice. "Daddy?"

Liam nodded, then took a long, deep breath as Edward Lee mimicked the seriousness of the occasion by offering Wyatt his hand without his usual smile. But the moment the handshake was over, he threw his arms around Wyatt's neck in a boisterous hug, and when he turned back around, the smile on his face was infectious. Everyone laughed. But not at him . . . with him. His joy was impossible to ignore.

"Then we'll be going," Liam said, and smiled gently at Glory. "Rest easy tonight, little girl. Your man just got himself some help."

"I don't know how to thank you," Wyatt said. "But be careful. Whoever is trying to harm Glory isn't giving up."

They nodded, then walked away. They were almost into the trees when Glory called out, then ran toward them. They paused and turned, waiting for whatever she had to say.

She stopped a few feet away, unaware that she'd stopped in a halo of late-evening sun. The blue of her dress matched the color of her eyes, and the hair drifting around her face and down her back lifted and fell with the demands of the breeze blowing through the clearing. More than one man had the notion that he was standing before an angel. Her eyes were brimming, her lips shaking with unshed emotion. But her voice was steady as she said what was in her heart.

"God bless you," she whispered. "My daddy was proud to call you his friends. Now I understand why."

Moved beyond words, they took her praise in stoic silence, and when they were certain she was through, turned and walked away without answering. Glory watched until they were gone, and then she turned.

Wyatt was waiting, and the look in his eyes made her shake. He was her man. He'd laid a claim before her people that they did not take lightly. And from the expression on his face, neither did he.

Chapter 11

Glory's eyes widened as Wyatt started toward her. Later, she would remember thinking that he moved like a big cat, powerful, but full of grace. But now, there was nothing on her mind but the look on his face and the way that his eyes raked her body.

She held her breath, wondering if she was woman enough to hold this wild, footloose man. And when he was close enough to touch her, he combed his fingers through the hair on either side of her face, and lowered his head. When his mouth moved across her face and centered upon her lips, the breath she'd been holding slipped out on a sigh. The impact of the joining was unexpected. She wasn't prepared for the reverence in his touch, or the desperation with which he held her.

Wyatt was absorbed by her love, drawn into a force that he couldn't control. It took everything he had to remember that they were standing in plain sight of whoever cared to look, and that she was still bruised and sore from yesterday's scrape with death. He groaned, then lifted his head, and when she would have protested, he silenced her plea by pressing his forefinger across her lips.

"Glory, I'm sorry. I almost forgot that you..."

"Take me to bed. Make me forget all this horror. Give me something to remember besides fear. I'm so tired of being afraid."

Ah, God.

She slipped beneath his arm, the top of her head way below his chin, and then looked up. Her silver-blue stare widened apprehensively as she waited for his response.

At that moment, Wyatt wasn't so sure that he couldn't have walked on water.

"I love you, Glory Dixon."

"I know," she said softly. "It's why I asked."

Hand in hand, they entered the cabin, for once safe in the knowledge that someone was watching their backs. The lock clicked loudly within the silence of the old rooms, and then there was nothing to be heard but the ticking of Granny's clock on the mantel, and the heartbeats hammering in their ears.

Glory was the first to move. She slid her hands beneath her hair, tugging at a zipper that wouldn't give.

"Help me, Wyatt. I think my hair's caught."

And so am I, he thought, but never voiced his fear.

He thrust his hands beneath her gold strands, moving the heavy weight of her hair aside so he could see. His fingers shook as he unwound a strand from the metal tab. When it was free, he lifted the tab and pulled.

Slowly. Lower.

Revealing the delicate body that was so much a part of the woman he loved. Impulsively, he slid his hands beneath the fabric, circling her body and coming to rest upon the gentle thrust of her breasts. Glory sighed, then moaned, arching into his palms.

He shook, burning with the need to plunge deep within the sweetness of the woman in his hands, and yet he resisted. She wasn't ready. It wasn't time. She wanted to forget, and he hoped to hell he could remember what he was supposed to do, because every breath that he took was driving sanity further and further from his mind.

"Glory."

Her name was a whisper on his lips as she moved out of his grasp. When her dress fell at her feet in a pool of blue, leaving her with nothing on but a scrap of nylon that barely covered her hips, he started to shake.

Twice he tried to unbutton his shirt, and each time, his fingers kept slipping off the buttons.

"Oh, hell," he muttered, then yanked.

Buttons popped and rolled across the floor. Boots went one direction, his blue jeans another. Before Glory had time to think, he had her in his arms and was moving toward the bed with a distinct gleam in his eye.

They fell onto the quilt in a tangle of arms and legs as the last of their clothes hit the floor. At the last minute, Wyatt remembered protection, and scrambled for the drawer in the bedside table.

There was no time for slow, easy loving, or soft, whispered promises. The passion between them was about to ignite. Glory's hands were on his shoulders, urging him down when he moved between her legs. When he slid inside, her eyelids fluttered, and then she wrapped her arms around his neck and followed where he wanted to go.

Rocking with the rhythm of their bodies, moments became endless as that sweet fire began to build. It was the time when the feeling was so good that it felt like it could go on forever. And then urgency slipped into the act, honing nerves already at the point of breaking.

One minute Wyatt was still in control, and the next thing he knew, she was arching up to meet him and crying out his name. He looked down, saw himself reflected in the pupils of her eyes, and felt as if he were drowning. A faint look of surprise was etched across her face as shock wave after shock wave ebbed and flowed throughout her body. Caught in the undertow, Wyatt couldn't pull back, and then didn't want to. He spilled all he was in the sweet act of love.

For Glory, time ceased. The problems of the world outside were momentarily forgotten. There was nothing that mattered but the man in her arms, and the love in his eyes. Seconds later he collapsed, lying with his head upon her breasts, and his fists tangled tightly in her hair.

Replete from their loving, Glory reached out with a satisfied sigh, tracing the breadth of his shoulders and combing her fingers through his hair, letting the thick, black strands fall where they might. Just as the sun sank below the horizon, she felt him relax and remembered last night, and how he'd stood watch while she slept.

Sleep, my love, she thought.

"Am I?" Wyatt asked.

Glory smiled. He'd done it again. "Are you what?" she asked, knowing full well what he was angling for.

"Your love."

"What do you think?" she whispered.

He lifted his head, his eyes still black from burned-out passion. "I think I'm in heaven."

She grinned. "No, you're in my arms, and in Granny's bed."

He rolled, moving her from bottom to top. "Like I said... I'm in heaven."

Before Glory could settle into a comfortable spot, Wyatt's hands were doing things to her that, at the moment, she wouldn't have thought it possible to feel.

She gasped, then moved against his fingers in a tantalizing circle. "I don't know about heaven," she whispered, and then closed her eyes and bit her lower lip, savoring the tiny spikes of pleasure that he'd already started. "But if you stop what you're doing anytime soon, you'll be in trouble."

He laughed, then proved that he was man enough to finish what he had started.

Carter Foster stood at the window of his darkened house, peering through the curtains and cursing beneath his breath as the patrol car moved slowly past.

It wasn't the first time it had circled his neighborhood. In fact, it was a normal patrol for the officer on duty. But in Carter's mind, he saw the police searching for clues that would destroy his world. Guilt played strange tricks on a criminal's mind.

He let the curtain drop and began to pace, wondering if he should pack and run before they got on his trail. With every day that Glory Dixon lived, his chances of getting away with murder decreased. And as a man who'd made his living on the good side of the law, he knew exactly how deep his trouble was.

He moved room by room through his house, jumping at shadows that took on sinister forms. Sounds that he'd heard all his life suddenly had ominous qualities he'd never considered. And the bed that he and Betty Jo had shared was an impossible place to rest. He sneaked by the room every night on his way to the guest room, unable to look inside, afraid that Betty Jo's ghost would be sitting on the side of that bed with lipstick smeared across her face, and a torn dress riding up her white thighs.

"When this is over, I'll sell the house and move," he reminded himself. He had started down the hallway to get ready for bed when the phone rang.

Panicked by the unexpected sound, Carter flattened against the wall, and then cursed his stupidity when he realized it was nothing but the phone. He considered just letting it ring, and then knew that with the condition his life was in, he'd better take the call. Yet when he answered, he realized that, once again, he'd made the wrong decision. He should have let it ring.

"It's me," Bo growled.

"I can hear that," Carter sneered. "Now unless you've called to tell me that you've finished something you so obviously botched last night, I don't think we have a damn thing to discuss!"

"I called to tell you that you owe me four new tires," Bo shouted.

Carter rolled his eyes. "Unless you get your butt in gear, I'm not going to owe you anything," he shouted back.

"Look, this job is more involved than you led me to believe. I ruined four tires today saving my own hide from some crazy hillbilly. You're gonna pay, or I know someone who'd be interested in my side of the incidents that have been happening to one Miss Glory Dixon."

Carter went rigid with disbelief. This was the last damned straw! The imbecile was trying to blackmail him. He took a deep breath and then grinned. Marker's gorilla brain was no match for his courtroom skills.

"Well, now, I'd be real careful before I went running to the law," Carter sneered. "They'd have nothing on me, and you have a rap sheet that dates back to your youth. You're the one who got bitten by a dog, and I'm a respectable lawyer. If some hillbilly took after you, why would they want to blame me? It wasn't my face that man saw, it was yours. And...to top that off, you're the one who stole a car and tried to run someone down, in front of the chief of police, no less. Now, you can talk all you want, but there is nothing...absolutely nothing...that links me to you. Not a dollar. Not a piece of paper. Nothing!"

Bo's response sounded nervous enough. "There's got to be a reason you want that Dixon woman dead, and I have no reason at all to care one way or another. If I tell them what I—"

Carter was so angry, he was shaking, but it didn't deter him from ending their argument with a resounding blow. One that got Bo's attention all too painfully.

"You do what you're told!" Carter screamed. "That crazy witch could ruin me. But so help me God, if you talk, I'll make it my personal responsibility to see that you spend the rest of your life behind bars."

"Now, see here," Marker growled. "You can't—"

"Oh, yes, I can," Carter said. "Now. Either do what you were hired to do, or leave me the hell alone. Understand?"

Bo frowned, then slammed the phone back on the receiver. That had not gone exactly as planned.

"Now what?" he muttered.

He frowned, cursing both Carter and bad luck, and started up the street toward his house. Somewhere between now and morning, he had to find himself four new tires, or he'd never be able to finish the job. And, if he had to steal them, which was his first choice of procedure, he could hardly be rolling the damned things down the street. He needed another pair of hands and a good pickup truck. As he walked, he wondered if his old friend, Frankie Munroe, was still around.

Anders Conway rolled over and then sat up in bed. He didn't know what hurt worse, his conscience or his belly. Grumbling beneath his breath, he crawled out from beneath the covers and started through his house in search of some more antacids. One of these days he was going to have to change his eating habits... or his job.

Today he'd faced the consequences of the law officer he'd become. With one year left to retirement, he'd let the office and himself slip. In spite of Glory Dixon's farfetched claims about her psychic abilities, the fact still remained that someone was out to do her harm.

The stolen car that they'd recovered had been wiped clean of prints... all except for a partial that they'd found along the steering wheel column. They'd already eliminated the owner and any of his friends or family. It only stood to reason that it would belong to the thief. But it was going to take days, maybe weeks, to get back a report from the state office. During that time, Glory Dixon could be dead and buried.

He'd sent the bit of fabric along to a lab with the faint hope that something could be learned, although what they could possibly glean from a bit of denim cloth was impossible to guess.

He popped a couple of effervescent tablets into a glass of water, waiting while they fizzed, and consoled himself with the fact that at least he was doing his job.

Minutes later, he crawled back into bed, more comfortable with the situation, and with his belly. On the verge of dreams, the memory of Carter Foster's hangdog face drifted through his subconscious. But he was too far gone to wonder why, and when morning came, he wouldn't remember that it had.

Miles away, in a cabin nestled deep in the piney woods above Larner's Mill, Wyatt slept, with Glory held fast in his arms. The fear that had kept him virtually sleepless for the past two days was almost gone.

They'd gone to bed secure in the knowledge that somewhere beyond the walls of this cabin, there were six mountain men who'd sworn to a vow that he knew they would keep. He'd looked at their faces. He'd seen the men for what they were. The steadfast honesty of their expressions was all that he'd needed to see. With their help, maybe...just maybe, there would be a way out of this situation after all.

It was the quiet peace of early morning that woke Wyatt up from a deep, dreamless sleep. Or so he thought until he turned to look at Glory's face and saw it twisted into a grimace of concern.

He'd never seen horror on a face deep in sleep, but he was seeing it now. And as he watched, he knew what must be happening. Somewhere within the rest that she'd sought, another person's nightmare was taking place and taking Glory with it.

Except for the day at the city dump when she'd had the vision of the body being disposed of, he'd never witnessed this happening. His heart rate began to accelerate with fear. He wondered if this was how she'd been when she'd come to his rescue, then wondered whose life was about to take a crooked turn.

Uncertain of how to behave, or what to do, he realized the matter was out of his hands when she suddenly jerked and sat straight up in bed, her eyes wide open and staring blindly at something other than the room in which she'd slept. Her eyes moved, as if along a page, watching a drama that only she could see. She moaned softly, wadding the sheet within her hands, rocking back and forth in a terrified manner.

Still. Everything was still. No wind. Not even a soft, easy breeze. Dark clouds hovered upon the early-morning horizon, hanging black and heavy, nearly dragging on the ground.

The outer walls of the white frame house were a stark contrast to the brewing weather. Fences ranged from barns to trees without an animal in sight.

And then everything exploded before her eyes, shattering the unearthly quiet by a loud, vicious roar. Trees bent low to the ground, and then came up by the roots, flying and twisting through the air like oversized arrows.

Windows imploded. Glass shattered inward, filling the air with deadly, glittering missiles of destruction. Everything that once was, was no more.

And then as quickly as it had come, it passed. Where there had been darkness, now there was light. The house was but a remnant of its former self. The limbs of a tree protruded through a window. Beneath their deadweight, a baby's bed lay crushed on the floor. And near the doorway, a clock lay on its side, the hands stopped at five minutes past seven.

Glory shuddered, then fell forward, her head upon her knees, her shoulders shaking as she pulled herself back to reality.

"Honey... are you all right?"

Wyatt's voice was a calm where the storm had been. She threw her arms around his neck, sobbing in near hysterics.

"The storm... I couldn't stop the storm."

Wyatt held her close, smoothing the tangled hair from her face and rubbing her back in a slow, soothing motion.

"There's no storm here, honey. Maybe it was just a bad dream."

Glory's eyes blazed as she lifted her head, pinning him with the force of her glare.

"Don't!" she sobbed. "Don't you doubt me, Wyatt! Not now! I don't *ever* dream. Either I sleep. Or these... things come into my mind. I can't make them stop, and I can't make them go away."

She rolled out of his grasp and out of the bed, desperate to see for herself what it looked like outside. Wyatt followed her frantic race for the door, grabbing for his gun as he ran.

Sunlight hit her head-on, kissing the frown on her face with a warm burst of heat, while an easy spring breeze lifted the tail of her nightgown and then flattened it against her legs.

"Oh, Lord," she muttered, and buried her face in her hands. "I don't understand. I saw the storm. I saw the...!" Her face lit up as she remembered. "What time is it?"

He looked back inside the house at Granny's mantel clock. "A little before eight. Why?"

Glory moaned, and began pacing the dewy grass in her bare feet. "This doesn't make sense. The clock had stopped at a little after seven. That time has already come and gone."

"Come here." He caught her by the arm, gently pulling her back inside the house. "Now sit down and tell me exactly what you saw. Maybe it was happening in another part of the country, and if it did, there's not a damn thing you can do to stop it, darlin'. You can't fix the world. I'm just sorry that you get pulled into its messes."

She went limp in his arms, and at his urging, curled up on the couch, tucking her bare feet beneath the tail of her gown to warm them. When she started talking, her voice was shaky and weak.

"It was so real. The house was white. And it's set on a hill right above a creek. There was an old two-story barn just below the house, and corrals and fences behind that stretched off into the woods."

Wyatt was in the act of making coffee when something she said made him pause. He turned, listening to her as she continued, the coffee forgotten.

"What else?" he urged.

She shrugged. "The sky. It was so black. And everything was still...you know what I mean...like the world was holding its breath?"

He nodded, although the description gave him a chill.

"And then it just exploded...right before my eyes. There was a roar, and then trees were being ripped out of the ground, and the windows..." She closed her eyes momentarily, trying to remember what had come next. Her lips were trembling when she looked up at him. "And then it was all over. There was a tree through a window, and a baby bed beneath it. And there was a clock on the floor that had stopped at five minutes after seven."

Wyatt shuddered. "Damn, honey. That's got to be hell seeing things like that and knowing you have no control of the outcome."

"Sometimes I do," she whispered. "Remember you?"

His eyes turned dark. "How could I forget?"

But the memory was too fresh to give up, and she thumped her knees with her fists in frustration.

"I just wish I'd recognized the place," she muttered. "It was so pretty. There was a rooster weather vane on the roof of the house, and it had a wide porch across the front, and a big porch swing. I love porch swings." And then she smiled sadly. "And there was the prettiest bunch of pansies growing in a tin tub beneath one of those old-fashioned water wells. The kind that you had to pump."

Wyatt paled. He listened to what she said as the air left his lungs in one hard gush. Panic sent him flying across the room. He pulled her to her feet, unaware that he was almost shaking her.

"Oh, God! Oh, God! What time did you say that clock stopped?"

Glory went still. The shock on Wyatt's face was impossible to miss. "Five minutes after seven," she said. "Why? What's wrong?"

He started to pace, looking at the mantel clock, then comparing the time that she'd stated.

"Oh, no!" He was at the point of despair when it dawned. "Wait! We're in a different time zone. It's not too late." Before Glory could ask what was wrong, he was running toward the bedroom, muttering beneath his breath. "The phone! The phone! I've got to find that phone."

Seconds later, she was right behind him.

His fingers were shaking as he punched in the numbers, and then he groaned as he counted the rings. Twice he looked down at his watch on the bedside table, and each time, the fear that had sent him running to call increased a thousandfold.

And then Lane's sleepy voice echoed in his ear, and Wyatt started shouting for them to get out of the house.

"Wyatt? What the hell's wrong with you?" Lane muttered, trying to come awake. He and Toni had spent sleepless hours last night with a sick baby, and when they'd finally gotten her earache under control and her back to sleep, they had dropped into bed like zombies.

"You've got to get out of the house!" Wyatt shouted. "There's a storm coming. You have less than five minutes to get everyone into the cellar. For God's sake, don't ask me why! Just do it!"

Without question, Lane rolled out of bed, grabbing at his jeans as he nudged Toni awake.

"Was it Glory?" was all that he asked.

"Yes," Wyatt shouted. "Now run!"

The line went dead in Wyatt's ear, and he dropped onto the side of the bed, shaking from head to toe as tears shimmered across his eyes. When Glory reached out, he caught her hand, holding it to his mouth, kissing her palm, then her wrist, then pulling her down onto his lap.

"It was my home that you saw," he whispered. "I'm glad you liked it. It was where I grew up."

Glory closed her eyes against the pain in his voice. "I'm sorry. I'm so, so sorry." She wrapped her arms around his neck and held him, giving him comfort in the only way she knew how.

Minutes passed, and then a half hour, and then an hour, during which time Glory tried to get him to eat, then gave up hoping he might talk. Wyatt sat, staring at the floor, with his hand no more than inches from a phone that wouldn't ring.

"Oh, God," he finally whispered. "What if I was too late?"

"Now you know how it feels to hold life and death in the palm of your hand," she said quietly. "I live with this every day of my life. Can you live with it, as well?"

He didn't answer, and she didn't expect one. He'd wanted to know all there was to know about her. And her heart was breaking as she realized that this might be too much to accept.

As Granny Dixon's mantel clock chimed, signaling the hour, Wyatt looked down at his watch. It was ten o'clock—nine o'clock for Toni and Lane. If they had survived, he would have heard by now...wouldn't he? He thought about calling his brother, Justin, and then couldn't remember the number. It was an excuse and he knew it. A simple call to Information would have solved that problem. But it also might have given him a truth he didn't want to face.

Seconds after he'd discarded the thought, the phone finally rang, startling them both to the point that neither wanted to answer the call. Glory held her breath and closed her eyes, saying a prayer as Wyatt picked up the phone.

"Hello?"

Lane's voice sounded weary and rough, but when it reverberated soundly in Wyatt's ear, he went weak with relief.

"It's me," Lane said.

"Thank God," Wyatt groaned. "I didn't think you would ever call. Are Toni and Joy all right? Did you—"

Lane interrupted. "I want to talk to Glory."

Wyatt handed her the phone.

"Hello?"

Lane swallowed a lump in his throat as he tried to put into words what he was feeling.

"How do I say thank-you for the only things that make my life worth living?" he asked quietly.

Glory started to smile. This must mean they were safe.

"I will never—and I mean, never—doubt a word you say to me again. Five minutes later and we would have been dead. All of us. A tree fell on Joy's crib. It smashed the—"

"I know," Glory said softly.

Lane paused, wiped a hand across his face and then smiled. "That's right, you do, don't you, girl?" He paused, then wiped a shaky hand across his face. "There's someone else who wants to talk to you." He handed the phone to Toni.

"Is this Glory?"

Glory's eyes widened. She put her hand over the phone and whispered urgently to Wyatt. "I think it's your sister."

He smiled. "So tell her hello."

Glory dropped onto the bed beside Wyatt, anxiously twisting a lock of her hair around her finger. Except for Lane, this would be her first connection with any of his people.

"Yes, this is Glory."

Toni caught her breath on a sob. "I'm Wyatt's sister, Toni. You saved our lives, you know." And then she started to cry, softly but steadily. "Thank-you is little to say for the gift that you gave me today, but I do thank you, more than you will ever know. If you knew what I went through to get this man and our child, you would understand what it means to me to know that they're safe."

A shy smile of delight spread across Glory's face as she caught Wyatt watching her. "You're very welcome," she said. "But it wasn't all me. Wyatt is the one who put two and two together. He's the one who made the call."

Toni sighed as exhaustion threatened to claim her. In another room, she could hear Joy as she started to fuss, and Justin's wife as she tried to console her. The call had to be short. With a trembling voice, she continued.

"When he comes back this way, I'd love for you to come with him. I've always wanted to hug an earthbound angel.

Now put that brother of mine on, I need to tell him thank-you, too."

Glory handed Wyatt the phone.

"Sis?"

At the sound of his voice, tears sprang again. "Thank you, big brother."

"You're welcome, honey," he said, and although he hated to ask, he needed to know. "Is the house gone?"

"No. It will take a lot of work, but it can be repaired."

"That's good," Wyatt said. "Are you at Justin's?"

She rolled her eyes as Joy's cries became louder. "Yes, but not for any longer than necessary. If you need Lane, call him here, at least for the remainder of the week. As soon as we get the glass out of the house and windows back in, we'll be able to do the bulk of the repairs in residence."

Wyatt grinned. He knew what a headache it would be for two separate families to be living under one roof, especially when two of the people were as hardheaded as Toni and Justin.

"Wyatt?"

"Yes, honey?"

"Don't you hurt that girl."

Glory saw the shock on his face and heard the pain in his voice, but she didn't know why.

"Why the hell would you say that to me?" he asked.

"Because I know you. You've got a kite for a compass. You go where the wind blows, and when her troubles are over, you'll be long gone again. Don't you leave her behind with a broken heart. If I find out that you have, I don't think I'll ever forgive you."

"That was never my intention," he muttered. "And I can't thank you enough for the vote of confidence."

"You're welcome, and I love you," Toni said. "Call if you need us."

The phone went dead in his ear.

"What's wrong?" Glory asked, aware that Wyatt was more than a little out of sorts.

He tossed the phone on the bed beside them, almost afraid to look at her for fear that she'd see the truth on his face.

"Nothing. She's just being her usual bossy self. She gave me a warning... and a little advice."

"And that was?"

He shrugged, then looked up as a reluctant grin spread across his face. He took her into his arms and dropped backward onto the bed.

"Something about hanging my sorry butt from the nearest tree if I didn't treat you right."

Glory laughed, and wrapped her arms around his neck. "I like the way that woman thinks."

Chapter 12

Just after noon, the sound of a car could be heard coming down the road to Granny's cabin. Wyatt watched from his seat on the steps as a black-and-white cruiser pulled to a stop only yards from the porch. When Anders Conway got out of the car, Wyatt couldn't resist a small dig.

"Are you lost?"

Conway had to grin. From the first time they'd met, he hadn't been as accommodating as he should have been, and yet this big, dark-eyed man didn't seem to hold a grudge.

"You might think so, wouldn't you?"

Wyatt motioned toward the single cane chair against the wall. "Have a seat."

Anders shook his head. "Maybe some other time. I just came out to update you on the investigation."

Wyatt made no effort to hide his surprise. "You mean there really is one?"

Conway frowned. He had that coming. "Yeah, there really is. And I came out to tell you that, no matter what I believe about Glory Dixon's *powers,* I do believe that someone is out to do her harm." And then he scratched his head and took the chair that was offered, in spite of his earlier refusal. "The thing is, none of this makes sense. Why would anyone even *want* to hurt her? Hell, half the town is afraid of her, and the other half thinks she's a little bit..."

"Nuts?"

Both men looked startled as Glory came out of the cabin. Embarrassed at being overheard, Conway jumped up from his seat and yanked off his hat as a flush colored his skin.

"Now, Miss Dixon, I'm real sorry you heard that, and I don't mean anything personal by it," Conway said. "I was just stating a fact."

It wasn't anything she hadn't heard a hundred times before, and it wasn't what interested her. "What was that you were saying about an investigation?" she asked.

Conway relaxed, apparently thankful that the conversation had changed.

"We found a partial fingerprint on the car that tried to run you down. Course it'll take a while for any results to come back, and you understand if the fellow that left it had no priors, then we have no way of identifying him, don't you?"

She nodded.

"And for what it's worth, I sent that scrap of fabric that you gave me off to the crime lab at the capitol. Don't think we'll learn much, but we'll at least have tried, right?"

He hitched at his gun belt, and studied a knot on the plank beneath his feet. "What I came out to say is, I'm sorry. When you came to me for help, I let you down, and I can promise it won't happen again."

When the chief offered his hand, Glory didn't hesitate. And when he shook it firmly, in a small, but significant way, she felt vindicated.

"Thank you for coming," she said. "I appreciate it more than you know."

He nodded. "So, that's it, then," he said. "I suppose I'd better be getting back into town. It doesn't do to leave my two deputies alone for long. On occasion, they get ticket happy, and then I've got some angry townsfolk wondering why they could make a U-turn on Main Street one day, and then get fined for it the next. Besides that, we had ourselves a burglary last night. Someone kicked in the back door to Henley's Garage and Filling Station, waltzed in and helped themselves to a whole set of tires. From what we can tell, the thieves brought their own rims and mounted 'em right on the spot."

Conway shook his head as he started toward the cruiser. "I'll tell you, crooks these days either have more guts or less brains than they used to. And finding any fingerprints as evidence in that grease pit is impossible. Nearly everyone in town is in and out of there. Ain't no way to figure out who left what or when they left it, and old man Henley's fit to be tied. See you around," he said, and then left.

Glory turned to Wyatt, a smile hovering on her lips as Conway drove away.

"I didn't think this day would ever come," she said.

"What day?"

"The day when someone other than my family would bother to believe me."

He cradled her in his arms, hugging her to him. "After this morning, how can you forget the fifty-odd members of my immediate family who think you hung the moon?" He tilted her chin, then kissed the tip of her nose when she wrinkled it in dismay.

"Fifty?"

He grinned. "I underestimated on purpose so I wouldn't scare you off."

Glory shifted within his embrace. "As long as I have you, I'm not scared of a living thing," she whispered.

Joy filled him as he held her. "Lady, you take my breath away."

A light breeze teased at her hair, lifting, then settling long, shiny strands across his hands. Unable to resist their offer, Wyatt combed his fingers through the lengths, entranced by the sunlight caught in the depths.

"Wyatt, there's something I want to talk to you about."

Play ceased immediately. The tone of her voice was serious, as was the look in her eyes.

"Then tell me."

She moved out of his arms, then took him by the hand and started walking toward the shade trees above the creek at the back of the cabin.

Wyatt went where she led, aware that when she was ready, she would start talking. As they reached the shade, Glory dropped down onto a cool, mossy rock, and then patted the ground beside it, indicating that Wyatt join her, which he did.

As she sorted out her thoughts, she fiddled with her hair. It was sticking to her neck and in spite of the shade, hot against her shoulders. Absently, she pulled it over her shoulders, then using her fingers for a comb, separated it into three parts, and began to braid.

"I have a theory," she said, as she fastened the end of the braid with a band from her pocket. "I don't know how to explain it, but I think that the body that was buried at the dump is somehow connected to what's happening to me."

A shiver of warning niggled at Wyatt's instinct for self-preservation as he gave Glory a startled look. "I don't like this," he said.

She shrugged, then stared pensively down the bank of the creek to the tiny stream of water that continually flowed. "I don't either. But nothing else makes sense."

"What made you think like that?" he asked.

"It was something that Chief Conway said, about people being afraid of me." She turned toward Wyatt, pinning him with that clear blue stare. "What if someone thought my gift was like some, uh, I don't know . . . a witch's crystal ball, maybe? What if someone did something bad . . . really bad, and they thought that all I had to do was look at them and I'd know it?"

Wyatt's heart jumped, then settled. "You mean . . . something bad like committing a murder and dumping a body?"

She nodded.

His eyes narrowed thoughtfully as he considered what she'd just said. The more he thought about it, the more it made sense.

"It *would* explain why, wouldn't it?"

"It's about the only thing that does," she said. And then her chin quivered.

"Come here," he said softly, and she crawled off the rock and into his lap, settling between his outstretched legs and resting her back against the breadth of his chest. When he pulled her close, surrounding her with his arms and nuzzling his chin at the top of her head, she savored the security that came from being encompassed by the man who'd stolen her heart.

For a time, the outside world ceased to exist. For Glory and Wyatt, there was nothing but them, and the sound of the breeze rustling through the leaves, birdcalls coming from the green canopy over their heads, the ripple of the water in the creek below and the raucous complaint of a squirrel high up in a tree across the creek.

Bo Marker was back in business. He had shells for his rifle, wheels on his truck and a renewed interest in finishing the job he'd promised Carter Foster he would do. Now he didn't just *want* the money Carter had promised, he *needed* it to pay Frankie for helping him last night with the heist.

But Bo wasn't a complete fool. He had no intention of going anywhere near that Dixon farm again. He still had nightmares about that man who'd run him off, and hoped he never saw him again.

As he drove along the back roads, he kept his eye out for a good place to conceal himself and his truck. A location that would be close to the main road that led down from the mountain. That Dixon woman and her man couldn't stay up there forever. They'd have to come down sometime, if for no other reason than to get food. When they did, he'd be waiting. This time, he'd make sure that there would be no Kentucky bigfoot with a gun at his back when he took aim.

Pleased with his plan, Bo proceeded to search the roads, while Carter Foster lived each hour sinking deeper and deeper in a hell of his own making.

Carter was running. His belly bounced with each lurch of his stride, and his heart was hammering so hard against his rib cage that he feared he was going to die on the spot. With every step, the sound of his shoes slapping against the old tile floor of the courthouse echoed sharply within the high, domed ceilings.

He burst into the courtroom just as the judge was about to raise his gavel.

"I'm sorry I'm late, Your Honor. May it please the court, I have filed an injunction against the company that's suing my client."

The judge leaned over the desk, pinning Carter with a hard, frosty glare.

"Counselor . . . this is the third time you've been tardy in my court this week. Once more, and I'll hold you in contempt."

Carter paled. "Yes, sir. I'm sorry, sir."

And so the morning passed.

When they recessed for the day, it was nearly three o'clock. Carter's belly was growling with hunger. He'd missed breakfast, and because of his earlier dereliction, had been forced to skip lunch. Right now, he wouldn't care if his client got drawn and quartered, the only thing on his mind was food.

He came out of the courthouse, again on the run. He tossed his briefcase into his car, and was about to get in when he heard someone calling his name. With a muffled curse, he turned, and then felt all the blood drain from his face. The chief of police was walking toward him from across the street.

"Hey there, Foster," Conway said, and thumped him lightly on the back in a manly greeting.

Carter managed a smile. "Chief, I haven't seen you in a while. I guess since the last time we were in court together, right?"

Conway nodded, while gauging Foster's condition. His supposition the other day had been right on target. Foster looked like he'd been pulled backward through a downspout. He needed a haircut. His clothes looked as if he'd slept in them, and there were bags beneath his eyes big enough to haul laundry.

"Say, I've been meaning to speak to you," Conway said.

"Oh? About what?" Carter's heart jerked so sharply that he feared he might die on the spot.

"Your wife and all," Conway said, a little uncertain how one went about commiserating with a fellow who'd just been dumped.

"What about my wife?" Carter asked, as his voice rose three octaves.

Conway shrugged and wished he'd never started this conversation. Old Foster wasn't taking this any better than he'd hoped.

"Well, you know, she's gone, and I heard that—"

"She ran off, you know," Carter interrupted. "She's been threatening to do it for years but I never believed her. I guess a man should believe his wife every so often. It might prevent problems later on, don't you think?"

The moment he said it, he gritted his teeth, wishing he had the good sense not to ramble, but when he got nervous, he always talked too much.

"I suppose you're right," Conway said. "Anyway, I just wanted to tell you I'm real sorry."

Carter sighed and even managed a smile. "Thanks. That's real nice of you, Chief."

Conway nodded, and then as Carter was about to get in his car, he asked, "Have you heard from her?"

From the look on Carter's face, the chief thought he was about to have a heart attack. Carter's mouth was working, but no words were coming out. Finally, he cleared his throat, and managed a small, shaky giggle.

"Daddy, Wyatt says I can have some of his cookies."

Liam Fowler grinned. "Then I suppose you'd better have some, son."

A wide smile spread across Edward Lee's face as he thrust his hand into the sack and came up with two cookies, one for each hand, then set about eating them.

"Had yourself any more trouble?" Liam asked.

Wyatt shook his head. "No, and I suspect that's thanks to you and your friends."

Liam nodded and absently stroked his beard, rearranging the thick, black curls without care for appearance.

"What puzzles me is why Glory is suffering with this," he said.

"She has a theory," Wyatt said. "It came from something that Anders Conway said. He said that a lot of people are afraid of her."

Liam nodded. "That's true. It's a shame, but it's a fact. Lots of people fear what they don't understand."

"Are you afraid of her?" Wyatt asked.

Liam smiled, then looked down at his son. "No more than I'm afraid of Edward Lee. So, what's she getting at, anyway?"

"Not too long after I arrived, she had a vision. She *saw* omeone hiding evidence of a terrible crime. But she only aw it in her mind. She believes that whoever committed this rime is afraid that, because of her gift, she will be able to oint the finger at him, so to speak. And that he's trying to t rid of her to keep his secret safe."

Liam frowned. "It sounds ugly, but it makes a lot of nse. I've known that girl since the day she was born. Rafe xon was one of my best friends. I've seen grown men say yers when she crosses their paths, just because she has sight."

Vyatt shook his head in disbelief.

Vith cookies gone, Edward Lee's attention wandered. yatt, where's my Mornin' Glory?" he asked, interrupt- the seriousness of their conversation.

was left of him surfaced months later in a fisherman's net off the coast of the Carolinas."

"Ooh, hell," Conway said. The image was startling, to say the least.

"Anyway, my point is, you might keep that in mind as you work the case."

"Yeah, right, and thanks," Conway muttered, and then disconnected.

He leaned back in his chair, propped his feet on the desk and locked his hands behind his neck, thinking as he did about what Monday just said. How did coincidence factor into a warning of impending danger? And how did...?

His feet hit the floor as his hands slapped the desk.

"Son of a..."

He jumped to his feet and stepped outside, staring across the street at the sign on Carter Foster's office.

Out To Lunch.

For a man who was supposed to be mourning the loss of a wife, he sure hadn't lost his appetite. "I wonder?" he muttered, then frowned, pivoted on his heel and stalked back into his office.

"Hey!" he shouted.

A deputy came running.

"I want you to check the bus station, the ticket counters in every airport within driving distance, and anyplace else you can think of that provides transportation."

"Yes, sir," the deputy said. "What am I checking for?"

Conway tapped the deputy on the shirt, lowering his voice in a confidential manner. "I want you to find me a paper trail. I want to know how and from where Betty Jo Foster left town, and if possible, who with. And I don't want to walk out of here this evening and find out that everyone in town knows what you're doing."

The deputy's eyes widened.

"What I'm saying is...do your job and keep your trap shut," Conway growled.

"Yes, sir," he said, and out the door he went.

* * *

Bo woke himself up when he snorted. The sound was so startling that he grabbed for his gun before he came to enough to realize that it was himself that he had heard. His legs were stiff, his butt was numb, and his belly was pushing uncomfortably against the steering wheel of his pickup truck. He yawned, then stretched as he felt nature call.

Satisfied that from where he had parked, he was perfectly concealed from the road, he opened the pickup door and then scooted out of the seat, leaving the door open for privacy's sake as he did what he needed to do. Groaning beneath his breath as his legs protested his weight, he went about his business.

At that minute, a car came flying around a corner and then headed back up the hill. Confident that he was safe from being seen, he turned to look.

His heart jerked as he cursed. In a panic, he grabbed for his rifle, forgetting that he'd been using that hand for something else. To his dismay, he was too late to take aim, and found himself watching the taillights of Wyatt Hatfield's car as it disappeared over the hill.

Disgusted with his bad luck, he kicked at the dirt. Now there was no telling how long it would be before they'd come back.

Wyatt was carrying in groceries while Glory, at his insistence, had gone to her bed to lie down. Ever since she'd had the vision about the storm, she'd had a dull, niggling headache. It wasn't uncommon for such a thing to happen, but this time, she hadn't been able to shake the feeling of malaise.

Her head had barely hit the pillow when he came into the room with a glass of water and a couple of pills in his hand.

"Here, honey," he said. "See if these will help."

Gratefully, she accepted the water and the pills and swallowed them in one quick gulp. She set the glass on the table, and then lay back down on the bed.

"Thank you for taking care of me," she said.

Wyatt leaned over and softly kissed her cheek. "I pleasure," he whispered. "Now see if you can get sleep."

She frowned. "I don't want to sleep. It's too late in day. If I sleep now, then I'll never get to sleep tonight."

A cocky grin slid across his mouth. "Oh, that's okay," said. "I can think of a few other things we might do i stead."

In spite of her pain, she laughed. And at his insistence, rolled over and closed her eyes. *I do love the way his mind works,* she thought.

"To heck with my mind, how about the rest of me?" he asked, and left her grinning.

In spite of Glory's determination not to sleep, she quickly succumbed, and she was still dozing when Wyatt wandered outside to get some air. It was hard to keep his mind occupied with anything but Glory's safety, but he knew that he needed to take a break from the tension under which they'd been living.

For a few minutes, he wandered around the imm vicinity of the cabin, but he was too cautious to go fa lack of anything better to do, he picked up a stick, back to the porch steps and then began to whittle. tivity had nothing to do with creativity. It was a thing the time.

He had a good accumulation of wood chips go he heard someone coming through the brush. Fo time since his arrival, he looked up with interest When Edward Lee came ambling out of the tr stood up.

"Ma said I could bring you some cookies." Wyatt the sack before adding, "They're my fav

Wyatt grinned, then opened the sack. "Wo some?"

Edward Lee looked back over his shoulder. right behind him, walking with the ease of a peace with himself, and comfortable with the rifle he had slung on his shoulder.

"She's taking a nap." As soon as he said it, he sympathized with the disappointment on the young man's face.

And then the door behind him suddenly opened, and Edward Lee bounded to his feet.

"Mornin' Glory! You woke up!" Delight was rich on his face as he threw his arms around her neck, hugging and grinning broadly as she greeted him with a kiss on the cheek.

"I thought I heard voices," she said, smiling easily at Liam and his son.

"Ma sent cookies," Edward Lee said.

Wyatt hid a grin. He could see where this was going and handed Glory the sack.

"They're my favorites," Edward Lee reminded her.

Glory laughed. "How many have you already had?"

"Only two," he said.

"Then maybe you could have two more?"

Liam laughed aloud at his boy's ingenious method of begging.

"Don't eat them all, boy!" he prodded. "Ma's got a whole cookie jar full saved for you at home."

Edward Lee nodded and chewed, unable to answer for the cookie in his mouth.

"Would you like to come inside?" Glory asked. "I could make a pot of coffee."

Liam smiled, and brushed his hand against the side of her cheek in a gentle, but testing gesture.

"No, thank you, girl. I just stopped by to say hello. We'd best be gettin' on home before my boy eats all of your food." And then he cast a long approving glance at Wyatt before tipping his hat to them both.

"You be careful now, you hear?"

Wyatt nodded. "Same to you, friend. Same to you."

When they were gone, Glory waited for Wyatt to say something, anything, to break the tension of the look he was giving her. But when he remained silent, she took the initiative.

"What?" she asked.

"I told Liam about your theory."

Her face lost all expression. She wouldn't allow herself to care if Edward Lee's father doubted her.

"So?" she asked.

"He said it made sense."

The tension in her body slowly disappeared as she dropped down to the porch steps and dug in the sack for a cookie.

"Want one?" she asked, and offered it to Wyatt.

He shook his head, then sat down beside her, slinging an arm across her shoulders.

"What I want is for you to be safe and happy. What I don't know is how to make it happen. This waiting is driving me insane."

She nodded in agreement, thoughtfully munching the cookie, savoring the spicy taste of cinnamon, oatmeal and raisin. When she was through, she brushed her hands on the sides of her jeans and then studied the toes of her shoes.

Wyatt could tell there was something on her mind, but he didn't know whether to ask, or wait for her to say it in her own time. Finally, impatience got the better of him and he tugged at her braid to get her attention.

"So are you going to say what's on your mind, or are you going to leave me hanging?" he asked.

"I think I should go back to the dump."

Wyatt flinched. He didn't like to think of what she'd endured before. Putting herself through torment again seemed more punishment than sense.

"But why, honey? You know what it did to you the first time."

She sighed, then leaned her head against his chest, relishing the comfort of his arms as he pulled her closer.

"Because if I'm right about why someone wants to harm me, then what happened there impacts my safety. When it happened before, I was so shocked by the horror that I pulled out of the vision before it had time to play out." Her voice deepened in dejection. "I don't even know, if we go back, that it *will* happen again, but if it does, maybe I will see something that will give us a face…or a name. As Chief Conway says, something solid to go on."

"I don't like it…but I'll take you."

She went limp in his arms. "Thank you, Wyatt. Thank you."

He frowned. "Don't thank me yet," he warned. "This mess isn't over."

Chapter 13

Wyatt was slipping the gun in the back of his jeans as Glory came out of the bedroom. He noticed her look of fear before she had time to hide it.

Watching him arm himself to protect her was a shock. She fiddled with the ends of her braid in embarrassment, unnecessarily tucked at the pink T-shirt already in place beneath the waistband of her jeans.

"It'll be all right," he promised, as he went to her side. "I won't take my eyes off you for a second."

"I know that." She let him hold her, relaxing against his chest, and focusing on the constant and steady beat of his heart. "It's just that the sight of that gun reminds me that I'm no longer safe."

He tilted her chin until she was forced to meet his gaze. "You say the word, and this trip to the dump is off."

Dread of what lay ahead was overwhelming, but she was firmly convinced that if her life was ever to get back to normal, it hinged upon finding the identity of the man who'd dumped that woman's body in with the garbage from Larner's Mill.

"No. I want this to be over with."

He nodded. "Then let's get started. The sooner we get there..."

He left the rest of the phrase undone as they started outside.

Glory paused in the doorway, allowing herself one last look at the inside of Granny's cabin, absorbing the familiarity of its simple decor. The old wooden floors. The papered and painted walls, peeling and faded. The pictures and knickknacks that Faith Dixon had accumulated over her ninety-one years.

Wyatt put his hand on Glory's shoulder. When she turned, there were tears shimmering across the surface of her eyes. Her pain broke his heart.

"We'll be back, sweetheart. I swear."

Glory lifted her chin, then straightened her shoulders and nodded.

"I knew that," she said softly. "I just needed to remember my people."

There was nothing else to say as he locked the door behind her. Moments later, they were in the car and on their way down the road. When they passed the site where her home once stood, she frowned at the remaining rubble.

"This place is a mess," she muttered.

"It will get better," Wyatt said. "One of these days, everything will be better."

Glory sighed, then made herself relax. *This, too, shall pass.*

Wyatt heard her thought and had to restrain a shudder. He hoped to God that he wasn't destined to be part of her past. He couldn't imagine a future... his future... without Glory in it.

Bo Marker sat in the midst of the ruins of a late-night run for food that he'd made to a local convenience store. Potato chip crumbs were caught in the fabric of the truck seat, as well as hanging on the front of his shirt and jeans, leaving grease stains wherever they clung. An empty box that once held half a dozen chocolate cupcakes was on the floorboard, and the wadded wrappers from two deli sandwiches lay on the ground where he'd tossed them out the window. An empty liter of soda was on the ground beside them, and a half-empty bottle of the same was tucked safely between his backside and the butt of his gun.

His eyes were red-rimmed; his face itched from a three-day growth of whiskers. But he was determined that this time, he would not miss his chance. So when he heard the familiar sound of a car coming down the mountain, his pulse accelerated. If it was them, he was going to be ready.

He lifted the deer rifle from the seat beside him, angling it until it was pointing out the window. Adjusting the telescopic sight until the cross hairs were in perfect alignment with a tree on the opposite side of the road, he drew a deep breath and took aim at the peak of the hill down which they would come. And when the car topped the hill and started down, he squirmed with pleasure. It was them!

"All right!" he muttered. "Now it's my turn."

The speed at which they were traveling allowed him little time for error. He squinted, adjusting the scope as he followed the car's descent. Now the cross hairs were in alignment with the middle of the driver's face. The image he had was perfect, right down to the scar on the big man's face. And then he swung the barrel a few inches to the left, firmly fixing upon the woman in the seat beside the driver.

The nearer they came, the more certain he was that, in seconds, it would be over. His finger was firm upon the trigger, his breathing slow and even. He was counting his money as he squeezed.

When the car came even with his location, he was still scrambling to find the safety he'd forgotten to release. And when the car passed the trees behind which he'd hidden his truck, and then disappeared around the curve in the road beyond, he was cursing at the top of his voice and hammering his rifle against the door in unfettered fury.

"By God, you won't get away from me this time," he screamed.

He started his engine, gunning it until blue smoke boiled from the rear exhaust. When he launched himself from the trees and onto the road, he left a wake of overrun bushes and broken limbs behind him.

Potato chips flew, while discarded paper scooted from one side of the floorboard to the other as he followed Wyatt around the curve. The partial bottle of soda tipped over and began to leak upon the seat. Bo couldn't have cared less. He was on a mission, and this time, there would be no mistakes.

Their ride down the mountain had been silent. Wyatt was concentrating on what lay ahead, and Glory was locked in the past, trying to remember everything she could of what she'd seen before. But when she saw the sign indicating the way to the dump, she tensed.

Wyatt sensed her anxiety, and when he slowed to take the turn, he gave her a quick, sidelong glance. Her face was pale, and her hands were clenched in fists.

"Honey, don't do this to yourself," he begged. "Either relax and let whatever comes, come, or just stop it all now."

"It's too late to stop," she said. "It was too late the day Daddy and J.C. died." Her chin quivered as she tried to get past the pain. "Besides, I can't stop what I didn't start. This is someone else's game. My fear comes from the fact that I don't know all the rules."

"Then we'll just make some rules of our own," he said, and moments later, came sliding to a halt at the edge of the pit.

For a time, neither moved as they stared down into the morass. Scavengers had dug through part of the dirt covering the latest loads. Bits of garbage were blowing around the bottom, caught in a mini-whirlwind of dust and debris, and the usual assortment of birds were circling and landing with no particular rhythm. Even though the windows on the car were up, the odor of rotting garbage was invasive.

"Here goes nothing," Glory said, and got out on her side of the car as Wyatt exited on his. When he came around to get her, the gun was in his hand.

"How do you want to work this?" he asked.

She shrugged. "I don't know. I guess go back to the place where I was when it happened before." And when she started walking, Wyatt was right beside her.

She paused, then frowned as she remembered. "No, Wyatt. If this is going to work, then everyone has to be in the same position. You were on the other side of the pit with the truck."

"Damn it, Glory. I don't want you out of my sight."

Smiling, she lifted her hand, caressing the side of his face, and tracing a fingertip down the scar on his cheek.

"Then don't close your eyes," she teased.

He groaned, then pulled her into his arms and tasted her smile.

Like Glory, it was warm and light, and Wyatt held her close, demanding a response that was not long in coming.

She bent to him like a leaf to the wind. Absorbing his strength, taking courage from his presence, when he trembled beneath her touch, she knew that she was loved.

The rough squawk of an angry crow disturbed the moment, and brought them back to the task at hand.

Wyatt held her face in his hands, gazing down into those wide, all-seeing eyes, and knew a peace that he'd never known before. His voice was rough and shaky, but he was certain of his feelings. "God in heaven, but I love you, girl."

"Remember that tonight when we've nothing else to do," Glory said, and tried to laugh through an onset of tears.

And then before he could talk himself out of it, he jogged back to the place where he'd parked, then turned and waved, indicating that he was ready for her to proceed.

Glory took a deep breath, said a small prayer and started to walk, trying to remember her frame of mind that day, as well as where she'd been when she stopped and looked back at Wyatt, who'd been standing on the bed of her daddy's old truck.

The air was thick and muggy, and she wished for a breeze to stir the constant and often overpowering smell that went with this place. As she walked, she tried to let her mind go free, discarding her fears so that she would be receptive to whatever might come.

Long, anxious minutes passed, while Wyatt stood beside the car, watching her as she walked farther and farther away from him. Twice he almost called her back, but each time he resisted, remembering instead why they'd come.

And while he waited for something to happen, he constantly searched the line of trees around the dump. Now that they were off the mountain, he was solely responsible for Glory's well-being. Just when he feared this might be a wasted effort, she paused, and then her posture changed. He could tell, even from this distance, that she was lost in a world he could not see.

Glory was at the point of believing that this would be a repeat of the day she'd stood in the rubble from her home without seeing any more of the man who'd caused its destruction, when everything shifted before her eyes.

The bright light of morning faded into night. Again, a quarter moon shed a faint ivory glow on the upraised trunk of a big gray sedan. A man stood hunched over the depths of the trunk, and then he straightened and turned. Again, Glory saw the long white bundle he held in his arms.

She shuddered, then moaned in fear—afraid it would stop and afraid that it wouldn't.

She watched through his eyes as the bundle toppled, end over end, then rolled down the deep embankment before coming to a stop against a mound of dirt. And as before, the wide-eyed but unseeing gaze of a dead woman's face stared back up at her.

She screamed, but it was inside her mind. No sound escaped her lips, and she remained motionless, waiting for a revelation.

A small cloud moved across the sliver of moon. Glory knew that it was so, because for a brief time, there was little to see but the darkness in the pit itself. And then as she watched, the cloud passed, and for a second, the copper glint of the woman's red hair was highlighted against the white spread in which she'd been wrapped.

Elizabeth.

The name slid into Glory's mind, and then suddenly, her vision switched from the pit to the man who was getting into the car. She fixed upon the stoop of his shoulders, the balding spot in the back of his head. He opened the door and began to turn....

Then, as instantly as she'd been drawn into the vision, she was yanked back out.

Glory gasped as the world about her returned to normal. The glare of sun against her eyes was suddenly too harsh to bear, and she shaded them with her hand. A dark and impending sense of doom was with her that had nothing to do with what she'd just seen. It came from here! It came from the now!

Glory spun.

"Wyatt!"

His name came out in a scream as she started toward him on the run.

Wyatt knew to the moment when she came out of the trance. But when she started toward him, shouting his name, he knew that something was wrong.

Years of military training kicked in, and he ran in a crouched position with his gun drawn, searching the thick boundary of trees that surrounded the dump as he tried to get to Glory before danger got to her.

And then out of the woods to his right, he saw the flash of sun against metal, and shouted her name. He heard the gunshot at the same time that he saw Glory fall.

"No-o-o!" he raged, reaching her just seconds too late to shield her body with his own.

A heartbeat after he fell forward and then across her, the second bullet plowed up earth only inches from his head. Afraid to look down and see something he couldn't accept, he scooped her into his arms, then rolled, taking them both to a nearby stand of undergrowth. Once there, he quickly dragged her through the trees until he was positive that they were momentarily concealed from the shooter's eyes.

But when he started to search her body for a wound, she gasped, then choked, and grabbed at his hand instead.

"Glory! Where are you hit?"

"Oh, God. Oh, God." It was all she could say.

Another shot pierced the limbs over their heads, and Wyatt knew they had to move, or it would only be a matter of time before a stray bullet hit its mark.

"Where are you hit? Answer me, honey, where are you hit?"

Shock widened the pupils in her eyes until they appeared almost black. "I fell. Dear God...the bullet missed me when I fell."

He went limp with relief, and had the strongest urge to lay his head down and cry. *Thank you, Lord.*

The sharp thump from a fourth shot hit its mark in a nearby tree. Wyatt grabbed her hand and started moving deeper into the woods, at an angle from where the last shot had come.

Yards away, Wyatt shoved Glory down between two large rocks.

"Stay here, and don't move. Whatever you hear or don't hear, don't come out until you hear me call." In fear for his life as well as her own, Glory started to argue when Wyatt grabbed her by the arm. "I said . . . don't move."

She stopped in the middle of a word. The look on his face was one that she'd never seen before, and she realized that this was the part of Wyatt that he'd tried to leave behind when he'd retired from the military. This was a man trained to kill.

She nodded as a single tear rolled down her cheek. And then he disappeared into the trees before her eyes. One minute he was there. The next, he was gone.

Periodic shots continued from the other side of the dump, and Glory could tell that the shooter was moving through the trees, circling the open pit. Overwhelmed by the horror of it all, Glory stretched flat in the dirt between the rocks, buried her face in her arms and prayed.

When Bo saw her fall, he was ecstatic. The fact that the man reached her seconds later was immaterial. He had a clear shot at a second hit, and took it without a qualm just as a gnat flew up his nose. One minute he was sucking air, the next, a bug. His finger twitched on the trigger, not much, but enough that it threw off his aim. And because it did, the bullet plowed into the dirt, instead of Wyatt Hatfield's head. By the time he could react, the man had rolled, taking himself and the woman's body into a cover of trees.

"Son of a hairy bitch!"

Just to prove he was still in charge, he fired another shot into the location he'd seen them last, and then waited, listening for something that would indicate that they still lived.

Sweat rolled from his hair and down between his shoulder blades as he waited, holding his breath as he sifted through the sounds on the air. He heard nothing. Not a scream. Not a groan. And more important, not a return shot.

He knew that the man had a gun. He'd seen it in his hand as he ran. That he hadn't once fired back was to Bo proof that he'd crippled, if not killed him, outright.

But while Bo's elation was high, he'd had too many misses on this job already. He was going to see for himself.

As he circled the dump, angling toward the area where he hoped to find their bodies, he continued to threaten with intermittent fire, unaware that he was no longer the hunter. He'd become the prey.

Cold reasoning took Wyatt deeper into the woods, honing instincts he had perfected years ago. He moved with the stealth of a hunter, running without disturbing the ground upon which he moved, choosing his steps and his cover with caution.

As he ran, he realized that the rifle shots were also moving in a clockwise direction. A spurt of adrenaline sent him into a higher gear. He had to get to the man before the man got to Glory.

Once he had a momentary fix on the man's location as he glimpsed a second flash of sunlight on metal. But by the time he got there, the man was already gone.

And then luck changed for them both, when Wyatt heard a loud and sudden thrashing in the underbrush ahead. Soft curses filled the air and Wyatt aimed for the sound with unerring instinct, hoping, as he ran, that the bastard had just broken his neck. It would save him the effort of doing it for him.

Bo was still trying to untangle himself from the rusting coil of barbed wire that he'd stumbled upon when he saw movement from the corner of his eye. Fear shafted, making his movements even more frantic and locking the barbs even deeper into his clothing as he staggered, trying to take aim without neutering himself in the process.

Wyatt came out of the trees at a lope. But when he saw Bo Marker struggling with the wire and the gun, he came to a stop and took aim.

"Drop the gun."

Bo gawked at the black bore of the automatic only yards from his nose, and could tell from the way the man was standing that he knew how to use it. But getting caught was not in his plan, and he feared jail almost as much as dying.

Wyatt could tell that the man was not in the mood to surrender. When he saw him shift the grip on his gun and tighten his finger on the trigger, Wyatt moved his aim a few inches to the right, then fired.

Pain exploded in Bo's arm, and his hand went numb as the rifle bounced butt first onto the ground.

"You shot me!" Bo screamed, and then fell to his knees, which considering where he was standing, was not the smartest move he could make.

"If you move, I'll do it again," Wyatt said.

Bo wasn't smart, but he knew when a man meant business. And from the look on this one's face, he considered a broken arm a minor inconvenience. It was the barbs on which he was sitting that were causing him the misery.

The calm that had led Wyatt to this man suddenly disappeared. He was shaking with anger as he pulled him to his feet and started dragging him, wire and all, through the woods toward his car.

"You're killing me," Bo groaned, as Wyatt tightened his hold on his good arm and yanked him past a blackberry thicket.

Wyatt paused, then looked back. "Don't tempt me," he whispered. "You tried to kill my lady. It would be all too easy to return the favor."

Bo shrank from the venom in the big man's voice. Suddenly, the idea of getting to jail seemed a bit brighter than it had before.

"It wasn't personal," he whined. "I was just doing a job."

His words froze the anger in Wyatt's mind as a chill went up his spine.

"Someone hired you to do this?"

Bo nodded.

"Who?" Wyatt asked.

Bo shook his head. "Unh-uh. I ain't tellin' until I get to jail. If I tell you now, what's to keep you from shootin' me where I stand?"

Wyatt smiled, and Bo felt his potato chips curdle.

"Look," he cried. "I'll tell you who he is, I swear. But I need doctorin' first. Okay?"

"You are lucky that my father taught me to be kind to animals," Wyatt said softly. "Because I have the biggest urge to put you in the dump with the rest of the garbage."

"Oh, God," Bo said, and started to snivel. "Please, just get me to the doctor. I'll tell you everything I know."

At that moment, Wyatt hated as he'd never hated before. But he thought of Glory, who was still in hiding, and if this man was to be believed, still in danger. Without another word, he continued toward the car as if they'd not exchanged a word.

Minutes later, he dumped a bloody Bo, barbed wire and all, into the trunk of his car, and then started at a lope to the place where he'd left Glory in hiding.

She'd prayed until she'd run out of words, and cried until she'd run out of tears. The fear that held her captive between the two rocks was worse than what she'd felt when she'd witnessed her family die. Then it had been sudden and overwhelming in intensity. Now it was the waiting...the interminable waiting, that was driving her mad. But she had no choice. She'd trusted Wyatt with her life. She had to trust that he knew how to save it.

It seemed a long time before she heard the shot and the accompanying outcry. Terror for Wyatt sent her to her feet, and then fear that she'd endanger him further sent her back to her knees. She dropped between the rocks, rolling herself into a ball, and pressing her fingers against her mouth to keep from screaming.

Seconds turned to minutes, and far too many of them passed as she listened for proof that he still lived. Finally, she could bear it no more.

Wyatt... Wyatt...where are you? she thought.

"I'm here, Morning Glory. I'm here."

She caught her breath on a sob, and in spite of her fear, began crawling to her knees. When she lifted her head above the rocks where she'd been hiding, she saw him coming through the trees.

Seconds later, she was on her feet and running with outstretched arms. He caught her in midair, and then held her close, loving her with his touch, as well as his words. When he could think without wanting to cry, he took her by the hand and began leading her out of the woods.

"Is it over?" Glory asked, and then took a deep breath, trying to steady the tremble in her voice.

Wyatt frowned, and slipped an arm around her shoulders as they came out of the woods. "Almost, sweetheart. Now if I can get the bastard in my trunk to a doctor before he bleeds to death, we'll find out who hired him."

Glory stumbled, as a new wave of fear crossed her face. "Someone hired him? Oh, God! That means..."

"It means that whoever wants you dead doesn't have the guts to do it himself," he said harshly. "Don't worry. The loser in the trunk is going to talk, even if I have to beat it out of him."

Glory got in the car, a little leery of riding in the same vehicle with a man who'd been stalking her every move. But when Wyatt took off in a cloud of dust, bouncing over ruts and fishtailing in the loose Kentucky earth, the loud and constant shrieks of pain coming from the trunk convinced her that, at the moment, the man was in no shape to do her any more harm.

A short time later, Anders Conway was on his way out to lunch when he heard the sound of a car coming around the street corner on two wheels. He was fishing for the keys to his patrol car, expecting that he would have to give chase, when to his surprise, the car braked to an abrupt halt only feet from where he stood.

"You in a hurry to spend the night in my jail?" Anders grumbled, as he watched Wyatt Hatfield emerge from behind the wheel.

Wyatt grinned, but the smile never reached his eyes as he started toward his trunk. "No, but I brought someone who is."

Anders frowned as he circled the car. But when the trunk popped, shock replaced his earlier disgust.

"What in the world?" he muttered, missing nothing of the man's bulk, the shattered and bloody arm and the nest of barbed wire in which he was lying.

"That—" Wyatt pointed "—is the man who's been trying to kill Glory."

Conway gave Wyatt a long, considering stare. "Bo Marker...you sorry bugger...is this true?"

Bo groaned, considered lying, then looked at Wyatt's face and nodded.

Conway frowned, waving at a deputy who was just coming out of the office. "Bring me them bolt cutters from the closet," he shouted. "And then call an ambulance to this location."

The deputy pivoted, hurrying to do as he was told.

At this point, Bo began to bawl, aiming his complaints directly at Wyatt. "You nearly killed me with that crazy driving."

Wyatt leaned over the trunk. "I told you, don't tempt me, remember?"

Bo sucked up a squawk and then gave the chief a frantic look, as if begging for him to intervene.

And while no one was looking, Glory got out of the car. She was already at the trunk before Wyatt noticed her, and when he could have stopped her, realized that she needed to confront a ghost or two of her own.

Bo Marker felt the tension changing. As he tried to shift his head to see what they were looking at, she walked into his line of vision. Everything within him froze. It was the first time he'd gotten an up-close and personal look at someone he'd spent days trying to kill.

He remembered what people said about her, and when he found himself staring straight into those pale, silver-blue eyes, he started to shake. There was no accusation, no demand. No shriek of dismay, no cry of fear. Only a long, steady look that seemed to see into his soul. Every black, rotten inch of it.

He shuddered as fear overwhelmed him. When she took a step forward, he shrank back into the trunk as far as he could go.

"Who?" she said.

His mouth dropped, and he stuttered out his own name.

"No," Glory whispered. "I want to know who wants me dead."

Bo stuttered again, then swallowed a knot of panic.

"I said that I'd tell when they fixed me up," he whined. "If I tell, what's to keep all of you from letting me die?"

"The same damn thing that's keeping you alive," Wyatt said. "I want to see you hang for what you did."

Bo shrieked. "They don't hang people no more! Chief, you got to help me! Tell this crazy sucker to leave me alone!"

Conway grinned to himself. Whatever Wyatt Hatfield had said and done to this man had made a believer out of him.

"Now, Bo, it was a figure of speech." Conway eyed the barbed wire snarling around Marker's body and shook his head. And when his deputy came dashing out of the office with the bolt cutters in hand, he grumbled, "Took you long enough," and began to cut.

An hour or so later, Glory and Wyatt, with the chief for added company, were waiting impatiently for Amos Steading to come out of surgery and tell them what they wanted to hear.

And when the doors at the end of the hall suddenly swung back, and he burst through with his usual gusto, Wyatt got to his feet.

"You could have aimed a little farther to the right and made my job easier," Amos growled, and then clapped Wyatt on the arm. "But he's fine, and will be in recovery for at least another hour. After that, you can have a quick go at him."

Conway nodded. "That's fine, then," he said, and then turned to Glory. "Miss Dixon, I'll be back at that time to interrogate the suspect. Rest assured that it will soon be over. Right now, I need to check in at the office. They're towing Marker's truck from the dump as we speak, and I want to take a look inside before I talk to him. See you in a while."

They watched as he walked away, and then Amos Steading took a good long look at Glory, gauging the lingering shock in her eyes against the paleness of her skin and the way she clung to the man at her side.

"Are you all right?" he asked gently.

Glory slumped against Wyatt. "I don't know if I'll ever be all right again," she said softly. And then Wyatt's arms tightened around her shoulders, and she felt the strong steady beat of his heart against her cheek. "But I'm alive, and it's thanks to this man."

Amos shook his head in disbelief. "Well, little lady, a few months ago, I think he could have said the same thing about you."

Glory turned, her eyes wide as she gazed up at the doctor.

"Amazing, isn't it?"

The doctor's laugh boomed in the confines of the hall. "That's hardly the word, girl. Hardly the word."

Chapter 14

Carter Foster was on the phone when his secretary, Bernice, burst into his office waving her hand, and mouthing for him to come look.

He covered the mouthpiece with his hand. "What? Can't you see I'm busy?"

"You've got to come see!" Her eyes were wide with excitement. "Some man just drove up in front of the police department and there's an ambulance on the way. I can hear it coming."

"So?" Carter growled. "It's the police department, for goodness' sake. Things like that happen over there."

"But that Dixon girl is there... and there's somebody screaming from inside the trunk of the car."

He blanched, and hung up the phone without excusing himself from the conversation. As he rushed to the door, he tried to pretend it was curiosity, and not horror, that made him move.

He and his secretary stood in the doorway, curbside onlookers to the scene being enacted across the street. Even as Carter watched, he began to sweat. He couldn't hear exactly what was being said, but that voice coming from the trunk of the car was all too familiar. When he saw the chief take a rifle out of the back seat, he started to shake. It was the same kind of gun that Bo Marker had carried in the gun rack in the cab of his truck, right down to that telescopic sight.

Oh, no.

"Look, Mr. Foster. There's a man in the trunk, and he's all tangled up in some kind of wire. What on earth do you suppose happened?"

That stupid Bo Marker got himself caught is what happened, he thought, but it wasn't what he said.

"I have no idea," he said, and made himself smile. "You know what, Bernice? It's nearly noon. Since we've been interrupted, why don't we just go ahead and break for lunch? I'll be in court all afternoon, so why don't you take the rest of the day off?"

And then the ambulance pulled up and the show was all but over. His secretary was pleased with his offer, and anxious to share the gossip of what she'd seen with the dentist's receptionist down the street. She didn't give him time to reconsider, unaware that her work schedule was the last thing Carter Foster was worried about.

As she went to get her purse, he slipped out the door and into the alley, leaving Bernice to lock up. But he wasn't going to eat. Food was the last thing on his mind. It would only be a matter of time before that idiot, Marker, started blabbing. Carter knew that if he was to have a chance of escaping, he had to be miles away when it happened.

His hands shook as he slid behind the wheel of his car, and although he wanted to race through the streets at full speed, he made himself take the trip home with his usual, poky ease.

Upon arrival, he began digging through closets, trying without success to find his big suitcase. It would hold all that he needed in the way of clothes. But the longer he looked, the more frantic he became. It was nowhere to be found.

He was at the point of hysterics when he remembered the last time he'd used it. It was the night Betty Jo had died.

He'd packed a portion of her clothes into it to back up the story of her having left him, then tossed it in the dump when he'd tossed her body.

"Okay...okay. I'll improvise," he muttered, and headed for the kitchen.

Moments later, he was back in the bedroom, stuffing shirts and underwear into a garbage bag and yanking clothes, still on their hangers from the closet. He had to get going.

Bo Marker came to in a frightening manner. One minute he'd been staring up at the bright lights of the operating room, and then everything went black. Now, light was reappearing at the periphery of his vision. A woman's voice was calling his name and urging him to wake. It was the nurse who'd put a needle in his hand earlier.

Struggling against the desire to stay where he was, he finally opened his eyes, and then wished he'd followed his own instinct. People were hovering around his bed, staring intently at his face as he awoke. In a drug-induced state, he imagined them vultures, hovering over a carcass, readying to take a first bite.

"No. Go 'way," he muttered, and tried to wave them away when he realized that one of his arms was in bandages, and the other was connected to an IV line.

"Bo, this is Chief Conway. I understand you promised Mr. Hatfield here a name."

Bo groaned. "Can't you let a man rest in peace?"

Wyatt shifted his position, leaning over the bed so that Marker could see him clearly. "If I'd known that's what you wanted, I could have aimed a little to the left and saved the county the cost of cutting on you."

Bo looked up into eyes dark with anger and then closed his eyes, partly in pain, mostly in fear.

Amos Steading stood to one side, judging his patient's capability to communicate against the need these people had to find out the truth. After learning what Glory Dixon had endured at this man's hands, he had to remind himself of the oath he'd taken to preserve life, not end it.

Wyatt leaned closer until he was directly over Marker's face. "Give me the name now...or face murder charges on your own!"

It could have been the tone of Wyatt's voice, or the fact that Bo was in too much misery to put up a fight, but when the demand was uttered, words spilled.

"I didn't murder no one," he cried. "The only thing that I put away was a dog."

Wyatt's voice was almost at a shout. "Glory Dixon's father and brother are dead because of what you did. And you tried your damnedest to send her with them today. You might also like to know that they found a partial print on that stolen car that someone used in an attempted hit and run. What do you want to bet that it's yours?"

Bo groaned.

"Just don't give me any more of your crap, Marker. I'm already wishing I'd left you in that stinking dump."

The machine monitoring Marker's heart rate began to beep in a wild and erratic pattern.

Amos Steading frowned. "That's about enough for now. You'll have to come back later for further interrogation."

"I didn't kill no one!" Bo said. "Them people was already dead before Carter Foster hired me. I didn't have anything to do with their deaths...I swear!"

The chief frowned. "Now, damn it, Bo, I don't think you're telling me the truth. Why would Carter Foster want to kill the Dixon family?"

"Who's Carter Foster?" Wyatt asked.

"He's the town lawyer," Conway said. "And as far as I know, he doesn't have a vicious bone in his body."

But as soon as he said it, he remembered the investigation he'd asked his deputy to initiate, and wondered if anything valid had turned up on the whereabouts of Betty Jo.

Wyatt spun, staring back at the doorway where Glory waited.

"Honey, what do you know about Carter Foster?"

Surprise reshaped her expression. "Who?"

"The local lawyer."

"Oh! Why, not much. I don't think Daddy ever used him. When we had to commit Granny to the nursing home in Hazard, Daddy hired a lawyer there. That's the one who's handling the probate on Daddy's will, remember?"

Wyatt nodded, then turned. He could tell by the look on the doctor's face that they were about to be ejected.

"Please," he urged. "Just one more question."

Finally, Steading nodded.

"All right, Marker, let's say you're telling the truth. Did Foster say why he wanted Glory dead?"

Consciousness was beginning to fade. Bo's attention was drifting and his tongue felt twice its normal size. He licked his lips over and over, and it took everything he had just to get the words said.

"I don't know," he muttered. "All he ever said was that the crazy witch could ruin him."

"That's enough," Steading ordered, and finally ushered the trio from the room.

Once they were in the outer hallway, Conway paused, and scratched his head. "I don't get it. This doesn't really make sense."

Wyatt grabbed the lawman by the arm, desperate to make him believe.

"Look, Chief, there's something we haven't told you. Glory thinks that there's a connection between what happened to her family and the vision she had of that body being tossed in the dump."

The argument he expected didn't come. Instead, a strange expression crossed the chief's face as he turned and stared at Glory, as if seeing her for the very first time.

"Is this true, girl?"

She nodded. "That's why we went back there today. I wanted to see if the vision I had the first time would recur. I hoped that if it did, I might *see* something that I missed seeing before, like a face, or a tag number on the car."

"Well, did you?"

"Yes, sir."

"Then who did you see?" Conway asked, and then couldn't believe he was considering the word of a psychic as an actual fact.

"I didn't see a face, but I saw the man's back," Glory said. "He was stooped and starting to go bald on the crown of his head. He also drove a dark gray sedan. And . . . I saw something else I hadn't seen the first time. The dead woman has red hair. And I think her name is Elizabeth."

Conway visibly staggered, then swiped a shaky hand across his face. "Good Lord, girl! Are you sure?"

"Yes, sir. Definitely sure about the red hair. Pretty sure about the name. It came to me out of nowhere, and I have no reason to believe that it is unconnected to what I was seeing."

Wyatt could tell by the look on his face that something Glory said had struck a chord. "Why? What is it you know that we don't?"

"It could be completely unrelated to what you saw. And it doesn't prove that what Bo Marker said is true. But . . ."

"Damn it, Glory has the right to know," Wyatt said. "Hasn't she endured enough?"

Conway looked at her where she stood, silhouetted against the bright backdrop of a wall of windows. Small in stature and fragile in appearance though she was, there was still something strangely enduring about her poise and the waiting expression on her face.

Finally, he nodded. "Yes, I suspect that she has." He made a quick decision and started talking. "A little more than a week ago, Carter Foster's wife ran off with some man. It wasn't her first indiscretion, and no one expected it to be her last. She's what you might call a loose woman."

Wyatt wasn't following this. If Foster's wife was gone, then why would he blame Glory?

"The deal is . . . to my knowledge, no one saw her leave. All we know of what happened is from Foster's version of the story. What gives me pause to wonder is what Glory just said. His wife was a redhead who went by the name of Betty Jo. But I've ticketed her myself on several occasions for speeding, and I distinctly remember that the name Elizabeth was on her driver's license."

Glory gasped, and then turned away. Wyatt came up behind her. His touch was comforting, but there was nothing he could do to ease the ugliness of what surrounded her.

"Why, Wyatt? Why did I get caught up in this?" she cried.

"Remember when you said the two incidents were connected?"

She nodded, then leaned against his chest, as always, using his strength when her own threatened to give. Wyatt's voice was low against her ear, but the truth of what he said was too vivid to deny.

"What if his wife didn't really leave him? What if he killed her, dumped the body and then feared you would *see* it and give him away? Bo Marker said that Carter claimed you could ruin him. Marker also claimed he had nothing to do with the explosion that killed your family. If he's to be believed, then that could mean Carter caused the explosion, and when he found out you escaped, he hired Bo Marker to finish what he couldn't."

She moaned and covered her face with her hands.

"Don't, honey," he said softly. "It's just about over."

"Look, I don't know quite know what to make of all this," Conway said. "But I need to get back to the office. I want to bring Foster in for questioning."

"I've got a cellular phone at the cabin," Wyatt said. "Here's the number. I'd appreciate it if you'd keep us abreast of what goes on, but right now, I think Glory needs to go home. She's had just about all she can take."

The trio parted company in the parking lot of the hospital, and when Wyatt seated Glory in the car, she looked like a lost child. Heartsick at what she'd endured, he was about to get in when he glanced across the street and noticed the drugstore on the corner.

Just for a moment, he had a flashback of another time when he'd been in this lot, sitting in a wheelchair and waiting for Lane to pick him up. In his mind, he could almost see the peace that had been on Glory's face that day as she'd stood between her father and brother, safe in the knowledge that she was right where she belonged. But that was then and this was now. Now they were gone, and God willing, she would soon belong to him.

She leaned across the seat, then looked out at him through the open door.

"Wyatt? Is something wrong?"

Quickly, he slid behind the wheel, then cupped the back of her head and pulled her gently toward him until their mouths were a breath apart.

"Not anymore," he whispered, "not anymore," and felt her sigh of relief as their lips connected.

Carter was at the end of the street and turning when he looked in his rearview mirror and saw a patrol car easing up his drive. There were no flashing lights or sirens squalling, but to him, the implications were all the same.

"Oh, my God," he gasped, and swerved, taking alleys instead of the streets to get out of town.

He cursed as he drove, damning everyone but himself as to blame. Once he barely missed a dog that darted across an alley, and then a few minutes later, slaughtered a pair of matching trash cans as he swerved to miss a pothole. On top of everything else, he now had a sizable dent in his left front fender.

"It's no big deal. I can handle this," he muttered, and then accelerated across a side street and into the next adjoining alley. When he realized he was on Ridge Street, he started to relax. He was almost out of town!

As if to celebrate his premature joy, a small dinging began to sound from the dash of the car. Carter looked down in dismay at the warning light near the fuel gauge. It was sitting on empty... and he had less than five dollars in cash to his name.

He slapped the steering wheel in frustration. He had credit cards he could use, but they left a paper trail. If he used them, it would be only a matter of time before they found him.

Frantic, he paused at a crossing and then saw salvation to his right. The First Federal Bank of Larner's Mill was less than a hundred yards ahead. Money was there for the taking. His money! And while he didn't dare enter, the automatic money machine in the drive-through beckoned.

Moments later, the decision made, he shot across the street and into the lane for the ATM, right behind a small brown coupé belonging to one Lizzie Dunsford, retired librarian. The moment he stopped, he realized he'd just made a mistake. Lizzie Dunsford was notorious for being unable to remember her own address. It was obvious by the way she kept punching numbers that she also could not remember her own personal identification number for her money card.

"No...oh, no," he groaned, and started to back out when a big red four-by-four pickup pulled in behind him. Although the windows were up, music could be heard as it reverberated loudly from the interior, marking time for the teenage driver and his young sweetie, who were making time of their own while they waited.

Carter waved at them to back up, but they were too busy locking lips to see him, and honking to get their attention was out of the question. Their music was so loud that they wouldn't have been able to hear, and honking his horn would only call attention to himself.

In a panic, he jumped out of his car, squeezing between it and the next car, until he was at Lizzie Dunsford's door.

"Miss Dunsford...it's me, Carter Foster. I see that you're having a little trouble. Maybe I could be of service?"

Hard of hearing, the old woman frowned. "I don't know any Arthur Fosser," she said, and started to roll up her window, certain that she was about to be the victim of a robbery.

By now, Carter was panicked. He stuck his hand in the gap between door and window, pleading his case with renewed vigor.

"I said, Foster! Carter Foster! You remember me. I'm a lawyer."

"Oh . . . why yes, I believe that I do," she said.

Thank God, Carter groaned inwardly. "Now... how can I be of service?"

"I just can't get this thing to work," she said. "I keep punching numbers, but nothing comes out."

Carter peered at the screen, then frowned. "I don't know what your identification number is, but this looks like a phone number to me. Are you sure you remember it right?"

She frowned, and then suddenly cackled in delight. "You know... I believe that you're right! Now, you run back to your car, boy. I'll try another. You're not supposed to watch me, you know."

"Yes, ma'am," he said, and jumped back into his car, praying that he hadn't been seen.

Afraid to kill the engine for fear there wouldn't be enough fuel to start it back up, he sat in horror as sweat rolled down his face and the gas gauge slid farther into the red. The only good thing about his location was that the patrol car cruising down the street didn't notice him sandwiched between the two cars.

In his mind, he was already preparing an argument to the court on his behalf when Lizzie's car suddenly sprang to life and bolted out of the lane and into the street, with Lizzie in less than firm control.

"It's about time," he muttered, and drove forward. Inserting his card, he began to withdraw all that he could from his account.

As Wyatt turned onto Main Street and headed out of town, he kept glancing back and forth at Glory. She was leaning against the seat with her eyes closed. More than once, he was certain that he'd seen her lips tremble. He kept watching for tears that never showed.

"Hey, little Morning Glory," he said, and slipped a hand across the seat toward her. "How about scooting a little closer to me?"

Glory opened her eyes and tried to smile, but there was too much misery inside of her to let it happen.

"What is it, baby?"

"Granny calls this...thing I can do a gift. But how can it be when it caused the deaths of my father and brother?"

"Your gift didn't cause them to die. Someone murdered them," he argued.

"Because of me," she whispered. "Because of me." Unable to accept his pity, she looked away.

There was nothing he could say to help. Only time, and a better understanding of the frailties of the human race were going to make Glory's burden easier to bear.

"Just rest," he said. "We'll be home in no time. Maybe it will make you feel better."

As they passed, the buildings seemed to blur one into the other. Glory was lost in thought and on the point of dozing, when the air inside the car suddenly seemed too close. And before she could react by rolling down a window, the skin on her body began to crawl. She went from a slump to sitting straight in the seat, searching the streets on which they drove for a reason that would explain her panic.

"Wyatt?"

Apprehension sent her scooting across the seat next to him, clutching at his arm.

"What is it?" he asked, and started to slow down, thinking she might be getting sick.

"No! No!" she shouted. "Don't stop. I think he's here!"

"You think who's h—" He swerved as understanding dawned. "Where?" he asked urgently, looking from one side of the street to another.

"I don't know," she said, and then pressed her fingers against her mouth and groaned softly. "I'm afraid."

"He can't hurt you, darlin'. I'm here."

Glory leaned even closer, her heart pounding, and let herself be pulled toward the fear. They had to find him. It was the only way she knew how to make it stop.

"Do I keep driving, or do you want me to stop?" he asked.

She closed her eyes, focusing on the fear, and then looked up with a jerk.

"Turn here!" she ordered, and Wyatt took the corner on three wheels.

Carter was stuffing money in his pockets when the sound of tires squalling on the street behind him made him look up in fright.

"Damn and blast," he groaned, and took off without retrieving his money card and receipt that were still hanging out of the machine.

"There!" Glory cried, pointing toward a dark gray car that was hurtling out of the drive-through at the bank.

Wyatt accelerated past the bank, and then swerved sharply to the right, blocking the car's only exit. Instinctively, he shoved Glory to the floor and then grabbed for his gun. He looked up just as the car came skidding to a halt. He jumped out with his gun aimed, unaware that Glory refused to stay put. The need to look into this man's face was, for her, overwhelming.

"Son of a . . . !" Carter's heart dropped.

But it wasn't the man with the gun who did him in. It was the sight of Glory Dixon, sitting up in the seat and staring back at him with those clear blue eyes.

"No-o-o," he screamed, and shoved his car in reverse. Rubber burned on the pavement as gears ground and tires began turning in reverse.

But no sooner had he begun to move, than the big red four-by-four that was behind them turned the corner and hit his bumper with a thump. It didn't make a dent in the big truck or its occupants, but it jerked Carter's head, popping his neck like the crack of a whip.

Whiplash!

He groaned. A lawyer's favorite injury, and here he was without a prayer of collecting on the deed. He looked out his windshield and saw the man with the gun, waving and shouting at the kids in the truck. He was vaguely aware of them getting out and running toward the bank, and then of someone dragging him out of the car.

He was choking from the hold the man had on the back of his shirt. Every time he tried to move, the hold tightened and he would be all but yanked off his feet. The reality of his situation came swiftly when he finally heard Wyatt Hatfield's angry voice.

"Glory. Is this him?"

In a daze, she stared at his face, looking past the plain appearance of an overweight and aging man, to the evil in his eyes. And when she looked, it was there. The guilt. The shame. The fear.

She looked down at his hands and, in her mind, saw the same hands turning the jets on the cookstove in her house, then breaking a knob so that it would not turn off.

"Yes," she said. "That's him. That's the man."

Carter cursed and made a desperate effort to jerk free of Wyatt's hands, but the man and his grip were too strong. In the struggle, his jacket fell open, and money dropped from his pocket and onto the ground. A draft caught the bills, shifting and fluttering them along on the pavement, farther and farther out of Carter's grasp.

"My money!" he cried. "It's blowing away!"

"You're not going to need money where you're going," Wyatt said.

Carter's mind was whirling in desperation as the sound of sirens could be heard in the distance. Moments later, when the chief himself slid to a halt and exited his car on the run, Carter started babbling.

"Conway, thank God you're here. This stranger just tried to hold me up. Look! My money! It's blowing away! You've got to help me."

Conway motioned for a deputy. "Handcuff him," he said.

"No!" Carter screeched as the steel slid and locked around his wrists. "You've got the wrong man! I didn't do anything wrong."

"That's not exactly what Bo Marker says," Conway drawled, and was satisfied with himself when all the blood seemed to drain from the lawyer's face. That was guilt showing, or his name wasn't Anders Barnett Conway.

"Who's Bo Marker?" Carter finally thought to ask, although he suspected his reaction might have come a little too late to be as believable as he'd hoped.

And then all eyes turned to Glory as she answered for them all. "He's the man you hired to kill me...isn't he, Mr. Foster?"

Carter looked away, unable to face her accusation.

But Glory wasn't through. "Why, Mr. Foster? Why would you want to harm me? I didn't even know your name."

He stared, unable to believe what she just said. She hadn't even known his name? Could that mean, if he'd let well enough alone, he would have gotten away with murder?

"Going on a trip, were you?" Conway asked, as he saw the bags and stacks of clothing in the back seat of the lawyer's car.

"Why, no," Carter muttered. "I was uh... I was going to..." He brightened. "I was about to donate all this stuff to the Salvation Army."

Wyatt picked up a handful of money from the ground and stuck it beneath Carter's nose. "What was this for? Were you going to donate all of your money, too?"

Carter glared, then focused his anger on the chief of police. "Exactly what am I being arrested for?" he muttered.

"For the murder of Rafe Dixon and James Charles Dixon. For hiring a man named Bo Marker to kill Glory Dixon. And when we get through digging in the city dump to find the body, for the murder of Elizabeth Foster."

Carter tried to fake surprise. "Betty Jo! Murdered! You can't be serious?" And then he tried another tack. "You have no proof."

"When we get through digging, I will. I'm going to go back to the office and take this little lady's statement, just like I should have done days ago. And when we get through digging through the garbage, if I find myself a redheaded woman by the name of Elizabeth, who's wrapped up in something white, then you're in serious trouble, my friend."

His eyes bugged. The description was so perfect that it made him sick. "That's impossible," he muttered, and then he thought to himself. *No one saw.*

Glory gasped, and answered before she thought. "Oh, but that's not true, Mr. Foster. I did."

Carter went weak at the knees. His mind was running on ragged, and afraid to stop for fear that hell would catch up with him while he was forced to face the truth of what she'd just said.

The witch, the witch. She'd read his damn mind.

Conway read him his rights as he dragged him away.

The ride home was quiet. Little was said until they pulled up in front of the cabin and parked. As they got out of the car, Liam Fowler and his friends walked out of the trees and into the yard.

"They've heard," Glory said.

"Already?" Wyatt asked.

She nodded. "It doesn't take long for word to get around up here."

Liam Fowler was grinning as he grabbed Wyatt's hand and gave it a fierce shake, then brushed the crown of her head with the flat of his palm.

"Glory girl, you choose your friends well," he said. "We're all glad you're safe, and if you want to rebuild, just say the word. We'll be here."

Tears shimmered on the surface of her eyes as she nodded. But the emotions of the past few hours were too much for her to speak.

"Excuse me," she said, and ran into the cabin.

"It's been a bad day," Wyatt said.

"It's been a bad week, friend. Real bad. We lost two good friends. Thanks to you, we didn't lose another. If you happen to be a mind to stay in these parts, we'd be real proud to have you."

Then without giving Wyatt time to answer, they disappeared as quickly as they had come. As soon as they were gone, Wyatt went to look for Glory.

He could hear her sobs as he walked into the room. Without pause, he locked the door, set the gun on the mantel, and followed the sound of her voice.

"It's all right, it's all right," he said gently, as he crawled onto the bed with her. "Cry all you want. I've got you."

When she rolled toward him and wrapped her arms around his neck, he groaned and held her close.

"Oh, Wyatt. His face...did you see that man's face? He's not even sorry for what he did."

Wyatt felt as if his heart was breaking. If he could, he would have taken her pain twice over, just to make sure she never suffered again.

"I know, darlin', I know. Sometimes the world is an ugly place." He pulled her closer against him, comforting her in the only way he knew how. With love.

He held her until her tears dried, and only the occasional sound of a sob could be heard as she slept. And when she was fast asleep, he eased himself gently out from her bed, then went into the other room. There was something yet to be done.

Justin Hatfield leaned out the front door of his house and called to his brother-in-law, who was loading tools in the back of a truck.

"Lane! Telephone!"

Lane dropped a tool belt and a sack of nails into the bed of the truck and came running. He cleared the four steps up the porch in one leap and reached for the phone just as Toni walked into the room.

"Hello," he said, and gave Toni a wink.

"Lane, it's me, Wyatt. It's over."

Lane dropped into the chair by the phone. "What happened?"

"One of them started taking potshots at us at the dump. We caught the other one coming out of a bank. It's a long story.

"I'll fill you in on the details later."

Lane was surprised by what Wyatt just said. "There were two?"

"So it seems," Wyatt said. "At any rate, it's over. I just wanted to let you know that she's safe and everyone's in custody."

"What happens now?" Lane asked.

Wyatt rubbed his eyes wearily, then stared out the window over the kitchen sink into the nearby trees. The beauty of what was before his eyes was in direct contrast to what lay ahead.

"Tomorrow they start digging through the dump for a body."

Lane sighed with relief. He'd been living with guilt ever since the day he'd left, knowing that Wyatt was more or less on his own.

"You did a real good job, brother. Have you ever considered going into my line of work?"

Wyatt's answer was abrupt, but concise. "No. In fact, hell no!"

Lane grinned. "Just thought I'd ask."

"Anyway, thanks for all you did."

"I didn't do anything," Lane said.

"Oh, yes, you did," Wyatt argued. "When I called, you came. A man couldn't ask for anything more."

"If there's one thing that living with the Hatfields has taught me," Lane said, "it's that...that's what families are all about."

Wyatt turned toward the bedroom where Glory lay sleeping. His eyes darkened. "I guess you're right," he said. "If you can't count on family...who can you count on?"

Long after their conversation was over, the heart of it was still with Wyatt. And as he lay beside Glory, watching her sleep, he felt the last of his uncertainties about himself slipping away.

Through a quirk of fate, he and Glory Dixon would be forever linked. He knew as surely as he knew his own name that he could not, and did not want to try to, exist without her. She was, quite literally, in his blood.

And with the acceptance of that fact, came the acceptance of his own future.

Chapter 15

Wyatt stood at the edge of the pit, watching as men scoured the dump below. With more than a week's worth of dirt and garbage to move, he did not envy them their task.

Along with the local law, officers from the state police were on the scene, and at last report, Bo Marker was recovering by the hour. The better Bo felt, the more he talked. He was perfectly willing to admit to two counts of assault with a deadly weapon, but not murder. For once, he was innocent of something vile, and fully intended that everyone know.

Wyatt knew that while Marker's testimony backed up the truth of Glory's life having been in danger, there was still only her word—the word of a psychic—as to why Carter Foster wanted her dead. Carter was sticking to his story about his wife having left him for another man. Unless they found a body, he knew her story would stand on shaky ground.

Yesterday had been bad...both for Wyatt and for Glory. But that was yesterday. This was today. And the despair that he'd expected to see on her face when she woke had been absent. In fact, she'd greeted the day with eagerness, ready to put the past behind her. *If only I was that confident about losing my ghosts,* Wyatt thought.

Someone shouted from the line of cars behind him, and as he turned to look, he realized Glory was nowhere in sight. Only moments earlier, she'd been at his side, squeezing his hand in intermittent bouts of anxiety as load after load of garbage was shifted down below. But now she was gone. A quick burst of nervousness came and then went as he reminded himself she was no longer in danger.

A hot gust of wind blew across the ground, stirring the air without cooling it as he moved away from the site. Just as he started toward the line of parked cars, he heard her calling his name.

"Wyatt!"

He spun, and when he saw her waving at him from the shade of the trees, he started toward her at an easy lope.

Glory watched him coming, looking at him as if seeing him for the first time, and marveled at the link they shared, as well as at the man himself.

In her eyes, he was as strong as the hills in which she'd been born. As brown as the earth upon which she stood. And he'd been as faithful to his promise as a man could possibly be. She wondered if after this was over, there would be anything left between them, or if he would consider this a promise made, a promise kept—and be on his way.

She said a prayer that it wouldn't be the latter. He was so deep in her blood that if he left her, he'd take part of her with him. How, she wondered, did one live with only half a heart?

Laughter was in his voice as he swung her into his arms and off her feet.

"I lost you," he said, nuzzling the spot below her ear that always made her shiver.

"No, you didn't, Wyatt Hatfield. You'll never lose me." She stroked her hand against the center of his chest. "I'm in here. All you have to do is look. I'll be waiting."

Whatever he'd been thinking died. All sense of their surroundings faded. The smile slipped off his face as he lost himself in a cool blue gaze.

"You would, wouldn't you?" he asked quietly.

But before she could answer, someone shouted his name. He turned, still holding Glory in his arms.

"Why, it's Lane!" Glory said, and then noticed the tall, pretty woman walking beside him. Neither the denim jeans and shirt nor the well-worn boots she was wearing could disguise her elegance.

"And my sister," Wyatt added.

Glory could see the resemblance in their faces, and the proud, almost regal way in which they held themselves as they walked. Both of them had hair the color of dark chocolate, and eyes that matched. Along with that, there was a similar stubborn thrust to their chins that made her smile.

Toni Hatfield Monday couldn't believe her eyes. Lane had said Glory Dixon was small. But she wasn't prepared for that fragile, fairy-looking waif who stood at her brother's side. And her hair! It was a fall of silver and gold that caught and held sunshine like a reflection on water.

But as she came closer, her opinion of helpless beauty disappeared. In spite of the fact that Toni was nearly as tall as Wyatt, she felt small and humbled by Glory's pure, unblinking stare. For several seconds, she was so locked into that gaze that she forgot why she'd come. And then Glory smiled, and the moment passed.

"So," Toni said. "We meet." A quick sheen of tears came and went as she spoke. "Do you remember what I said I wanted to do when that happened?"

"About wanting to hug angels?" Glory asked.

Toni nodded.

"Good. I could use a hug today," Glory said, and let herself heal in Toni Monday's welcoming arms.

Toni smiled at the nervous look on Wyatt's face, and then turned and kissed him on the cheek.

"Don't worry, big brother. I won't give away your secrets. I just came to see your lady, face-to-face."

Wyatt was playing it safe and accepted her kiss as his due. "I have nothing to hide," he drawled.

Toni laughed aloud at her brother's audacity. "God save us from pretty men who lie as easily as they make love," she said, and winked at her husband as she took Glory by the arm. "Let's walk," she said. "I came a long way to say thank-you."

Glory held the joy that was in her heart, savoring this moment to herself. It gave her a feeling of belonging to someone again.

"There was no need to say it again," Glory said. "I'm the one who's thankful that Wyatt could make sense of what I'd seen."

It was impossible for Toni to hide her amazement. "I won't pretend to understand," she said. "But I will never doubt your ability, of that you can be sure." And then her voice softened as she took Glory by the hand. "Lane told me what you've had to endure. I'm so sorry for your loss, but at the same time, thankful that you and Wyatt have found each other."

Glory savored the words, hoping they were true. Had she and Wyatt truly found each other, or would he be saying goodbye now that she was safe?

"So, what are your plans now that the worst is behind you?" Toni asked.

Glory shrugged. "I have none, other than to rebuild my life."

A little surprised by the singular way in which she'd expressed her plans, Toni couldn't help but ask, "You sound as if you're planning to do this alone."

Glory paused, considering the best way to express her feelings, yet unashamed to admit what they were.

"I don't know," she finally said. "What happens between us now is not up to me. It's up to Wyatt. He knows how I feel." And then she smiled slightly. "In fact, most of the time he also knows what I think. I'm supposed to be the psychic and he reads *my* mind."

Toni's eyebrows arched, and she squeezed Glory's hand just a little, as if in jest. "You're kidding, of course."

"No, I'm not."

Toni gasped. "Really? He can do that?"

Glory shrugged. "For some reason, we now share more than a few pints of blood."

"Good Lord!"

Toni looked back at Lane as he stood talking to her brother, trying to imagine what it would be like to live with someone and have him know her every thought. And then something occurred to her, and she started to smile.

"So...my big brother knows what you think?"

"He sure does."

Toni put her hands on her hips and gave Glory a wicked smile. "Then give him something to think about. Let him in on some...uh, innermost thoughts, then see if he's man enough to take them."

The idea was audacious, just like Toni. She couldn't help but grin. "You're a lot like Wyatt, aren't you?"

"How so?" Toni asked.

"You don't waste time on details. You just jump in with both feet?"

Toni grinned even wider. "Well now, I didn't know I was so transparent, but if you need an answer, then I guess all you need to do is look at Lane Monday. I wanted that man from the time I pulled him out of a flood." And then she paused, and grinned even broader. "I need to amend that slightly. I wanted *him,* but I was willing to settle for making a baby with him."

Glory couldn't hide her shock. "Good Lord, Wyatt was right."

"How so?" Toni asked.

"He said once Lane met you, he never had a chance...or words to that effect."

"Like I said," Toni reminded her. "If you want something but don't give it a try, you have only yourself to blame."

"Hey, you two, time's up," Wyatt shouted. "You've had time enough to plot the fall of man."

"Just about," Toni whispered, and winked at Glory.

Glory shivered with anticipation, and then started to smile.

"I'm glad you came," she said softly.

Toni hugged her. "So am I, Glory. So am I."

* * *

It was well toward evening on the second day of the dig when the revelation came. Birds, disturbed from their normal scavenging, were circling the air above the pit where the garbage was being moved. Yard by yard, earth was scooped then dumped as they continued their search.

Anders Conway stood on the precipice, wondering if he'd made a mistake by putting his cards on the table too soon by calling in the state police, and wondering how he was going to explain his mistake when someone shouted, and another man started running toward him, waving him down.

Wyatt stood alone, watching from a distance away as the men began to converge upon their latest location. Even though he was high above the spot and hundreds of yards away, Wyatt could tell they'd found what they'd been looking for.

He took a long, slow breath, and said a quiet prayer, thankful that Glory wasn't here to witness it. Even from this distance, he could tell that what they found wasn't pretty. The once-white spread she'd been wrapped in was a stiff, dirty brown, and what was left of Betty Jo Foster was even worse. He turned away. He didn't need to see anymore.

"By God, Hatfield, they found her!" Conway said, as he came up and out of the pit a short time later.

Wyatt nodded. "I saw."

Conway looked around, expecting to see Glory Dixon somewhere nearby with a satisfied expression on her face.

"She didn't come with you today?"

"No," Wyatt said. "We were up late last night visiting with Lane and my sister. They left for home early this morning. Glory wanted to sleep in."

Conway nodded. "I guess it's just as well, but I thought she'd be here...wanting to know if the body was down there after all."

"You still don't get it, do you?" Wyatt said. "She didn't need to come for that. It was making you believe enough to look for the body that mattered. When your people started to dig, her worries were over. It was inevitable that you'd find what she already knew was there."

"You came," Conway said. "Does that mean you didn't believe her?"

Wyatt's smile never quite reached his eyes. "Oh, no. I came to make sure you didn't quit on her."

Conway flushed. "I suppose I had that coming."

"I think I'll be going now," Wyatt said. "Looks like you've got everything under control."

"Looks like," the chief said, but when Wyatt started walking away, Conway called him back.

"Hey, Wyatt!"

He paused, and then turned.

"I don't know how she does it," Conway muttered.

This time, Wyatt's smile was a little less angry. "Neither does she, Chief. Neither does she."

By the time they had Betty Jo Foster bagged and out of the pit, Wyatt was already gone.

Glory was down in the creek below the cabin, wading through the ankle-deep water with her jeans rolled up to her knees and her shoes in her hand. The soft, gentle breeze that had come with morning did not blow down here. Leaves drooped silently on heavily laden branches as an occasional dragonfly dipped and swooped only inches above the water. She moved without purpose, content only with the cool, constant flow between her toes and the ease that comes from knowing she belonged.

A squirrel scolded from somewhere in the canopy above her head, and she closed her eyes and took a slow, deep breath, realigning herself with the world in which she'd been born. Enclosed within the confines of the steep rocky banks, once again she felt safe and cleansed.

It would take longer for the anger to go away, and even longer before she learned how to live with the pain of her loss, but the guilt that had held her hostage was gone.

Something brushed against her ankle. She opened her eyes and looked down, smiling as tiny tadpoles wiggled past. And then something else, just below the surface of the water, caught her eye. As she stooped to look, her braid fell over her shoulder, baptizing the ends in the cool, Kentucky stream.

Her heart began to beat with excitement as she lifted a perfect arrowhead out of the creek.

"Oh, my gosh! J.C. is going to love..."

Realization struck. Staggered by the pain of loss, her lip trembled as she clutched it tightly in her fist. The time had come and gone for adding to her brother's beloved collection. Glory held it between her fingers, staring down at the cool gray piece and its perfect triangular shape.

Someday, there'd be another boy who was as fascinated by the past as her brother had been. The arrowhead should be there, waiting for him to find. She held her breath and let it go, watching as it turned end over end, dropping into the water and then settling, once again, into the rocks.

And then she heard someone calling her name and looked up. Wyatt was standing at the top of the bank. She could tell by the look on his face that it was over. Without looking back, she stepped out of the water and started up the bank with her shoes in her hand. He met her halfway.

"I got your mail when I came by the box," he said. "There's a letter from your lawyer. It's on the table."

Refusing to cry anymore, she stifled a sob, and just held him.

"Are you all right?"

She nodded. "I am now," she said. "Help me up the bank."

But before they moved, he tilted her chin, forcing her to look him in the face.

"Would you like to go see your granny again?"

A smile of delight spread from her eyes to her face.

"Could I?"

"Honey, you name it, it's yours."

"Be careful what you say," she warned. "I may ask for more than you want to give," then laughed at the shock on his face.

It was as if the old woman hadn't moved since they'd been there last. She sat in the same chair, in the same clothes, with the same lost expression in her eyes. Staring out a window into a world from which she'd withdrawn, she rocked without thought, moving only when the urge struck her.

"Granny."

Faith Dixon blinked, and then turned her head toward the pair at the door.

"Comp'ny? I got comp'ny?"

"It's me, Granny. It's Glory."

Identity clicked as she smiled. "Well, come on in," she said. "I've been waiting for you all day."

As before, Glory knelt at her granny's feet as Wyatt took the only other chair.

"Did you bring my gingersnaps?" she asked, and then cackled with glee when Wyatt promptly handed over a small white sack bulging with a fresh spicy batch straight from the bakery in Larner's Mill.

"I'll save some of these for your daddy," she said. "My Rafe does love cookies."

It hurt Glory just to hear his name. But she knew that keeping silent about the truth was the best thing for all concerned.

"Yes, he does, doesn't he, Granny?"

The old woman nodded, and then patted Glory's head. "He's lookin' real good, don't you think?"

A frown marred Glory's forehead as she tried to stay with her granny's train of thought. She supposed she must be referring to Wyatt, although they'd been discussing her father only seconds before.

"Who, Granny? Who looks good?"

"Why, your daddy. Who else?" She smiled to herself, and then looked up at the sky outside. "He was here jest a day or so ago," and then she began to frown. "At least I think it was then. I lose track of time, but I'm sure it warn't no longer than that."

Oh, Lord, Wyatt thought. *Maybe this wasn't such a good idea after all.*

"Honey?" He touched her shoulder, asking without saying the words.

Glory shook her head, and then whispered, "It's all right, Wyatt. It's not so bad."

Unaware of their aside, Faith was still lost in thought about her son's visit. Suddenly the frown slid off of the old woman's face.

"No! I'm right. It was only a day or so ago cause I 'member askin' him why he didn't come with you before."

Glory froze. What kind of tricks was her granny's mind playing on her?

Granny started to rock, happy that she'd settled it all in her mind. "Said he was goin' on some trip." She slapped her leg and then laughed. "I swear, that boy of mine ain't been out of Kentucky three times in his life and now he's goin' on some trip."

"Oh, God," Glory said, and rocked back on her heels. When she felt Wyatt's hand on her shoulder, she all but staggered to her feet.

Faith frowned a little, continuing to talk to herself, even forgetting that they were still there.

"I'll be seein' you soon, he said." She nodded confidently, as her tiny white topknot bobbed on her head. "Yep. That's what he said. I'll be seein' you soon."

Glory turned. Her eyes were wide, the expression on her face slightly stunned.

"Wyatt?"

There was little he could say. The implications of what Faith Dixon was saying were almost too impossible to consider. And then he thought of the connection that he and Glory shared. It was a bond stronger than love, that even death would not break.

"I heard."

"Do you suppose . . . ?"

He pulled her to him. "It's not for us to wonder," he said. "Whatever happened is between that woman and her boy. If she believes she saw him, then who are we to question?"

Glory went limp in his arms.

"Are you all right?" he asked.

She nodded, and then looked back at her granny as she rocked. The scene was one that Glory had seen a thousand times before. But this time, she was struck by the peaceful, almost timeless quality of the sight. And as she looked, in a small way, she began to accept the inevitability of the circle of life. One was born. One died. And life still went on when yours was gone.

Suddenly, she reached out and took Wyatt by the hand.

He felt the urgency with which she held him. "What is it, sweetheart?"

"Take me home, Wyatt. I want to go home."

Moonlight slipped through the parted curtains, painting the bodies of the couple upon the bed in a white, unearthly glow. As they moved together in a dance of love, the sounds of their sighs mingled with those of the wind outside the door. Sometimes easy—just above a breath; often urgent—moving with the force that was sweeping them along.

With nothing but the night as a witness, Wyatt destroyed what was left of Glory Dixon's defenses. And when it was over, and they lay arm in arm, trembling from the power of it all, he knew that he would take the same road that he'd taken before. Risk losing his life all over again, for what he now held.

Wyatt smoothed the hair from her face, gentling her racing heart with his words and his touch. "I love you, Glory Dixon."

Weak from spent passion, Glory still clung to him, unwilling to let him go.

Ah, God, Wyatt thought. *Making love to you every night for the rest of our lives would be heaven.*

Glory gasped. She'd heard that! For the first time since their relationship really started, she'd read *his* mind. He'd said it couldn't happen. That he never let down his guard.

She turned her cheek, hiding her smile against his chest. He didn't know it yet, but he'd done more than let down his guard.

When he let her into his mind, he let her into his heart. Now she knew there were no more walls between them.

"Wyatt..."

The sound of his name on her lips was sweet music. "What, darlin'?"

"You're more than welcome to try... if you think you're able."

For a moment, he couldn't think past the shock. The little witch! She just read his mind!

"Oh, my God!" He sat straight up in bed. "What did you just do?"

She only smiled, then stretched enticingly, arching her body like a lazy cat.

"You heard what I thought... didn't you?"

"Why, yes... I believe that I did," she said.

"That does it," Wyatt said, and then pounced, pinning her with the weight of his body, and with the dark, hot fire in his eyes. "I'm done for." His words were rich with laughter, the kisses he stole from her smile were warm and sweet.

Glory shivered with longing. Even though they'd just made love, she wanted him all over again. And then she remembered his sister's advice about letting him know what was in her heart.

"Are you sure you're done?" she whispered.

"Lord, yes," he laughed.

I'm not done, Wyatt. I've only just begun.

The laughter stopped. And when he looked in her eyes, his heart almost followed suit. Although her lips didn't move, he heard her whispers as clearly as if she were leaning next to his ear. The surge of desire that came with the words made him shake with longing. What she said...what she asked... what she wanted to do!

"Have mercy," Wyatt muttered. "Not unless you marry me."

Glory blinked slowly as she began to refocus. "Is that a proposal?"

He raised himself up on his elbows and began to grin. "Why do I feel like I've just been had?"

Her eyes widened in feigned innocence. "Oh, no, Wyatt. You're the one on top. I believe it's me who was just had."

His eyes twinkled as he scooped her into his arms, rolling until the mattress was at his back and they were lying face-to-face.

"Now, then, where were we?" he whispered. "Oh, yes, I was waiting for an answer."

"I will marry you, Wyatt Hatfield. I will love you forever. I will make babies with you and share your life until I draw my last breath."

Tears came unexpectedly. The beauty of her vow stunned him.

"And I will be forever grateful," he whispered.

"So what are we waiting for?" Glory asked.

I guess I'm just waiting for the sound of your voice.

Glory paused, gazing down at the face of the man she'd come to love, and lightly traced the path of the scar across his cheek.

Quietly...in the dark...in the tiny cabin in the deep Kentucky woods, she called his name aloud.

A single tear rolled down his cheek, following the path of the scar. It was the sweetest sound that he'd heard on earth. Someone was calling him home.

Epilogue

Spring had been a long time coming. Kentucky had wintered through more snow than it had seen in years, delaying the finishing touches that Wyatt and Glory Hatfield kept trying to put on their new home. It hadn't been so bad, wintering in that tiny cabin nestled deep in the woods, but the ground had long since thawed, and Glory had already seen the first Johnny-jump-ups beneath the trees around Granny's cabin.

Their dark, shiny green spikes with a single white flower suspended at the end of a miniature stalk were among the first woodland flowers to part the mat of rotting leaves. They were nature's signal that it was time to work the ground and plant the crops.

And for Wyatt, spring was a homecoming in more ways than one. He'd started out a child of the land, and despite a lot of lost years between then and now, it had called him home, just as his wife had done. He couldn't wait to put plow into ground, and he'd been thinking of buying some Hereford heifers to start a herd of cattle.

And then finally, three days ago, the last nail had been driven in the house. Yesterday, two trucks from a furniture store in Hazard had delivered, and then set up, an entire houseful of brand-new furniture, which now resided in the rooms in shiny splendor, waiting to give comfort and ease.

A wide, spacious porch framed the entire front of the house, and along each side, brand-new lattice gleamed white in the noonday sun, waiting for the first tendrils of a vine…or a rose…to breach the heights. Hanging from the underside of the porch, and rocking gently in the breeze, was a white wooden swing just big enough for two.

Wyatt pulled into the yard with the last load of their clothes from the cabin and started carrying them through the back door. Inside, he could hear the frantic patter of Glory's feet as she scurried from room to room, making sure that everything was in its proper place. At any moment, the first attendees to their housewarming might arrive, and Wyatt knew that Glory would skin his hide if he wasn't dressed and waiting.

She gasped when she saw him coming through the kitchen. "Give those to me. I'll hang them up while you get dressed."

Wyatt's chin jutted as he lifted the hangers high above the reach of her hands. "No, darlin'. I've got them. I told you before, you're not carrying anything heavier for the next few months than my baby."

In spite of her anxiety, she savored the adoration in his eyes, as well as his tender care, absently rubbing the slight swell of belly barely noticeable beneath her white gauzy dress as he disappeared into the back of the house.

The dress, like the house, was new and bought especially for this day. The neckline scooped, almost revealing a gentle swell of breast. The bodice was semifitted, and hung loose and comfortable against her expanding waistline. The skirt hung midlength between knee and ankle, and moved with the sway of her body like a tiny white bell. The sides of her hair were pulled away from her face and fastened at the back of her neck with a length of white lace.

Minutes later, as Wyatt came out of the room buttoning a clean shirt and tucking it into his jeans, he looked up, saw Glory standing in the doorway, anxiously looking down the long, winding road, and had to take a breath before he could speak. She stood silhouetted against the bright light of day. For a moment, he thought an angel had come to bless this house. And then he smiled. What was wrong with him? One already had. Her name was Glory.

She spun, her eyes wide with excitement, a smile wide upon her lips. "Someone's coming!" she cried.

Wyatt swung her off her feet and stole a quick kiss, aware that it would have to last him a while. "They're supposed to, darlin'," he teased. "We're having a party, remember?"

He clasped her hand, and together, they went out to meet the first arrival.

An hour later, the party was in full swing and the air full of laughter. A game of horseshoes was in progress over near the barn. A long picnic table had been set up underneath the shade tree at the edge of the yard and with every carful of well-wishers who arrived, more food was added to what it already held.

Children ran and climbed, shrieked and cried, and while Edward Lee was the only six-foot child in the midst of the play, he was having as much fun as the smallest.

Gifts for their new home were piled to overflowing on the porch, and Glory basked in the joy of knowing she was loved. Just when she thought there was no one left in Larner's Mill who could possibly come, more cars began to arrive.

But when the occupants started spilling from every opening, she started to smile. It was Wyatt's family.

"My goodness! Who are all of those people?" a woman asked.

Glory smiled. "My husband's family."

"Well, my word," the lady said. "I had no idea." She glanced down at Glory's belly, then back up at the brood moving like a groundswell toward the food and frivolity. "Fruitful lot, aren't they?"

Glory laughed aloud. "Yes, ma'am. I believe that they are."

Babies were napping on their mothers' shoulders and the older children were playing quietly in the shade. Typical of the mountains, men sat in one spot, gathered together by the bonds that made them head of the families, while women gathered in another, secure in the knowledge that they were sheltered by more than the breadth of their husbands' shoulders. And as one, they watched while Glory and Wyatt sat side by side on the front porch steps and began opening the gifts that had been brought to bless this house.

The thoughtfulness with which each gift had been chosen was obvious. Everyone knew that the newlyweds had literally "started with nothing." The fire that had destroyed Glory's family had also destroyed everything she owned.

Stacks of new linens grew with every package they opened. Often a gasp would go up from the crowd as Wyatt would hold up a particularly fine piece of glassware meant to be put on display. Mouth-watering jars of homemade jellies and jams lined the porch like fine jewels, their colors rich and dark, like the sweets themselves, waiting for a hot biscuit to top off. From the hand-embroidered tablecloths to the colorful, crocheted afghans, everything came from the heart.

And then Justin and David Hatfield, two of Wyatt's brothers, came around the corner of the house, carrying their gift between them.

"It's been in the family for years," Justin said, setting it at Wyatt's and Glory's feet. "Nearly every one of us has used it for one baby or another, little brother. We thought it was time you had a turn."

Glory was overcome by the symbolic gesture. The rich, dark grain of the wood was smooth and warm to the touch. And when she pushed on the side, the old wooden rockers rocked without even a squeak. They hadn't just given her a cradle. They'd made room for her in their hearts.

"Oh, Wyatt, a cradle for the baby! It's fine! So fine!"

And so are you, darlin'. So are you.

Glory turned, and for just a moment, the rest of the crowd shifted out of her focus. There was nothing in the world except Wyatt's face, and the love he felt for her shining out of his eyes.

"Thank you, Wyatt."

"There she goes. She's doin' it again," Justin grumbled. "All I can say is, thank God Mary can't read my mind or I'd be in trouble from sunup to sundown."

Everyone laughed, and the moment passed as they opened their next gift. The box was small, and the crystal angel figurine even smaller, but before she ever looked at the card, Glory knew that it had come from Lane and Toni. She'd been nicknamed the family angel, and took pride in their love and the name.

"It's from Lane and Toni," she said, holding it up for the people to see. "I'm going to save it for the baby's room. He'll need a guardian angel."

"He?" Wyatt leaned over and kissed the side of her cheek. "Do you know something I don't?"

"Figure of speech," she said, and everyone laughed.

But as she set the angel back in the box, Wyatt wondered at her secretive smile. He'd already learned that the less he knew about what she was thinking, the better off he was.

The next gift was quite heavy and bulky. And when the wrapping came off and they realized it was a large sack of dog food from Liam Fowler and his wife, they tried to find a way to say thank-you for something they didn't need.

And then Liam grinned at the blank smiles on their faces and pointed toward his truck. Edward Lee was coming across the yard with a squirming black-and-white pup in his arms. He knelt at their feet, then set the pup down on the ground.

"He's a pretty one, ain't he, Mornin' Glory?" His long, slender fingers caressed the pup's ears with gentle strokes. "I'll bet he'll make a real good watchdog, too."

Glory held back tears, although it was hard to do. He was marked so like her brother's pup that she could almost hear J.C.'s shout of laughter. When Wyatt slid an arm around her shoulder, she leaned into his strength and found the courage to smile.

"Thank you, Edward Lee. It's just what we needed to make this house a home."

Pleased that his gift had been a success, he scooted back into the crowd, teasing the pup with a string of ribbon lying on the ground, while Glory and Wyatt continued to unwrap.

When all the gifts had been opened, and thanks had been given for the fellowship that they'd shared, as well as for the presents, Wyatt held up his hand. He had a gift of his own for Glory, and he'd been saving it for last.

"Wait," he said, "there's one more left to open," and ran to their car.

Surprised, Glory could only sit and wonder what he'd done now. But when he came walking back to the house, carrying a box so big that he could barely get his arms around it, she started to smile. Just like Wyatt. He did nothing halfway.

He placed it before her like gold on a platter, then stepped back, becoming one of the onlookers as he watched her shredding the ribbon and paper.

Twice she laughed and had to call for his help when the knots in the ribbon wouldn't come undone. And then finally, there was nothing left but to open the top and look in.

At first, she could see nothing for the folds of tissue paper. And then the paper finally parted and she peered inside. The smile of expectation slid sideways on her face.

"Oh, Wyatt."

It was all she could say. As hard as she tried to stop them, the tears still came, filling her eyes and running down her cheeks in silent profusion.

Stunned by her reaction, the guests shifted uneasily on their feet, uncertain whether to watch or turn away, yet wanting desperately to know what had sparked such a reaction.

And then as they watched, they saw. Handful by handful, she began to pull the contents out of the box, piling them in wild abandon into her lap. By fours and sixes, by ones and by threes. And with each handful she took, her movements became more eager, laughing through tears while they spilled out of her lap and onto the steps beside her. As nothing else could have ever done, they filled her hands and her heart.

And when there was nothing more to take out, she wrapped her arms around the lot as Wyatt knelt at her feet and began wiping the tears from her cheeks.

"I couldn't give you back what you lost," he said softly. "But it's something to remember it by."

"Will you help me plant them?"

Wyatt grinned, and then stood. "We all will. Why do you think I got so many?"

And then he grabbed the packets of seeds by the handfuls and started tossing them to the crowd.

"Plant them anywhere. Plant them everywhere," he shouted. "By the barns, along the fences, down by the well. Run them up the mailbox and the old windmill. But not here." He pointed toward the two, shiny new trellises on either side of the porch. "Glory and I will plant here."

Caught up in the fantasy of the moment, people began claiming their spot, and before long, the place was crawling with gardeners on their hands and knees, planting the tiny seeds with makeshift tools in the rich, spring earth.

Wyatt took Glory by the hand, and led her to the side of the porch.

"I'll dig, you drop," he said.

Careful of her dress, she went to her knees, and through a veil of tears, planted the seeds that, weeks later, would grow into vines. And from the vines, would come flowers that gave bloom in the mornings. Blue as a summer sky, she could almost see the fragile little trumpets that would hang from these walls like small bells.

They were the morning glory, her daddy's favorite flower, and her namesake.

Like nothing else they'd been given this day, these would make their house her home.

Glory's hands were shaking as she dropped the last of her seeds into the ground. When she looked up at the man at her side, she knew that she was loved.

"I wish Granny had lived to see this day," she said softly.

Tenderness colored his words and his touch as he cupped her face with his hand.

"What makes you think she didn't?" Wyatt asked. "Remember, darlin', time doesn't break the bonds of love."

* * * * *

COMING NEXT MONTH

#691 MACKENZIE'S PLEASURE—Linda Howard
Heartbreakers
Zane Mackenzie lived and breathed the soldier's life. Nothing—and no one—had ever shaken his impenetrable veneer. Then he rescued Barrie Lovejoy, a woman who desperately needed a savior—needed *him.* And suddenly Zane's responsibilities included the role of expectant father....

#692 PERFECT DOUBLE—Merline Lovelace
Code Name: Danger
She was a dead ringer for the vice president, which was why Omega agent Maggie Sinclair discreetly assumed the other woman's identity. But impersonating an assassin's target was child's play compared to her *pretend* love affair with boss Adam Ridgeway. Because Maggie had done a lot of things undercover...except fall in love.

#693 GUARDING RAINE—Kylie Brant
Mac O'Neill took his job very seriously. After all, he was in the business of protecting people, and Raine Michaels was one woman who needed him more than she would ever admit. But somewhere, somehow, Mac crossed the line between simply wanting her alive and desperately wanting her in his arms.

#694 FOREVER, DAD—Maggie Shayne
Alexandra Holt knew she had secrets men would kill for—or die for. And secret agent "Torch" Palamaro was one man she alone could save—with love...and the truth. Because Torch's heart had died the day he believed his sons were murdered. But Alexandra knew *nothing* was quite what it seemed....

#695 THE MAN FROM FOREVER—Vella Munn
Spellbound
Anthropologist Tory Kent was a scientist foremost, a woman second. So when she came face-to-face with a century-old Indian warrior, she reacted at first with disbelief, then with uncontrollable passion. Loving Loka should never have been possible, and Tory had to wonder: how long could it possibly last?

#696 FATHER FIGURE—Rebecca Daniels
It Takes Two
Like father, like son. Only Marissa Wakefield saw the resemblance between Sheriff Dylan James and the teenage troublemaker he'd busted. After all, Josh was as stubborn as the man who'd fathered him, the man who'd once left Marissa for deceiving him. So how could she tell Dylan the truth now...especially when she'd fallen for him all over again?